THE
COUNTERSTIRKE

JOSHUA T. CALVERT

aethonbooks.com

THE COUNTERSTRIKE
©2022 JOSHUA T. CALVERT

Aethon Books
www.aethonbooks.com

Print and eBook formatting, and cover design by Steve Beaulieu.

Published by Aethon Books LLC.

ALSO IN SERIES:

THE ARRIVAL
THE COUNTERSTRIKE
THE EXTINCTION

PROLOGUE

THE AIR TASTED of cement and acrid chemicals, and he couldn't tell if that impression came from the filtration systems designed to protect him from the alien biosphere or from the environment itself. Tom Bijleveld led his team of Dutch soldiers from the fast reconnaissance units in a westerly direction around a rugged ridge. He could have almost imagined he was on Earth. However, he only managed that when he looked at the ground, which was covered in knotty plants and moss in shades of yellow and green. As soon as he lifted his gaze, he saw the concentrated strangeness of this place. The hazy, ochre daylight that struggled to force its way through the brown mountains of clouds high above them, where lightning flashed incessantly, looked like something out of the horror of a nuclear holocaust. At least, that was exactly how he would have imagined a post-nuclear war sky. The clouds seemed unnaturally distant, and yet he worried about what would happen should these artificial formations decide to rain down their moisture. There had been no reconnaissance data for Tom and his team to obtain. For the first two days of their mission, they had been constantly dousing themselves with disinfectant and wearing their camouflaged chemical suits, but by now, they were slinking through the alien biosphere in their normal uniforms with combat helmets and breathing masks. As a soldier, you quickly reached a point where you threw prescribed precautions overboard because they made the mission you had been sent on impossible. The chemical suits had fallen into just that category: uncomfortable, with poor visibility, acting as a miniature greenhouse that left them drowning in their own sweat. If alien microbes were to be their downfall, they still preferred that to drowning in their own juices or suffering a fainting spell before they could send the first dataset home.

If we can send data home, he thought, mouth agape as his over-acidified muscles pushed their way to the forefront of his attention. The planet they were marching on possessed about one and a half Earth masses, according to the eggheads in Brussels, and was a suitably unpleasant gravity sink. The miles they covered each day would have been exhausting even on Earth, without his body being one and a half times as heavy as it was here. He would probably have to gnaw on this action for a long time – should he survive.

Tom looked up as a mighty shadow fell in front of him and regarded the huge mushroom that blocked their path. The dark brown thing was at least twenty feet tall, and with its thick trunk and white gills under the cap, looked as if it were cast from rubber. In its shadow, the cool temperatures dropped even further, and at first glance, he thought he saw movement in the undergrowth. So far, they had been able to observe hardly any animals, except for a few hand-sized critters that had looked like a cross between squirrels and lizards. The acid rain was most likely getting to them. Anders and Jasper had already suspected during their first night here, which had been less than six terrestrial hours, that something like a climate change event must have taken place, because everything seemed as it had been predicted for the Earth in the next hundred years: the ground was quite dry under the plants, the trees and mushrooms, reminiscent of his homeland yet strangely wrong-looking, made a withered, morbid impression on him. The sky was permanently overcast, and when it rained, it was better to look for the nearest mushroom as an umbrella, as the acid rain quickly made one realize where the weak points in the rain cape were. When they'd taken samples on the first thirty-hour day, he'd picked up a nasty rash in a spot where his rubber gloves hadn't been properly connected to the chemical suit. All the more reason to forgo that precaution. Whatever he could contract here had surely found its way into his bloodstream long ago — and he could still walk upright and hadn't developed a fever.

Tom peered past the giant mushroom to the jagged ridge to the north and raised his binoculars to his eyes. The mountain range seemed to form an inverted U to the west, where their target was supposedly located, if the approximate indications of Central Defense were to be believed. However, since these had largely consisted only of directions and distances, he hadn't expected to actually end up finding a mountain formation that resembled an inverted U as in the description. As far as he could estimate the distances, he guessed three or four more days before they would reach the entrance to the oddly shaped valley.

A quick glance at the sky told him that the dirty brown clouds were moving north, toward the mountains. If his guess was confirmed that the peaks reached six to eight thousand feet, quite a bit of the lowest cloud layers would get caught on the slopes and rain off. There would be no joy in that, that much was certain. On the other hand, along with the other European Defense Force teams, they were the first humans to ever set foot on a planet other than Earth. Tom had not only volunteered for this mission because he was quite willing to accept the risk of an untimely death on alien soil for the opportunity. His ancestors had been explorers involved in the founding of the colonies in the Caribbean, and apparently that spirit of discovery continued in his genes.

The alien nature sent shivers down his spine, but he wasn't afraid like the rest of his team. That was good, because it meant he could reassure them and count on the genuineness of his words getting through to them, even unspoken. When they lay together during the short nights at the bivouac, mumbling into their breathing masks in suppressed voices, they had to inject each other with antibiotics, and that was usually the only time they had to talk besides their forced marches over hill and dale. That was helpful too, because constantly exchanging their own fears and fantasy stories that accumulated throughout the day didn't do them any good either way. So he had stopped such talk early, preferring instead to listen to the strangeness of this place. The nocturnal animal sounds, for example, which barely stood out against the rustling of the wind in the treetops and mushroom slats. If one listened closely, however, one could discern that something like hoarse bird calls — if there were such a thing as birds — resonated in the rustling. It sounded like cawing that had been unnaturally drawn out and distorted by some device, but once you listened in, there was no doubt that it was not the wind and that some kind of melody was resonating. It seemed creepy, but just about everything here was creepy. They had been prepared for this by the psychologists and he knew that anything his brain didn't know or couldn't place was bound to result in an inevitable fear reaction. He had grown used to all the hot and cold shivers of adrenaline kicking in by now.

"Wachtmeester," Anders growled behind him, and Tom stopped.

"What's up?"

The young soldier had stopped behind him and was just

taking his binoculars from his eyes before he pointed diagonally forward to where there was a hole in the roof of jagged leaves above them. "See that on the mountain? What's that?"

Tom motioned Jasper to stop too, and took his binoculars to his eyes. At first, he found nothing to attract his attention. The mountain slopes still lay there like gigantic sandcastles of extinct giants that had tried to conquer the clouds. They looked downright boringly normal, like they could have been anywhere on Earth except for their very plain shape. But then a movement caught his attention. What he had thought was a reflection of the sparse sunlight a moment before turned out to be movement. Something large was rolling over the eastern slope of the hillside, and with three more zooms, he realized that it appeared to be a gigantic gray vehicle lowered by a pulley. The movements seemed slow, downright ponderous. But when he recalled the scale of the flattening slopes, he realized that this apparent slowness only emphasized how large the object must be.

"That must be huge," Jasper gave shape to his thoughts. Through the breathing mask, his mumbling was barely understandable.

"Looks like a giant garbage can," Anders agreed with him.

"Guess they use it to haul away the stuff they mine." Tom pursed his lips and sniffled as he dropped his binoculars back to his chest and turned around. "Don't give a shit. We're here to do our own recon, not just rely on the Morphs' words, and that's exactly what I intend to do."

"Since we're here anyway." Jasper shrugged, as if he had a choice and didn't care.

"Here's the deal. We march into that valley, snap a few pictures, and radio them back."

"And when the corrosive rain comes down?" Anders queried.

"Then we'll clench our butt cheeks or stand under one of those mushrooms." Tom made a nod, half to interrupt the burgeoning conversation and half to point in the direction he intended to march in. "Less talking, more walking."

While they quietly made their way back through the alien undergrowth, somewhere on a distant spiral arm of the Milky Way, Tom kept thinking about the video footage that had been presented to him at Central Command in Switzerland. The huge mine complex that already looked like a gigantic military camp from a distance. As if that impression hadn't been enough, he knew that this camp would have already given him respect if it had been guarded by humans and not unknown aliens. Added to that was the knowledge that the video had merely been a perfect simulation by the Morphs of what they imagined the mine to be like based on ancient reconnaissance data. What was really there in the deep valley they would find out soon enough, and Tom wasn't sure if that should scare him or excite him.

———

Major Denize Chazelle of the French Air Force steered her EADS Harfang reconnaissance drone further north over Planet X's thick cloud mountains. The toxic-looking mixture of water vapor and sulfur seemed to glow yellow from within, as if there had been a reactor accident below. Of course, such an accident would hardly give clouds a yellow glow, but in her imagination, it would still look exactly like that. That impression only added to the queasy feeling she had as she piloted her drone — one of five — through the thin layers of air in the alien planet's upper atmosphere. Since the clouds here were quite high in altitude and were quickly damaging the material of the drones, the mission commander had decided that they should just lay out radar maps. Flying by sight under the cloud masses had not been an option anyway, lest they risk detection.

The flight had been quite smooth so far and she rarely had to use her joystick as the AI took care of most of it. Still, she was excited, knowing that she was piloting a familiar device in a completely unfamiliar environment. Not only that, the Harfang was tens of thousands of light years away, and yet the sheer work felt exactly the same as usual. Only the yellowish clouds and knowing what she was doing gave her a sense of rapture, as if something completely surreal was happening at that moment. Worse than all that, though, was her extreme fatigue. In her mid-forties, Denize was no longer the youngest soldier at the Recon Center, and fifty-eight hours without sleep was taking its toll. There were already a dozen empty energy drink cans beside her, making her function like she used to at a LAN party when she'd been playing for so long that it was all like a trance. But she had to concentrate, she couldn't make any mistakes, since they'd put her in the field because she was the best. She didn't want to betray that trust of the military leadership under any circumstances.

A glance at the fuel consumption at the lower left corner of her center screen warned her that she was nearing reserve. Planet X's high gravity was driving fuel consumption to new heights, just to keep the bird in the air. Denize blinked a few times to clear the sleep from her eyes, which was trying to wedge itself under her lids as a viscous, sticky mass.

"Putain," she muttered quietly enough that her two colleagues to the right and left couldn't hear, and reached with trembling hands for another can of the vile energy drink. The taste, supposedly reminiscent of blueberries, had by now turned into something that tasted like she had licked over a rusty iron bar.

"Major." Lieutenant Haby snapped her out of her brief trance.

"Oui?" she asked without looking up from her central screen. Her drone's eye shot over the clouds like lightning at an altitude of more than thirty kilometers, and yet it seemed too slow as she initiated a turn to begin the return flight.

"There is an anomaly in the cloud cover fifty clicks to the south," the younger officer replied with Brittany's mumbling accent. "You're the first on the return flight; you might want to check it out."

"What kind of anomaly?" she asked rather mechanically, scolding herself for it. If he had known what it was, he probably wouldn't have said *anomaly*.

"I don't know, Major. Either a pretty big object or a pretty big hole."

"The enemy has no air force, we were told," she replied, more to herself. The gravity of the planet, which ESA scientists had estimated to be a super-Earth, with its great mass, made it all but impossible to escape it with rockets. The mass of propellant that would have been needed to reach escape velocity was simply too great to set up a satellite network. Air travel didn't seem to have caught on for the same reason. However, she wondered how, with one and a half times Earth's gravity, the reports could be true that there were huge mountains on the surface. They should have been smaller in her estimation, the planet pulling harder on them. But surely this would not be the last mystery of this alien world to be uncovered.

"I'll look into it," she promised, and entered the coordinates she'd received on the left screen from her subordinate. Her heart pounded violently as she made the entry, and she knew it wasn't from excitement. Sullenly, she looked to the half-empty can of the disgusting energy drink and then to the image frame as it aligned itself to the southeast. Sure enough, there in the far distance, she found an area in the clouds that was less luminous, and leaned forward with interest. As she did so, the feeling that she was missing something wouldn't let her go. It had been gnawing at her since her brief pause fifteen minutes ago, and yet she could not quite put her finger on it.

I'll have to sit out the next shift or I won't be doing anyone any favors, she thought sullenly, blinking again to clear her vision.

"Remain cautious, Lieutenant. We must not be discovered under any circumstances – this is top priority."

"Roger that, Major."

The area the lieutenant had apparently spotted on radar was found after a few moments. It was not an object, but a hole in the cloud cover the size of a small town. It must have formed spontaneously, although their instruments indicated no change in wind conditions.

"Merde!" she muttered, bringing her drone into an evasive turn too late. Top priority, according to the mission briefing, was to remain undetected. Her operating altitude and the clouds had made that fairly easy, but now she was making a mistake. She could already make out the green-brown landscapes in the depths as the camera image turned away.

Her heart hammered uncomfortably hard in her chest, as if trying to force its way through her ribs.

Why am I getting so nervous? she asked herself irritably. She knew herself to be calm, but now not only was her heart about to burst, but another feeling, as if her back were being squeezed by a red-hot iron, joined in.

Breathing heavily, she stared at the readouts, barely noticing them, but thinking everything was fine as she looked down at an angle with her bow telescopes. She was about to turn away, when she noticed a reflection.

An object? That looks artificial, she thought in alarm, panic spreading even further inside her. Panic? Was it really panic? She was finding it harder and harder to breathe, that much was certain. Had the aliens just spotted her? A random hit?

This is a catastrophe! But even if it had been discovered, wouldn't one dismiss a device in the sky that really shouldn't exist with the same nonchalance as one did in this country with alleged UFO sightings?

Before she could even answer her question, she remembered what had been gnawing at her: she had forgotten to press the record button, so the last few minutes since her break hadn't been recorded.

With a horrified curse on her lips, Denize Chazelle began to twitch twice in quick succession before freezing in a deadly heart attack. Her right index finger had almost reached the record button, resting motionless on it in a sort of frozen attempt to compensate for a mistake that could no longer be erased.

She had seen something and died knowing it was important if Operation Rolling Thunder was to be a success, but no one would ever know what it was. When the medics rushed into the underground room a short time later, any help was too late and her superiors never learned that they had missed a potentially important spy clue.

CHAPTER 1

NIKOS

NIKOS WAS JOLTED out of a nightmare by the penetrating warble of the old-fashioned clock radio, half of which was about a giant glowing blue needle hurtling toward the earth and trying to impale him, and the other that he was on his way to his kindergarten and had forgotten something important — but since his hands weren't hands but sandwiches with the edges cut off, he couldn't turn the wheel of his car. So, as he groaned and slapped one hand on the alarm clock, he didn't quite know whether to be relieved or incensed at the cool penetration of the little device.

There was a deep rumbling in his stomach — a rumbling of the same kind that he had heard and felt before he fell asleep. He had initially glossed over the rationing of food by remembering his therapeutic fasting days, which he had taken twice a year on the advice of his naturopath. Before the alien invasion and all the resulting upheaval, of course. But after more than a month, he found it harder and harder to keep downplaying the latent malnutrition, and instead felt uncomfortably transported back to his days in the ruins of Athens. There was no comparison, of course, as he had been severely malnourished among the ruins of his former hometown, always on the verge of starvation. Now, a caloric deficit was bothering him, but it was still within acceptable limits. He had thought that nothing could be a nuisance to him anytime soon after his ordeal and deprivation in Greece, but it turned out that one apparently hastily forgot what one was capable of once living a reasonably comfortable life again.

Comfortable living, he thought, snorting as he flipped the covers aside and sat up. A ridiculous idea. Then again, anything was more comfortable than Athens, and he would do well to keep recalling that to mind.

Yawning, he stood up and wiggled his cold toes before placing his feet on the old hardwood floor of his bedroom. After rubbing his sticky eyes, he got up and shuffled to the small bathroom off to the left. He quickly washed and brushed his teeth as he circled his arm and shoulder. The feeling was still not the same as before the Congo, but at least he could move his arm again. A torn bicep tendon was obviously not something that healed in two months. On the other hand, he'd been luckier than others in his situation, since a physical therapist had taken care of him exclusively for the first month.

As he strolled back into the bedroom, and from there, into the combined kitchen-living room, the doorbell rang, right next to the entrance to the kitchenette. Irritated, he frowned and checked the fit of his pajamas, which had the logo of a local football club sewn on them.

"I'm coming," he said in broken German, pondering for a moment whose visit he should be prepared for. His physical therapist wasn't due until Friday. It was Wednesday. Another PR appointment for the war bonds was scheduled for the weekend and he had a date with Jacek, Uffe, Hardy, Knut, and Pill in the evening. "Hmm."

When it rang again, the ringing sounded downright impatient, though it was exactly the same tone. Nikos took two steps to the door, pulled the attached latch to the side, unlocked it with the key, and pulled the door handle.

"Well, princess? Sleep well?" a cheery voice greeted him in English, and the smell of cereal spread around his nose as Sönke Teunen sidled past him. He'd known Sönke since his release from the military hospital six weeks ago, when he'd been transferred. *Transferred,* in this case, meant that JEMCOM, the Joint European Military Command, which had since been relocated to the incorporated Switzerland, had recalled him to a new position.

Place, Nikos thought indignantly and heaved a long sigh.

"That bad, then?" asked Sönke, setting the fragrant paper bag down on the bar that separated the kitchenette from the living room. The little German grinned mischievously and placed his coral army beret beside it before rubbing his short-cropped brown hair and pointing disapprovingly at the improvised den between the sofa and the television. "Isn't there some kind of therapy for that?"

Nikos eyed the structure of blankets, two old lamps, and the TV's wires, and pursed his lips. "In my defense: I moved to the bed last night for the third time in a row."

"So, was it that bad?"

"I had nightmares and went back to the cave."

"Nightmares?" Sönke frowned. "We've all been having them since the beginning of the year."

"My hands were sandwiches."

"Oh. Well, at least you can eat those." The soldier from military intelligence *MAD* shrugged and pointed to the cereal-scented bag. "Not buttery, but Kraft cereal. Cashed in a favor."

Nikos walked over to the paper bag and peeked inside as if it was too precious to touch. The smell of oatmeal and baked cereal rose seductively to his nose, making his mouth water.

While he disappeared into the kitchenette in search of two bowls and orange juice, Sönke continued to speak. "How's your arm? Are you reasonably fit again?"

"I can brush my teeth and lift light things, but that's about it," Nikos explained between the clatter of doors and drawers. "The others are already back to target practice. I really don't know how they do it."

"These are KSK soldiers. They are made of special metal. Besides, they were injured in a completely different physical condition. You were nothing more than a skeleton."

"I guess you're right." Nikos placed the two bowls and two tablespoons, which he quickly rubbed against his pajamas, on the bar, and the orange juice next to them after sniffing it with careful scrutiny.

"Oh no, no, I've already eaten," the little intelligence soldier said, making a dismissive hand gesture. Nikos ignored that and poured half of the muesli into the bowl he had prepared for Sönke.

"Nobody can eat enough in these times."

With ARD, there was only one German television station left after the EU confiscated all media satellites and granted each language area only one state-controlled station. Since Nikos spoke only broken German, although he had been able to use his free time between public appearances and physio-therapy to learn feverishly in the hospital and in the weeks after-wards when Sönke had been assigned to assist him, progress had been manageable. Still, he'd turned on the TV every day, between eight and nine p.m., when the power grid was most stable. The reports were sobering. The collapse of international trade in goods had caused severe shortages of many foodstuffs, even in the world's largest single market, the EU. The complete halt in soya supplies alone was a major problem that had led to the animal industry effectively ceasing to exist. Europe had become a vegetarian continent overnight, as it were, as energy- and food-hungry factory farming could no longer be sustained once stocks were depleted. Since Europe was a very fertile continent, its agricultural capacity was indeed sufficient to feed its population, especially since it had shrunk by about ten percent due to the showers of rubble, epidemics, riots, and all those other things that come with a world ending. But the problem of the globalized world economy, which had collapsed overnight, could not also be solved overnight. Structures had to be changed, regulations and laws had to be redesigned or abolished, and all that was done in a hurry only a month ago, after the EU Commission, as a puppet of the EU Council, had effectively taken over indefinitely. Since then, things had moved really fast, and the new planned economy, focused on armaments and agriculture, was heading full steam ahead toward a bleak future. Every man and woman of military age was gradually conscripted and worked for the military in one way or another, whether in arms production or direct service to the weapon. Everyone else, however, was conscripted to help produce food and medicine. To be sure, there were still many who worked in subcontracting firms — all nationalized in the wake of the 2023 Disaster Relief Act — to make rubber seals for armed forces vehicles, for example, and the many little things that hardly anyone thought about. All this had affected people much less than expected. The unrest had quickly subsided once the mass influx of civilians had begun.

"What is it?" asked Sönke, and when Nikos looked up, the look on his counterpart's face seemed as if he had been staring at him questioningly for a long time.

"Oh, I'm just thinking about what's going on out there." He shoveled a spoonful of cereal with orange juice into his mouth, savoring the taste of cereal between the slightly bitter orange juice. There hadn't been any milk for a long time, but that didn't bother him, since he'd always found milk tasted about the same as a cow barn smelled.

"Our new Green Revolution, you mean?"

"Green Revolution?"

"Well, everyone's eating vegetables and seitan now, and all the private vehicles have been confiscated and stripped down to their raw materials one by one. That sounds like every Green's wet dream at Thanksgiving, don't you think?" said Sönke, smacking his lips.

"I'm amazed that people would flock together without complaint to confront a common enemy, but I'm even more amazed that there was no real revolution in Germany when they bagged the cars," Nikos returned. "I guess that's proof that miracles do exist."

"Don't forget that we've had full employment for a month now. There's no one left to be lazy or bored."

"Compulsory service, great stuff." Nikos snorted contemptuously, though at times, he wasn't sure how he really felt about the drastic measures taken by the EU Council. His logical working mind applauded the unusually swift and drastic measures taken by the leadership in Brussels, but his moral self-screeched in despair at the thought that there was hardly any personal freedom left, any attempt at self-development and individuality. Europe had mutated into a strict ant state and in record time, which frightened him.

"At least no one can complain about social inequality anymore," Sönke pointed out. "Everyone gets the same rations and allotments of hygiene items and clothing. And everyone works for a good cause."

"Since when is war a good cause?"

"Since war is the only option; otherwise, it is certain to be doom."

"I guess you're right." Nikos sighed again and wolfed down

the last of his cereal with some disappointment. "I can't quite get used to all this yet."

"Hey, you became a star overnight. That's normal. At least you don't have any airs and graces yet and only drink out of pink cups or eat croissants cut in half or something."

"What are you talking about?"

"Well, that's what stars are like sometimes, isn't it?"

"I'm not a star!" grumbled Nikos.

"Let's see. Three rallies a week, an average audience of five thousand..."

"They only come because there's free bread."

"Plus constantly changing television appearances of the hero from the Congo, broadcast around the clock," Sönke continued, regardless of Nikos' objections. "Every kid knows you."

"Yes, because the Chancellor is using me as his advertising mascot," Nikos grumbled in frustration and put the two bowls in the sink. In an hour, there would be water again, then he could wash them, but he would probably forget again and be annoyed in the evening. "I'm nothing but a figurehead, a story to be embellished and cannibalized so that as many people as possible will buy war bonds. But that doesn't make any sense. Money can't buy anything anyway because there are no more shops and no more consumer goods being produced. What's the point?"

"You're quite right. It's not about the money for the war either; it's about getting the money out of circulation. If we survive it all as a species, as Europe, there will be money again at some point, and then the state will just want to have a finger on how it's all done. If no one has anything anymore, no one can complain," the soldier explained, unimpressed. "Besides, you're far more than an advertising mascot. You're a sign of hope. An ordinary social pedagogue who ran a kindergarten and had to rise above himself to become an alien expert. A Greek in

Germany who bled with our soldiers to save the continent and form an alliance with the Morphs."

"I'm not an alien expert!" shouted Nikos a little too loudly, chewing furiously on his lower lip to stop himself from rumbling on.

"You've been in an alien ship twice, both in one of the Morphs and one of the Tears. You survived both times and were the only one to capture one. That makes you very much an alien expert in my eyes," Sönke countered.

"I wasn't the only one after all! The whole team..."

"Consisted of KSK soldiers, a special unit whose missions are as secret as the Queen's underwear. No one knows about them and no one ever will, so that leaves you!"

"That's unfair, and besides..."

"The whole fucking world is unjust. The piece of rubble that wiped out Bruges: unjust. That the aliens showed up over our blue orb, of all places, to settle their conflict: unfair. That we were ripped from our lives overnight: unjust. That the Constitution is suspended: unjust. That the entire Saarland is contaminated: unjust. That we will send soldiers into battles we cannot win: most unjust. What is just at the moment? Nothing. But complaining doesn't get us anywhere, so we keep doing our best and don't give up hope, it's as simple as that," Sönke explained, leaning over the bar to put a finger on Nikos' chest as if to impale him. "And you, my Hellenic friend, are the face of a new Europe. A Greek who bled with our people and works for the Chancellery. One from our midst who has suffered as few others have, and yet goes beyond his limits, whether in the Congo or on the stage. A European face who stands for the new future without borders, for a Europe united by a common purpose and no longer interested in the petty things of the past."

"That doesn't sound so bad," Nikos admitted, muttering. If it helped people to have a figure to identify with, then at least that was a positive, even if he still felt uncomfortable playing a role that didn't suit him. "I'm just trying to help."

"I know. See," Sönke said lightly, grinning broadly as if this was just another ordinary day. "The Chancellor didn't make you into a story. He's hyped you up as a dutiful, self-sacrificing do-gooder. While some of it may have been perfected a bit for audience custom, that's far from a lie, it's an exaggeration of the truth. Come here, I want to show you something."

Nikos raised a brow and frowned as the soldier stood up and walked toward the window. When he turned and noticed Nikos wasn't following him, he waved impatiently. "Come on!"

As they walked around the improvised cave, without which he wouldn't have been able to sleep for the last few weeks without having violent nightmares, his heart went cold for the first time at the sight of the ceiling structure. Of course, he knew he'd needed it to feel safe. Of course, he knew that had to sound paradoxical and sick; after all, it reminded him of his time in hiding in Athens, a place that had been anything but safe or even homey. When he'd worked with traumatized children, he'd often clashed with parents who hadn't believed him that there had to be some kind of break from traumatizing circumstances. Abandonment of even the worst but familiar circumstances, in some cases, was worse than slow change. Now that he had experienced this principle firsthand, it almost disturbed him more. The horror one knew was often simply less terrible than the unknown.

Reaching the window, Sönke, who just barely reached his shoulder, stopped and pointed into the cold spring morning. Berlin's Friedrichstraße was deserted, except for the occasional military jeep passing by and a few passersby scurrying back and forth as quickly as if there were a curfew.

"Looks just as bleak as yesterday," Nikos observed dryly. In the distance, above the sea of rooftops, he could see the many columns of smoke from the industrial plants on the outskirts of the city, mingling with the thick gray cloud cover. "I wonder what's the point of all this."

"A lot of people wonder that," Sönke agreed with him before Nikos realized he'd said the thought out loud.

"What do you mean?"

"What's the point of us rearming so heavily? If one thing has become clear, it is the fact that we have no chance whatsoever against the aliens. Their technology is indistinguishable from magic to us and plays on no horizon tangible to us in terms of physics, materials science, and engineering prowess. We are ants trying to mess with humans. We now produce over five thousand tanks a week in Europe and at least five times that many missiles. Don't even get me started on small arms and artillery. What are we going to do with that? Huh?" When Nikos didn't answer, Sönke continued unapologetically. "The aliens are up there, not down here, and whether we shoot at them with one howitzer or ten thousand when they land — it won't make the slightest bit of difference. But sometimes the direct route isn't the only route to victory."

"Victory?" asked Nikos incredulously.

"Well, let's say: Survival."

"Now I'm curious because I don't see a way and I'm the *alien expert* after all."

"Our allies..."

"You mean the Morphs?" Nikos snorted. "Since when do the boot and the ant form alliances?"

"Well, we need ants to maintain the ecosystem. It's not out of the question that the Morphs need us too, and that puts us in a good position."

"Sounds like wishful thinking."

"Oh, it was," Sönke admitted, grinning wolfishly. "But as it turns out, that's exactly what happened. They need us for something they can't do themselves, and you're part of it."

"What?"

"You will be one of those who forge the alliance."

"What, me? What alliance? Forging? What are you talking about?"

"I won't explain that to you, the General Staff will, and it will be at the Chancellery." The soldier from the Military Counterintelligence Service pressed a finger against the windowpane and pointed in the direction of the modern building on the right behind the Brandenburg Gate.

"You want me to forge an alliance?"

"Yes. Oh, and I'll be there too, alongside about forty thousand other men and women."

Nikos looked with tingling hands to the headquarters of the Federal Republic's power. "I swear to you, if I have to make one more appearance this week, then…"

"No, no, my big, bearded friend! Not only are you going to be part of a tour group, but you're going to get a new job."

"That's exactly what I've been wanting to hear for a month, and now that I hear it, it scares me," Nikos muttered glumly, not taking his eyes off the Chancellery, which was little more than a cream-colored outline against the gray city.

"It should," Sönke said, and as Nikos eyed his friend suspiciously, any apparent nonchalance had drained from his features.

IT FELT good to be back in Calw. They had left the Graf Zeppelin barracks behind them that day to visit a place that shouldn't even exist: a pub. In the middle of the tranquil pedestrian zone of the small town in the heart of Baden Württemberg, which consisted mostly of old half-timbered houses that had survived the Second World War relatively unscathed, was the "Ratskeller." Jacek liked to think back to the days when every town had a Ratskeller, plus dozens of other restaurants and pubs where people went in and out, where they socialized. Not that he had ever had much time for it, but it had been a sight he had enjoyed every now and then.

The original Ratskeller had, of course, been shut down like all other catering establishments and barricaded with boards and iron chains. Public life was now almost non-existent, as every man and woman worked in some way for the new European superstate. It didn't exist formally, but it did exist factually, which meant that there were no corresponding laws and no regional Constitution, but everyone was in fact governed from Brussels. Jacek thought that was a good idea, as it was still the Council of Heads of Government, who were now de facto autocrats due to emergency laws, who were in charge. That made for short decision-making paths and quick reactions — both foreign words to politics until a few months ago. But what he found most useful was that children and young people were in school from early morning until late at night and, in addition to compulsory basic education, were taught mainly emergency procedures, first aid, handicrafts, and all sorts of useful things. This kept them off the streets where they could commit stupidities like he had done then. Besides, they learned something that could really help them.

There was an old cellar vault under the Ratskeller, accessible through a hatch in the barricaded former taproom, where the military police could not find it. Jacek had learned of this location through his attending physician, Colonel Ferdinand — along with the knock by which he could identify himself as a confidant. Ferdinand was certainly a drunk, that was certain, for the gray-haired fellow had smelled slightly sour every morning. But since he was obviously a social drinker, and had done a splendid job to boot, Jacek didn't even think of reporting him.

"Hey, are you brooding again?" Uffe snapped him out of his thoughts and he shook his head to clear it. The sharpshooter, as well as Hardy, Knut, and Pill, stared at him questioningly. They were sitting in a small seating area of the secret taproom, in the middle of which was the ladder that didn't exactly inspire confidence, leading up through the hatch, into the authoritative taproom. The ten tables that existed down here were filled with men and women in uniforms and those in the blue and gray coveralls of the various manufacturing lines. Although it was so crowded, the volume remained manageable and added to the impression that they were doing something forbidden, which was indeed the case.

Jacek let his gaze wander around the table. His team had already looked quite deep into their glasses and gotten rosy cheeks, but the big beer steins, which he had declared to be the last of the evening, were still well filled. They weren't even thinking of sneaking back to the barracks prematurely, and he could well understand them. The two months of hospital and rehab that had ended only the day before had tugged at all their nerves. They weren't made to be bedridden at first and then mothered all day and only do functional training like old grandpas and grandmas.

"Old grandpas and grandmas? That's a whole new sound," Knut laughed, his frozen grin looking even a little more crooked than usual. Jacek cringed a little when he realized that he had obviously spoken his thoughts out loud.

"He's right, though," Hardy grumbled. "I can't see all those walkers and TheraBands and yoga mats anymore. And if anyone tells me what rhythm to breathe in and out with one more time, I'm going to kill a small animal."

"A small animal?" asked Uffe with narrowed eyes. "What do you mean?"

"Well, a rabbit or something. Something cute."

"Why would you do that?"

"Well, because then that will shock someone?"

"Me, for instance. A rabbit didn't do anything to you, did it? If it did, please kill your therapist!" the sniper growled, and Hardy threw his hands in the air in surrender.

"Man! I'm still gonna..."

"If you kill a small animal, I'll kill myself. This time for real," Knut intervened and made a serious face.

"I wish you'd stop doing that," Pill cut in, rolling his eyes. "That's really disturbing. Why do you keep saying that?"

"I don't know." Knut shrugged with a grin. "At least the two small animal people shut up."

"Amen." Pill raised his massive pint glass and toasted his comrade.

"Anyway, I'm glad we got it all over with," Jacek said, slurping the froth off his glass. "The hard part's still to come, but I'd still rather have that than rotting uselessly in rehab while everyone around us rehearses for the real thing."

"What do you mean?" Hardy wanted to know.

"Well, something's coming. We were released from rehab a week early. Sure, with round-the-clock therapy, progress can be made very quickly, but it's still unusual. The rapid changes due to politics, the massively ramped-up production volumes, and all the general's secrecy. I'm telling you, There's something brewing."

"Maybe it's connected to Scotland. They're the ones who supposedly took our captured Tear to where that Morph thing landed, right?"

"If this Bachara is to be believed, that's exactly what happened, yes." Jacek nodded thoughtfully and took another sip of his beer.

"I think it has something to do with the Shard that's stuck in the Athens Containment Zone."

Now all eyes turned to Pill, who shrugged and stared into his pint glass. "Heard that thing regenerates."

"Regenerates?" asked Hardy incredulously. "The thing's a scrap heap, isn't it? Yeah, a still twitching pile of junk with some real weird stuff going on around it, but a pile of junk."

"Of course, the wreck is broken, or it would have blown away long ago, I guess," Pill agreed with him, but didn't sound fully convinced. "But I hear that some of the holes have closed up. When I talked to Nikos on the phone yesterday, he told me that an acquaintance of his who works in the Greek military said that the hull crack he went through in the thing in January is gone now."

"Disappeared?"

"Yeah! I mean, that means this thing is somehow rebuilding itself. Maybe it sucks raw materials out of the ground and rebuilds itself, like nanites with some kind of material memory or something." Now Pill leaned forward, his voice taking on a conspiratorial undertone. "I'm telling you, this thing regenerates and flies off. What happens then, I don't even want to imagine."

"Do you know what else renews itself?" Knut wanted to know.

Pill sighed and gave a wave. "No, please tell me so you don't kill yourself."

"The foreskin."

"Seriously now?" Hardy snorted and rolled his eyes.

"Oh, come on," Pill chimed in, much to his colleague's frustration. "We're trying to have a conversation here."

"I read that in South Korea, the cells of freshly cut baby foreskins are used to make a serum that Hollywood stars use to rejuvenate their facial skin. The stuff is supposed to support collagen formation and elastic or something. Well, at least that's what they used."

"*Elastin*," Uffe corrected him.

"Yeah, because of me. Kate Beckinsale did it and Sandra Bullock did it. I think it's called Fibroblast, supposedly smells like semen, and it's done through little needles..."

"I'm trying to drink a beer right now!" scolded Hardy indignantly.

"Does that only go with baby boys' pelts?" Uffe wanted to know, bending over her tankard of beer with interest.

"Seriously?" asked Pill, staring at the sniper, shaking her head.

"She's encouraging him too." Hardy lowered his head to the table.

"Where are you going with this disgusting shit anyway?" asked Pill, turning to Knut and making a face as if he already regretted the question.

"One, that you shouldn't cut the fur off little babies, and two, that just because something can regenerate doesn't mean it's going to fly away afterwards."

"He's right. All this speculation about the Shard is pointless. Strange things are happening in all the containment zones in Europe. Sometimes it's a glow in the night, sometimes it's a weather phenomenon, sometimes a small town nearby loses all its power. Wrecks or not, whatever comes from the aliens remains active in some way. In ways, mind you, that not even our brightest minds can comprehend. Maybe the thing in Athens will fly away eventually, maybe not. Knut brought up a good point, albeit a disgusting one, that inferences are useless if they are made by us. Since we don't know anything anyway, it all remains speculation, and it may well be that there is simply an automatic regeneration program going on, much like a — no, Knut, I'm not saying *foreskin* now — human body. That's what normal cells do," Jacek explained to end the discussion. He had already experienced many evenings where his team had gotten bogged down in seemingly pointless discussions. More than once fists had almost flown, and he wanted to prevent that at all costs. It didn't do either of them any good to be without a weapon in their hands for so long and cut off from any adrenaline. They were usually on drills all year when they weren't currently deployed, and whenever one of them got injured, he could watch them slowly perish. That didn't give him much hope for after duty, but they could deal with problems like that when the time came. Chances were, after all, that none of them would live long enough to experience what life after service felt like.

"I just wanted to give an example where this mongrel at least listens to me," Knut grumbled sullenly.

"Have you heard of Rolling Thunder?" Hardy abruptly changed the subject.

"Rolling Thunder?" Uffe raised an eyebrow and half emptied her beer. After a suppressed belch, she shook her head. "Sounds like an AC/DC album I would have bought in a heartbeat."

"This is some big thing being cooked up in Switzerland. I'm telling you, there's something big coming. Maybe a backlash? We've got to do something with all this manufactured stuff," Hardy was undeterred and bent over the tabletop with a lowered voice. "I'll give you a letter and a seal that this is why we got out of rehab early. General mobilization! That's Rolling Thunder."

"Up your ass!" Uffe waved it off. "It's just another epically titled paper tiger from Brussels because they think it sounds like AC/DC and AC/DC is cool."

"I don't think a general mobilization is likely," Jacek interfered again, trying to bring some calm to the bunch. He could already see his comrades getting the next spat going, and he didn't fancy having to settle a full-blown argument just because they were bored. "I rather think it has something to do with the unexplained raids on military installations and black sites."

"Muggings?" asked Pill curiously.

"The major from B1 dropped something like that. Apparently, many of our comrades have been deployed all over Europe in the last six weeks as unknown persons have attacked secret hideouts and camps. Nothing was stolen or captured, but all the guards were either killed or disappeared without a trace, as if they never existed." Jacek raised a finger in admonishment. "You keep that to yourselves, though, all right? I don't fancy the major ending up in trouble and not telling me anything."

After they nodded one after the other, he relaxed a bit, knowing he could rely on their word one hundred percent.

"Do you know anything more specific?" Knut's permanent grin had faded a little and his eyes had narrowed to little slits.

"No, not really. Rumor has it that Russians or Chinese might be behind this. Word has certainly gotten out that we have our hands on alien tech and taken a prisoner. The EU propaganda machine, while not making this public, has hinted that we are making great strides. That will not have escaped the notice of foreign countries one way or another. However, that only explains some of the raids where our people have been found with bullet wounds and gunpowder residue. The cases where there weren't even bloodstains or the slightest traces that a guard was once on duty haven't been explained."

"Maybe those were Tears task forces trying to get their man back," Uffe thought aloud.

"It's possible, of course, though I'd be surprised that they know so much about us that they can raid black sites that even the regular troops or most of the Defense Department don't know about. There's something fishy about this."

"The Tears outnumber us so much that it's within the realm of possibility that they've X-rayed our entire fucking planet from top to bottom, and there's no secret left that they haven't revealed." Pill was sure, grunting contemptuously. "I'm sure we'll all get cancer from it soon."

"I'd look around before I..." put in Knut, but Pill silenced him with a raised index finger.

"Ah, ah, ah, friend, not again!"

"After all, if they could scan the entire planet, they wouldn't have to attack the very obviously wrong black sites," Jacek pointed out. "No, I think it's more that we don't know enough pieces of the puzzle yet to figure out the big picture. But the fact is that something is going on, and my guess is that's why we've been recalled."

"You may be right about that, Sergeant Major," a deep voice confirmed, causing Jacek to immediately freeze. It belonged to Major Brandt, the commander of their Command Company One.

"Shit," muttered Uffe, who had jumped up to take a stance like the rest of the team. If you were going to get caught, at least keep your back straight.

"Major, I take full responsibility for..." Jacek began, but Brandt made a gruff hand gesture, silencing him. The major was wearing civilian clothes, a dark jacket and tight denim pants, but his sparse fringe of hair and scarred face left no doubt that it was him.

"Save it, Sergeant Major." Brandt, without asking, pulled up a chair from the next table and sat down. "We live in crazy times, so I'll let you get away with a slip like that. Don't take it as a free pass, though. You know I always try to be fair, but don't like to repeat myself."

"Yes, Herr Major," they answered in chorus — but in hushed voices. Perhaps out of shame, because they had been caught like children doing something they shouldn't have been doing, but perhaps also so as not to alert the other guests that they had also been discovered. If word got out, the place would be shut down and they would be blamed.

"Good. You're going into the field tomorrow, and I strongly advise that after our conversation, you head to the barracks as soon as possible to get ready. Get as much sleep as you can; you're going to need it."

"With respect, Major," Uffe spoke up sullenly. "We've done almost nothing but sleep and Pilates for two months. We couldn't be more ready to kick some alien ass than we are right now."

"Alien asses, " the major growled with raised brows. "You disappoint me. I thought that, as commandos, you would be more realistic about the situation. We have no say in this war. You must have realized that."

"We captured one of them, after all, and destroyed one of their combat drones," she replied with her lower lip thrust forward defiantly, and Jacek hoped she would calm down and shut up soon.

"Oh yeah, I read the report. You shot down the drone after that anti-tech field took it out. I hope you carved a notch in your rifle for that heroic deed. And you pulled an unconscious alien out of his half-shot UFO," Brandt sneered, and Uffe's face turned a shade of red so dark, Jacek was beginning to fear she might explode at any moment. The others on his team were getting more tight-lipped too.

The major waited a moment, eyeing them in turn before a thin smile curled his lips.

"Look at you. Two months of rehab and you're nothing more than a bubbling barrel of gasoline. You're KSK soldiers, for crying out loud. You're not going to be rattled by a couple of provocations thrown your way!" their superior officer huffed, shaking his head. "You did a good job in the Congo and the entire barracks pays you respect. Make sure you earn it, and don't squander it with childish crap like this, understand?"

"Understood, Major," they replied again in chorus, and the faces that had been tinged with anger had turned pale, like those of teenagers who had just been shamed.

"I'm going to get up now and head back to the barracks. I want to see you in the briefing room in six hours. The Brigadier General himself will be leading the briefing and I want to be proud of my soldiers, do you understand?"

"Yes, Major."

"Good. I don't know what this is about — this thing is being negotiated at levels well above mine, so it's going to be something big. If one of you thinks you're not at a hundred percent yet, I expect an honest statement." The major looked at them in turn, scrutinizing, and nodded meaninglessly when no one responded. "All right, then. Don't disappoint me. I have a hunch that the weal and woe of us all may depend on it."

CHAPTER 3

NIKOS

NIKOS FOUND the drive to the Chancellery exceedingly lavish. An SUV in grey Bundeswehr livery with the EU's new defense emblem — the star-spangled banner with the stylized eagle holding a knife in its talons — picked up him and Sönke at the roadside. Nikos thought he recognized a former Nissan Pathfinder under the paintwork. In the old days, before all the vehicles had been confiscated and melted down, you would never have been able to get a parking space here, but now the street was deserted. The pavement was covered in old leaves, brittle through the winter and now muddy in the spring. No one cared about details like clean sidewalks anymore when murderous aliens were up in orbit doing their thing. Public life had fallen so silent and diminished that now little really mattered except surviving and somehow saving one's loved ones and species into the next day.

"You know the legend of the Sword of Damocles?" asked Nikos, not taking his eyes off the window as their driver sped up Friedrichstraße toward the Brandenburg Gate.

"The sword that hung on a rope over Dionysius?" speculated Sönke beside him.

"It was a horsehair."

"Excuse me?"

"The sword hung on a horsehair, and it hovered not over the tyrant Dionysius, but over Damocles. For he was not the one who had fastened the sword, but Dionysius, its ruler," Nikos explained thoughtfully.

"Oh, I didn't know that. I just know it's a metaphor for a seemingly comfortable situation where you overlook an imminent threat."

"That's not quite right either."

"Well, all the better that I have a genuine Greek sitting next to me as a colleague, and hopefully also as a friend. What does it really mean?" Sönke wanted to know and Nikos could almost hear him grinning.

"Damocles was a favorite of Dionysius of Syracuse, a king who may have lived around 400 BC. Damocles lived as a courtier in his court and envied his master's power and wealth. He flattered Dionysius to be near him, and if not to have power, at least to taste its flavor by his presence. When Dionysius realized this, because Damocles kept buttering him up about how great his wealth and power were, the king decided to teach him a lesson. He invited him to his table for the first time to revel in luxury with the princes but attached a sword to a horsehair directly above the young Damocles. The latter could no longer enjoy the opulence around him because he kept squinting upwards to see if the sword would come down on him. So, he could not enjoy the luxury and understood what Dionysius was trying to tell him: Power and wealth come at a price and are always threatened. They provide neither pleasure nor security, but bring dangers all their own."

"Sounds like a pretty wise king," Sönke agreed, nodding with pursed lips as Nikos looked at him, before looking out the window again and eyeing a group of children being led frantically along the sidewalk by two governesses as if every second outdoors meant imminent death. "But didn't you call Dionysius a bully?"

"Yes, he always oppressed his people and was unpopular, but he also wanted to use the lesson to convey to Damocles why he did it: namely, to protect himself. Everyday dangers of losing one's power tempts the powerful to protect it as best they can."

"Why are you even telling me this?"

"I don't know; my ancestors were wiser than me."

"You think it has something to do with the current situation."

Nikos squinted at the driver, a burly older sergeant with a green beret who didn't seem interested in them — or else was particularly good at acting.

"Possibly. The powers-that-be have secured absolute authority to do as they please. That's probably a good thing, keeping in mind the sword of Damocles of the two alien fleets in our solar system. Now the skies are clear, but they were at the turn of the year, then suddenly, they were there, laying waste to half our planet. I have such an inkling of what's about to befall me, and the more I pursue this conjecture in my mind, the more I feel like Damocles being summoned to court by Dionysius, only I'm standing in for all the other civilians."

"There are no more civilians, my dear," Sönke corrected him.

"Well, that's what worries me. What if we actually get through all this, a miracle happens, and we can fight our way free? Not that we could do it on our own." Nikos turned his head and looked at his new friend promptly. "Huh?"

"Then Earth is saved, and we can rebuild our civilization?" Sönke grimaced questioningly, as if he feared being scolded.

"How can that be when, for years, everyone wears a uniform and knows nothing but war and constant danger? How is it possible when art and science have stood still, to say nothing of social progress? Who will still find a painter meaningful or recognize the touching value of a poem or good literature if all that has ceased to matter? *It is not the beautiful, the human that has brought us victory, but cold weapons,* it will then be said. Perhaps artists will even be ostracized?"

"I think you're painting a pretty bleak picture." The soldier sighed, shaking his head.

"Yes, I am, but someone has to do it so we don't make serious mistakes that can't be undone. A large number of weapons that are no longer needed have a habit of being used again soon. As it was after the collapse of the Soviet Union. All those tanks and firearms went to crisis regions that have since been shaken by crises even more brutal than those before," Nikos continued, but Sönke raised a finger in warning.

"It's not comparable because those crisis regions may no longer exist. Thanks to the aliens, by the way. We all have a common goal now that unites us as never before in the history of mankind: namely, the survival of us all. And what you say about science is not entirely true. The new EUSFOR has a budget of specialist personnel and material allocations that would have been considered unimaginable before the war."

"European Science Force?" Nikos snorted contemptuously. "Not only does that sound stupidly martial, they also do research exclusively in one direction: military, military, military."

"Yes, but World War II also saw huge leaps in technology due to military research. Jets, rockets, nuclear energy, materials science, chemistry..."

"Nuclear weapons, breakthroughs in medicine through bestial *research on* Jewish concentration camp prisoners..." Nikos interrupted him, and Sönke put on an offended expression.

"Hey, I didn't say everything went perfectly, but it's not like this compares to World War II."

"I'm just saying that when you march tightly in one direction, you quickly lose sight of alternatives to the right and left of the path, and in the case of our current direction as a species, I think that's a great danger," Nikos opined, feeling a knot of oppression forming in his stomach and growing heavier.

"You may be right about that, but I don't think we have an alternative. Not with these war-mongering aliens in our front yard." Sönke sighed as the car pulled up in front of the Chancellery and the driver rolled down his window to show his ID. All the doors were opened and soldiers with dogs examined the car and its occupants. Since they already knew this procedure from other places, Nikos continued talking.

"I know I don't see a better alternative myself and that's what worries me so much. If you have no leeway to make decisions, others will make them for you." Before Sönke could answer, the doors were closed again and they were waved through into a garage that led directly under the Chancellery and was not visible from the outside. Once in the basement, the doors were opened again and four soldiers in black combat fatigues and hooded faces led them with quick steps across the small parking deck where only armored military vehicles with government identification were parked. Limousines no longer existed; they obviously wanted to send a signal that even the suits in the capitals were now part of the military, though of course that was factually incorrect. They were still technocrats, juggling numbers and dates, except that they were from the former civilian society, which was certainly a thorn in the side of many a general.

The soldiers led him and Sönke into an elevator and got in with them. It descended quickly after the heavy doors closed, and no one said a word. To Nikos, the hooded soldiers, all nearly as tall as him, were an unpleasant threat, though he knew they were not his enemies. He had never felt comfortable being surrounded by weapons.

When the elevator finally chirped and the doors moved aside, a young woman with a brown ponytail and big horn-rimmed glasses was already waiting for them, looking as dressed up as a mannequin in her flimsy camouflage uniform. She certainly wasn't a soldier, that was for sure.

"Hello, gentlemen, I'm Susanne, one of Chancellor Leopold's personal assistants. If you'll follow me, please?" The young woman greeted them with a rehearsed smile and pressed the clipboard to her chest. She went ahead and then pointed to the left. Nikos nodded at her and followed Sönke down a narrow hallway with doors leading off at regular intervals. The cold LED light from the overhead spotlights created a ghostly mood and made his tanned skin look oddly colorless.

"Next door on the right, please," the assistant in front of them said, stopping at a gray door with a code lock, but one that stood ajar. A muffled conversation could be heard from inside. "There you go, go in."

Sönke obeyed and pushed the door open. Nikos followed him with the same sinking feeling in his stomach that had been with him since they left his apartment. The room they were led into was windowless and gloomy. A single oval table was lit by cool spotlights in the ceiling, as well as a large display wall on the opposite side, on which the eagle crest of the Federal Republic of Germany was embedded in the European star-spangled banner, rotating leisurely against a black background. There were only four people present: two wore baggy uniforms and hung in their chairs more than they sat, and the other two were Chancellor Günther Leopold and a high-ranking military man with plenty of tinsel on his chest and epaulets. Together with the short-cropped grey hair and the downright professorial narrow glasses, all the clues could probably be summed up by the title "General."

"Ah, here are our last guests," the Chancellor rejoiced and got up from his seat, whereupon the rest of those present did likewise. Leopold came around the table and shook hands first with Nikos and then with Sönke, who stiffened a little. Unlike Nikos, his friend from the Abschirmdienst had not yet met his head of government in person.

"Hello, Nikos, are you alright? How's the arm?" Leopold asked and smiled chummily before waving him closer and pointing to an empty seat next to the two uniformed men — a man and a woman, he now realized.

"Thank you, I am already feeling much better than I did in the hospital when you visited me. Thank you again for this honor," Nikos thanked him artfully and walked toward the offered chair next to the two obviously reluctant civilians in uniforms.

"Ah, the honor was all mine. It's not often that a foreign citizen takes the fall for me and the entire continent. You're a hero whether you like it or not." Leopold paused and seemed to think. "Yes, you most certainly are, and I can see in your face that you're already protesting and trying to talk this down again. But you won't get away with it this time." The Chancellor winked in apparent amusement and returned to his chair. "Well, the reason you're here is also directly related to your exploits in the Congo. It's something of a delayed gratification, if you will." Leopold looked at Sönke, who still remained in a guarded position in front of the table. "Ah, you may step away, Captain Teunen. Thank you very much."

Sönke saluted briskly and paused in irritation when Nikos cleared his throat.

"Um, Chancellor," he spoke up in English. "Sönke Teunen has been a great support to me over the last few weeks.

Honestly, I wouldn't have made it through all this hoopla without him. If this is about something you want me to do, it would be a very great help to me if he would continue to be responsible for me."

Leopold was silent for a moment, looking thoughtfully back and forth between him and Sönke, while the general raised an eyebrow critically. Sönke seemed visibly uncomfortable and avoided eye contact with anyone in the room, staring at the floor. Finally, Leopold clapped his hands and Nikos startled at the sudden volume amidst the slightly tense silence.

"You are a hero; how can I refuse you anything? If Inspector General Werhahn has no other pressing obligations for his officer..." Leopold looked to the highly decorated commander-in-chief of the German Armed Forces and waited for his nod before fixing his eyes on Sönke. "You must realize that if you stay here and listen, you will no longer have any decision whatsoever as to whether or not to participate in what we are discussing here?"

"I understand, Chancellor," Sönke assured the politician, nodding as Leopold gestured for him to take one of the chairs pushed up against the wall.

"Good, then we're ready to go." The Chancellor pointed to his seatmate, the portly general. "That's Inspector General Werhahn, as you probably know, and next to you," he pointed to the two civilians in disguise, a young man with freckles and sassy curls and a woman in her forties with shoulder-length blond hair who smiled politely at him, "sit Rooney Schneidfelder and Karin Getzsch. Mr. Schneidfelder was previously a cameraman for ARD and Ms. Getzsch a reporter. The two are a well-rehearsed team and will be your faithful companions for the next few days."

Nikos' eyes widened as he looked at his seatmates with a whole new look. A camera crew? Had he been wrong after all, and it was just another round of staged PR gigs to extract cash from people and mobilize them for war?

"By being able to bring in a prisoner from the Congo, dear Nikos, which we would never have dared hope in our wildest dreams, our diplomats in Scotland were able to make a major breakthrough in negotiations with the Morphs." Leopold sounded excited now, smiling expectantly as he leaned over the table like a vulture and raised his eyebrows. When Nikos finally opened his mouth, his expression darkened a little.

"I would like to emphasize that I did not accomplish this alone, Chancellor. On the contrary, I was rather a follower and I see hardly any reason that I would have been particularly helpful. Jacek and..."

"Oh, Nikos, you know we can't talk about that." Leopold smiled conciliatorily, but his voice had taken on a sharp tone as his eyes twitched briefly to the two former journalists.

"Yeah, I'm sorry." Nikos sighed.

"Oh, bygones!" The politician immediately seemed in high spirits again. "In any case, you played a part in making sure we had something viable to offer the Morphs! You helped make us no longer mere ants, but respected negotiators, and that should be appreciated."

"There's no need for that," Nikos quickly assured his counterpart, striving for a disarming smile. Before his appointment as a European integration and motivational figure for the masses, the Chancellor had sounded similarly enthusiastic, hyping it all up as a wonderful reward for his services. If that was what a reward looked like, he was happy to forgo any more. Others might like being in the limelight; he certainly didn't.

"Oh, you haven't heard what it's all about." Leopold winked at him and gave the Inspector General a wave.

"You will be one of the first humans to set foot on an alien planet," the veteran general with the four stars on his epaulets stated succinctly, and Nikos nodded casually before realizing the significance of his words, and gasped.

"Excuse me?"

"More specifically, you will be traveling to planet P3X-888, commonly referred to in the force as *Planet X*, as part of a military operation codenamed *Rolling Thunder*." The Inspector General picked up a remote control and pointed it at the display wall. As if controlled by a puppeteer, all the faces at the table turned. A representation of the Milky Way appeared. The spiral arms rotated seemingly inertly around the black hole at the heart of the galaxy until the image stopped and a blue dot was marked in one of the spiral arms.

"That's Earth," Werhahn commented on the image, and a second dot — this time in red — appeared on the display, opposite the massive center of the Milky Way on another spiral arm. "That's P3X-888, the target location of Operation Rolling Thunder."

"Sir," Nikos said in English with a dry mouth, and had to swallow before he could continue. "You're not kidding, are you?"

"No," the old soldier replied gravely, frowning as if he didn't understand the question.

"But... how is that even possible?" Nikos looked at Sönke, who, however, was staring at the huge statue with widened eyes, then at the two journalists, who were sitting there with their mouths open and also seemed unresponsive.

"Through a wormhole," Werhahn explained, and pressed another button, whereupon camera shots of an almost unreal environment ran across the wall. They showed a forest landscape in which huge mushrooms and oversized tree trunks grew, their leaves looking strangely jagged and dark. The daylight possessed a striking yellow tinge. "It's in a secret tunnel in Switzerland."

"A wormhole?" Sönke finally joined the conversation. "Since when do we have such technological possibilities?"

"We didn't." It was Leopold who spoke now. "But the Morphs have, and they have agreed to open such a wormhole to Planet X for us."

It didn't escape Nikos' notice that the general snorted disapprovingly at the name *Planet X*.

"That means the negotiations with the aliens were successful?" asked Nikos incredulously. "I thought communication was impossible until now?"

"It was too. Or at least difficult. But Colonel Bachara has assured me that it was accomplished by means of some mathematical constellation." The Chancellor raised his hands in surrender. "Don't ask me, but it's worked since the Morphs have gone out of their way to return communication attempts, and for that," he paused briefly and pointed a finger at Nikos, "we have you to thank. As soon as we brought the prisoner into play, all of a sudden, there has been progress. Now it looks like the first fencer in the forest is taking the ants seriously for the first time." Leopold grinned triumphantly and propped his elbows on the back of his chair to place his fingers together in front of his mouth.

"I still don't understand," Nikos confessed. The knot in his gut was now big enough to feel like he'd swallowed a medicine ball — a medicine ball that kept growing.

"As it turns out, P3X-888," the Inspector General gave the Chancellor a quick sideways glance, "is a world allied with the Tears, mining a particularly important raw material that is of critical strategic value to the Tears' war machine. However, there is a sort of anti-technology sphere there, like the one you found in the Congo on a small scale. It makes it impossible for the Morphs to penetrate there and cut off supplies."

"They want us to do it for them, with our primitive chemically powered weapons," Sönke speculated aloud.

"They want to use our special position to cut off the Tears' supply of the rare ore mined there by the Tears' allies," Werhahn corrected him with a warning look.

"And that's exactly what we're going to do," Leopold gloated. "Because in doing so, the Morphs have not only made us an offer of alliance, but they have promised us two things in return. One is a transfer of technology. For the time being, only in the fields of medicine and materials science, but that would be a huge step forward. The debris is piling up in the EUSFOR camps, and yet we still have no clue what we're dealing with. All those aliens could be mages, and we'd believe them. The drone you brought back from the Congo has shed some light, but not as much as we'd hoped. Maybe there hasn't been enough time since then either, but if there's one thing we don't have, it's time."

"And what's the second?"

Leopold looked questioningly at Nikos, then nodded in understanding. "The second thing they promised us is... well, a little delicate. We made a mistake that they won't hold us accountable for, for now; let's put it that way."

"So that means we're supposed to attack a planet that's on the other side of the Milky Way on behalf of the Morphs?"

"We're cutting off the Tears' supply," Leopold corrected him with an indulgent smile.

Politicians, Nikos thought and would have liked to grunt in frustration, but at the last moment, he was able to force himself to present a neutral expression. *They can wrap everything up in beautiful words.*

"But, sir, we don't know anything about these aliens we're supposed to be attacking? We don't know the first thing about the Morphs and Tears, the reason for their conflict, or their motivations. With that, you're going to take sides, is that..." Nikos tried to pre-sort his words in his head so that they sounded polite and careful but didn't know exactly how to go about it. "Isn't that a little unwise? We don't even know what horse we're betting on, do we? No, we don't even know what the horse race is."

"I understand your concern, Nikos. But then, you are not fully in the picture on this matter, and I can assure you that we have reviewed all the information and made a decision in several committees. It was not only the best way out of our dilemma of helplessness, but the only way."

Nikos exchanged a glance with Sönke and could see that his friend was also thinking about their conversation before they reached the parking garage. *When you have no alternatives, others decide for you.* Since the Chancellor's firm expression left no doubt that this little question session was over and Nikos had used up all his hero credit, he merely nodded.

"I understand, sir."

"Very well. You'll accompany the first two European space divisions assembled specifically for this mission and assist the staff on the ground as an alien expert."

I'm not an alien expert, Nikos wanted to protest, but he had already experienced often enough what effect that would have: None at all, except that he was praised as being particularly modest.

"But, Chancellor, I am a civilian. For a war zone, I am not..."

"Oh, you're being modest again, Nikos." Günther Leopold shook his head as if he were lovingly scolding a child. "You did two years of military service in Greece before you went to college. I read your record, which I got from Thessaloniki."

"That was a long time ago, and I wasn't particularly..."

"Oh, fiddle-dee-dee, you're a hero, a soldier, *and* a civilian. If anyone can explain to the folks back home what a heroic effort our men and women are making hundreds of light years away, it's you!"

Nikos turned his head to the two journalists, who were looking at him at least as much as he was looking at them. Apparently, he wasn't the only one who had come to this meeting completely clueless.

So that's what this is all about. I'm supposed to be there as the familiar TV face when our soldiers invade a hostile world and show everyone how heroic it all is. The thought of what that really meant made him dizzy all at once.

CHAPTER 4

JACEK

JACEK HAD BEEN SITTING in silence with Uffe, Knut, Hardy and Pill in the briefing room of their barracks for a while, when the door finally opened and they scooted up from their uncomfortable wooden chairs. Brigadier General Georg Driedler, commander of the Special Forces Command, rushed past them to the small lectern in front of the screen with a sizable stack of files under his arm and, with an absent nod of his head, motioned for them to take their seats.

Jacek found that he had aged considerably in the last few months. Deep crow's feet furrowed the skin around his eyes and the gray hairs on his short-shaven skull were not only more numerous, but also thinner.

"Glad to see you're sober," the general said without looking up as he arranged his papers and turned on the projector.

Uniforms rustled as his team lolled about uncomfortably. Jacek wondered if their commander really knew about their excursion or was merely throwing an innuendo into the room to infer something from their reaction. If the latter was the case, they had already revealed enough to him. He decided to remain silent.

"As you can probably guess, I took you out of rehab early, not because I wanted to spare you further vegetation, but because I need you. You proved in the Congo how far you're willing to go for your homeland, and even if your reports read like a pure accumulation of coincidences..." Driedler paused and smiled thinly. "I am of the opinion that coincidence is what comes to us by virtue of being so. So, you have my trust." He looked Jacek straight in the eye for the last words. "You have earned it. But you shouldn't use that trust to hang garlands on your balls; you should use it to worry. Because when I trust a team, it's like having the sharpest knife in the drawer: I like to use it on everything, but I'm safest using it on the hardest shells I can find. One such very hard coconut has now come our way."

"Are we going to kick the aliens' asses?" gloated Uffe, raising her hands when Jacek gave her a hard look. "What?"

"No, you aren't."

"But I've heard that there's going to be an operation against the aliens that..."

"I don't know," Driedler interrupted her sternly, "where you got your classified information, Private, but I advise you to shut up now or I'll invite you into my office and then we'll see how long it takes you to reveal your sources."

To Jacek's relief, Uffe actually remained silent, though her eyes blazed with anger. How such a temperamental woman had made it through the selection tests was a mystery to him until now. Or rather, it was a mystery to him how she could control her temper like a robot time and time again, especially in crisis situations, but fail that control in more unimportant situations.

"Good. You're being transferred to Russia."

"What?" Hardy burst out. "To Russia?"

"Right," the general confirmed and pressed a button on his remote, revealing a satellite image showing a bird's eye view of a snow-covered landscape. In the middle of a seemingly endless forest were two helipads, a hangar, and a boxy building. Jacek thought he could also make out thin lines that appeared to represent fences. "This is a former Soviet nuclear missile silo near Angoya, north of Lake Baikal. The Russians stole something from us that we want back."

"The Russians?" It was Hardy again, who could not conceal his curiosity. "I thought they didn't exist anymore."

"Apparently, they do. They evidently coped well enough with the shower of debris from Voronezh, despite large civilian casualties, to still be able to conduct targeted espionage and commando operations in Europe."

"Baikal," Jacek thought aloud. "Isn't the entire lake and the area around it a containment zone? Isn't there a huge wreck that crashed into the lake and contaminated the entire area?"

"That is also correct," Driedler confirmed. "Apparently, the Russians thought this was a particularly good place to hide. If we hadn't gotten a little help from the Morphs, our satellites wouldn't have seen anything there either."

"Help from the Morphs?" asked Knut, his perma-grin now looking more like the sad-faced smile of a Pierrot.

"Yes. They helped us recalibrate our infrared telescopes to compensate for the strange interference from the containment zone. Don't ask me how."

"Since when do the Morphs help us?" Uffe wanted to know.

"Since we made a declaration of intent for an alliance with them," Driedler said tersely, and Jacek sat up a little straighter. He exchanged a few glances with his comrades and cleared his throat.

"General... an alliance?"

"Yes. Our diplomats in Scotland have apparently made a breakthrough in their attempts to communicate with the aliens, and it looks like we're siding with them in return for their protection from the Tears and, of course, the promise that they'll try to keep all fighting off our planet and provide us with a technological aid or two." Driedler showed a new image over the beamer, showing a Morph standing in front of a figure in a chemical suit with an oxygen tank, whom they all knew as Henry Wilson. In the image, they were apparently in a dark room with no outlines or obvious light sources. The Morph reminded Jacek of an octopus with countless tentacles, or rather, legs that looked like intertwined cables. The relatively small torso at the end of the many tentacles, which constantly changed shape, length, and form as they moved and had given them the nickname *Morphs,* looked like a mouth torn open into a silent scream with the eerie opening at the front. More tentacled tubes extended from this torso-head structure like oversized dreadlocks that seemed to rigidly defy gravity. The alien was at least three heads taller than Wilson and looked like it had come straight out of a horror movie.

"This is one of Mr. Wilson's negotiators and he would like a gift back that we gave them." Driedler pressed a button again and a pure white humanoid figure with a slightly too small head made of a formless hard mass was visible on a stretcher.

"That's our ET!" shouted Uffe indignantly, leaning forward. "Our fucking alien from the Congo!"

"Yes, that is the prisoner you extracted," the general confirmed, nodding. "Thanks to the prisoner, we had something to offer the Morphs, which was apparently enough to get them to pay attention to us and respond to our attempts at communication. We don't know why, but we can assume that the Tear who landed in the Congo and tried to install that anti-technology field has some special significance to the Morphs."

"Were they able to tell our people *exactly* what this Tear was up to in the Congo? I mean the anti-tech field is all well and good, but *why*?" Pill wanted to know, making his presence known for the first time after having remained silent until now.

"Not that I know of. What we can tell from your reports is that the prisoner certainly wasn't acting in the best interests of his species, or they wouldn't have tried to shoot him out of the jungle. We need answers to questions like this, but to do that, we need our prisoner back." Driedler paused for a moment. "Or rather, the Morph's prisoner."

"Don't tell me the Russians stole it," Hardy growled.

"I'm afraid that's exactly what happened." Driedler pressed his remote again and a grainy video played without sound. It showed an explosion in false color and then a vaguely discernible group of dark-clad commando soldiers that Jacek recognized by their running image. They held a long stretcher and disappeared into a dense patch of woods, while explosions — also in false colors — flashed further back. "A Russian commando team was able to take control of the prisoner two weeks ago. Apparently, they had infiltrated some key areas of Operation Overlord, thus taking control of the alien. Fortunately, we were able to unmask one of their spies, and Military Counterintelligence is currently investigating further. From the looks of it, they haven't been able to find the transmitter the Morphs planted in the prisoner's suit. The signal didn't disappear until they arrived at the containment zone at Lake Baikal. That's where Recon suspects the alien's location is in this old nuclear weapons silo."

"Why don't you send a whole airborne division?" Uffe wanted to know.

"Because Russia still has a nuclear arsenal ten times the size of the European Union," Driedler replied tersely. "We can't risk a war with the Russians in the current situation, and they can't risk one with us."

"Politics," Hardy grumbled. "Both sides know what it's about, but you act normal so nobody has to make a mistake they regret."

"And instead, we send our special squads to fight the battle under the radar," the general surprisingly agreed with him, gritting his teeth. "But that's the way it is. You will be leading the operation. Assisting you will be Teams Four and Six from Company One. The air force will bring them in. Radar coverage of the airspace over the containment zone is spotty at worst, according to our recon. At best, it's almost nonexistent. They will jump in, extract the prisoner, and take him to the destroyed Ulan-Ude, where they will board a train that our engineers will pick up north of Ulan Bator. The train, should the pincer fighters get there as planned, and it is in as good condition as the satellite imagery suggests, will take them to Ulan Bator, where we will fly you out on a Luftwaffe A400M. The Mongolians have been informed of a relief shipment."

"What do we know about the containment zone we'll be operating in?" asked Jacek quietly. Going to Russia didn't appeal to him because, even in training, he had hated the cold far more than the heat of the jungle or the desert. In April, it could still be sub-zero there, in the double digits.

"It is one of the largest in the world — at least of those we have marked. Large chunks of water from Lake Baikal burst its banks in a huge tsunami when the debris crashed, forming new lakes in the surrounding area that have since frozen over. The water level is believed to have dropped significantly, destroying the surrounding towns. Nothing is known of the wreck itself, as it is thought to have disappeared completely into the depths of the lake, which is still a kilometer and a half deep. There are mostly dense clouds over the immediate lake area and there is no longer any electricity. The silo you are to enter is probably supplied by Russian Army diesel generators."

"So effectively, we know next to nothing." Jacek summed up what he'd heard, nodding slowly.

Driedler shrugged. "No more than in the Congo."

He's right again, Jacek thought.

"Can we have our Greek back?" asked Uffe after a short pause.

"No. Nikos Antoniadis is deployed elsewhere. Sorry. Besides, he's a civilian. I didn't think you'd want to go back to babysitting so soon."

"Oh, he was all right."

"Once you've brought the prisoner back to me, I'll see what I can do, if Antoniadis is back on Earth by then."

"On Earth?" the sniper asked, puzzled. "Has the media frenzy caused him to take off enough to leave the gravity well yet?"

Driedler waved her question away with a gruff gesture. "Make sure the prisoner gets back, preferably alive and in one piece. This thing is making the entire leadership of the EU nervous and could cost us our alliance with the Morphs."

"One more question, General," Jacek spoke up again, as he couldn't get one thing out of his mind.

"Yes, Sergeant Major?"

"You've assigned us and two of our comrade teams. Why are only German special forces involved? That's highly unusual if I may say."

"You may. The Chancellor in particular, and the Ministry of Defense in general, are extremely incensed by the fact that the British refused to involve us in the protective measures for the prisoner after it was we who extracted him in the first place. Now the Chancellor apparently has no intention of repeating the mistake. He wants our prisoner to *remain* our prisoner this time."

"Are the intrigues in the new Union starting so soon?" grumbled Hardy sullenly. "Well, it was pretty quick."

"Do you know what the hardest part of a soldier's life is,

Sergeant?" demanded Driedler, fixing the telecommunicator with a penetrating stare.

"Rehab," he immediately replied and the others chuckled. Jacek left it at an amused smile, as his thoughts were already mostly about their mission.

"That we have no say in politics. We know what it's like on the ground and what the burning issues are at a flashpoint of conflict that no politician will ever see, even though he or she makes the decisions that cost, among other things, our lives at worst. It's unfair, but the world is simply an unfair place." The general paused for a moment, and a barely perceptible smile played around his thin, wrinkled lips, which seemed to have lost all red decades ago. Raising his palms expectantly, he continued, "No decision in a complex world like this is ever simple, and we are in a position that does not allow us to make decisions beyond purely operational issues. We follow orders, that's all. I, for one, consider that a great relief."

"I guess you're right," Hardy agreed, tapping his epaulet. "That's why you have an asterisk on your shoulder and I have an arrow."

"If you keep connecting all the dots like that, you may get a star on your epaulet too."

The others laughed again and even louder when Driedler added, "But I don't think you'll live past ninety."

"When do we leave?" asked Jacek into the general merriment, which he knew was not fueled by real amusement at all, but by overtiredness and a touch of nervousness. From his team, he knew such behavior, and it was typical of soldiers, whether in the special forces or the regular force. From Brigadier General Driedler, however, he was not familiar with this behavior. It could only mean that there must be a lot at stake for him personally, or that he was worried — which worried Jacek even more —

about Earth, should they not bring back the prisoner and thus appease the Morphs.

"Tonight, you will be flown by helicopter to Pforzheim, where you will be flown out by an A400M with their escort teams. Teams Four and Six are currently being briefed in tandem. They will take over the tasks of insertion and extraction and will be on standby in case you call for reinforcements. You bring that prisoner back to me, do you understand?"

"Understood, General," Jacek assured him.

"And no tracks."

"No leads."

"Do you have any questions?"

"Pforzheim was a Yankee airfield, wasn't it?" Uffe spoke up. "We're not being flown by a Yankee, are we?"

"As you well know, the US soldiers stationed in Germany, along with their equipment, were integrated into the Bundeswehr after the collapse of the US. So if one of your pilots is American, that's just as good for us as if he'd been trained in a decent army, got it?" Driedler didn't bat an eyelid as his soldiers chuckled.

"What about the recon data?" Jacek pointed to the satellite image that was back on the screen.

"You get everything on your tablets. You'll have plenty of time to study everything on the flight. We know from our informant that most of the silos were built four stories underground with readiness crew quarters. There's at least one radiation shelter, and we're assuming that's where the Russians are holding the prisoner."

"Do our informants and the analysts also assume that the guard force is very well trained and equipped, but the area is not extensively mined?" Jacek huffed, frowning as he looked at the downright tiny-looking building next to the two helipads. "No armored brigade lying in wait in the woods?"

"What are you getting at, Sergeant Major?" Driedler crossed his arms in front of his chest.

"All I'm saying is that we've snatched away arguably the most valuable object — or subject, as the case may be — on the planet. If I were Putin, I'd probably be presented with two strategies. Number one is to barricade the prisoner in the most secure place in Russia and post all the tanks, howitzers, and soldiers around so that no one would dare take him back. Number two is to get him somewhere stealthy and quiet. With number one, everyone knows where to look for the prisoner, but the hurdle to getting him is great. In number two, nobody knows where to look for him, but the hurdle to getting him is small. What I'm saying, General: are we really sure that the Russian president has decided on strategy number two?" Jacek looked at the satellite image one more time. Everything looked very peaceful and manageable in the whites and grays of the infrared image. Presumably, thanks to all the snow there, it looked about the same in the normal light spectrum.

Driedler seemed to be about to respond and sighed before tightening and nodding. "I understand your objections, Sergeant Major, but both recon and informant have assured the Army Staff that the number two strategy you mentioned is the most likely. Massive troop movements would certainly have been picked up by our spy satellites, and we should have been able to detect something on the infrared data as well. Everything points to the Russians trying to make the prisoner disappear as inconspicuous as possible. There's a containment zone. Hiding an armored division there would not only be almost inconceivable, but highly dangerous for the soldiers involved."

"With respect, General: they're Russians," Uffe objected from the side, and Jacek instinctively wanted to whistle her back, but in this case, he had to agree with her.

"If the Kremlin has managed the extraction of the prisoner,

it will also factor in that one of its people will be caught and questioned. And they will have prepared the whole thing for a long time," Jacek added.

"The Russians lost most of their oil reserves in the Voronezh disaster. Their infrastructure around Lake Baikal was mostly destroyed, and the earliest they could have known about the prisoner was two months ago, because you and your team didn't get him out of the Congo until then," Driedler explained matter-of-factly. "Don't be too paranoid. The Kremlin was forced to act quickly, and when that happens, you make mistakes."

"I hope you're right, General." Jacek sighed softly, rising to salute as Driedler stepped back from his desk.

"We only have this one shot, so don't screw it up. Everything is decided by the will!"

"All is decided by the will." They repeated the KSK motto in chorus and saluted as the general nodded with a serious face and left the room.

"I have a feeling that after the stunt here, the Congo thing will seem like a walk in the park to us." Uffe spoke the thoughts in her smoky voice, which made Jacek stare thoughtfully at the still image on the screen.

CHAPTER 5

"WHAT WOULD you say makes you an alien expert?" asked Karin Getzsch, and Rooney Schneidfelder panned his shoulder-mounted camera away from the ICE window and straight at his face like a gun.

"I'm not an alien expert," Nikos objected, doing his best to hide his discomfort.

"But you did survive the containment zone in Athens and entered the alien wreckage commonly referred to as *the Shard*. No one else survived that," the reporter objected, looking at him with interest as she kept taking notes on her tablet. He wished she would stop doing that, because every time her fingers touched the display, he felt judged, or at least analyzed.

"Yes, I survived it, but it is a common misconception that no one has ever gone in and out of the Sklithra. Few have made it, but some have," Nikos clarified. Catching himself staring into the yawning mouth of the camera pointed at him, he looked back at the blonde reporter. She'd spent the last few hours making him aware of proper camera behavior, and apparently, looking directly into the lens wasn't part of good interviewee 101. *Eyes to me, never at the camera,* she'd said. *It all had to be organic*. Whatever that meant. Anyway, nothing about any of this was normal. At least they both spoke very good English and misunderstandings didn't happen too often.

"Are there any other survivors today who can claim to have done what you did?"

"Yes," he said without thinking, biting his lip a moment later. *Matteo*. But Matteo had asked him not to talk to anyone about him before his inpatient psychiatric therapy in France. Since their last contact a month ago, a brief email, that hadn't changed. Apparently, he was getting better, slowly but surely, but he didn't seem to be comfortable with the hype surrounding Nikos' person, and he'd asked again not to talk about him to anyone.

Karin Getzsch had raised an eyebrow, indicating to him that she had probably asked something he hadn't heard.

"I'm the only one," he finally said with a sigh.

"Can you tell us anything about your experience inside the Shard?"

"No, I'm afraid that's classified. I'm not authorized..."

"You don't have to give details," the reporter insisted, keeping him hooked like a wriggling fish with her penetrating gaze. Nikos looked at Sönke, who was sitting next to him, but he merely shrugged and continued to go through the mission specifications that had been played on his tablet. The entire occupants of the former Deutsche Bahn express train, now full of military personnel and equipment, seemed to be doing nothing else. It was quiet as a graveyard, which didn't help his comfort level.

"It was very dangerous, I can tell you that. I was the only one who got out alive and there were four of us when we went in. Those pieces of debris, they... they..." Nikos searched for the right word. "They're alive, somehow. Everything around them seems to be changing and no longer obeying the laws of nature we're used to. It's really hard to describe. But what everyone should know is that the government's quarantine measures make sense. Anyone who goes into a containment zone against the military's prohibitions and warnings is not in danger of simply passing away, but dying in the most agonizing way possible. Believe me, this is not an exaggeration, rather the opposite!" He thought back to Giorgos, who had been amputated by a sunbeam that had stopped in time, and Eleni, who had been turned to mush by the strange analyzer at the heart of the Sklithra.

"You're not feeling well?"

"I... it... I'm fine," he retorted, trying to catch his breath as the brutal memories mingled with the realization that the two runners he had been pushed into the abyss with were emblematic of what he had continued to lose: his ex-wife Konstantina and his little boy, who had been killed by the alien debris on impact, their apartment having been near the Acropolis.

"Thank you for sharing your experience with us," the reporter said with mock gratitude. He could tell by her eyes that she was focused on her notes and already thinking of the next sentences.

"I'm glad to. But I'd like to..."

"What do you think of this expedition we're currently on?" she interjected, smiling as if he hadn't said anything.

"Excuse me?" he asked, perplexed. "I don't think we're allowed to talk about that, that's..."

"Oh, we're just recording and editing together a finished film after the expedition that takes our viewers right up close to the front lines. That won't air until it's been vetted and approved." The reporter shrugged. "We're just gathering footage, but I'm sure the EU Council will want to get it all out there as soon as possible so some whistleblower doesn't beat us to it."

"I understand," he grumbled.

"So, what do you think of the expedition?"

"First of all, I think the term *expedition* is a misleading euphemism. We are talking about a military offensive on an alien planet. I would have liked the first foot that a human set on a planet other than Earth to not be in a military boot," he replied bluntly, fueled by a subtle anger at his counterpart, who apparently didn't care about him in the slightest, but solely about the material she was hoping to get. He might as well provide her with ammunition. If she didn't like it, then she could delete it all again. He preferred that anyway. Noticing the surprised look on her face, he continued with even more motivation, "We've let ourselves get backed into a corner we can't get out of. We're threatened by two alien species that we're no more a match for than a mayfly is for an elephant, and now we're supposed to be a mayfly on behalf of one of the elephants draining the other elephant's water source. Not only do I wonder how we're supposed to do that, I wonder why."

"Clearly the Morphs need our help because they can't do it themselves." Getzsch dutifully repeated the Chancellor's words.

"I even believe that part, because otherwise there would be no reason whatsoever to rope us in and lure us with technological promises," he agreed with her, but shook his head at the same time, which obviously irritated her and made him happy, because she evidently wasn't as detached as she wanted to appear after all. Or else she had simply underestimated him. "However, I don't think it's a good idea to send two divisions of our soldiers into battle on an alien planet against a third alien faction we know absolutely nothing about."

"Well, there's recon data from both the Morphs and some drone and scout missions that have been conducted in the last few weeks," Sönke cut in, and the reporter gave her cameraman an impatient wave, whereupon he turned off the camera and shrugged it off on his lap.

"So, what did they find out?"

"Details on the ore mine we've been ordered to destroy. It seems to be pretty well guarded. There were also photos snapped of the aliens." Sönke held out his tablet to him and Nikos saw a humanoid figure with a squat build that, unlike a human, was not elongated but rather boxy with knobby arms and legs and a barrel-shaped torso. Even though the photo was washed out, he could clearly see that the creature must be wearing a suit, for the "skin" was bluish throughout and the face was hidden by a mirrored visor. What caught his eye the most, however, was the weapon the alien held in its hands: an elongated object that clearly had a handle and a muzzle, like a rifle, only significantly bulkier and more misshapen.

"What kind of suit is that?" The cameraman, Rooney, wanted to know.

"The atmosphere is toxic. Data could be obtained from the protective suits of the first reconnaissance teams from the Netherlands, Spain, and France, which detected elevated sulfur concentrations. The atmosphere in general is not that dissimilar to ours. The oxygen content of 22 percent is only slightly higher than ours but can already lead to increased oxidation in the body's cells. In addition, there is 71 percent nitrogen and 5 percent sulfur dioxide. Due to oxidation processes of the sulfur dioxide, the rain becomes acidic and affects the entire climate. If we had this concentration in the air, we would no longer go outside without breathing masks and full body protection. The flora seems to have adapted; otherwise, it wouldn't exist anymore, but animals have hardly been encountered by our teams. Besides, some scientists seem to agree that it's possible, based on geological measurements, that the natives are putting out a greenhouse effect like we're causing right now. Except that they are already experiencing much more severe consequences than we are. Possibly for several generations already, which would result in the aliens' immune systems degenerating as they become highly sensitive to bacteria and viruses of all kinds through constant use of air filters and protective suits."

"Wait, that would mean that even indoors they might be forced to wear those disguises?" Nikos frowned, trying to picture what that life might be like. It wasn't a scenario he liked to imagine.

"At least, unless all the rooms are kept sterile, which would be really elaborate and costly," Sönke said, taking the tablet back to his lap. "The General Staff's plan calls for a rapid advance on the target, to surprise the locals as much as possible and give them little time to mass forces. The mission is militarily very difficult because the native forces will know immediately what we are targeting. So, it's not about tactics. It's about speed, and that could become a problem since we're operating on unfamiliar ground."

"A Blitzkrieg, then," the reporter summarized, nodding as if she understood something.

"I don't think it compares," Nikos objected.

"Like this?"

"The term Blitzkrieg is commonly misused by civilians. The Nazi concept was to overrun Poland so quickly that it could not become a full-blown war. To do this, strategies based on reinforcing those formations that met the most resistance were jettisoned. Instead, motorized units were sent deep into enemy territory in large numbers to encircle and destroy the sites of greatest resistance as quickly as possible. The current plan of the General Staff looks more like that of Major General Erwin Rommel in the French campaign," Sönke answered in Nikos' place.

"Do you need to know this plan?" Rooney wanted to know

with a bored expression and turned back to Lake Constance rushing past her window.

"Should have. His 7th Armored Division was nicknamed the *Ghost Division* by the French because it broke through the Maginot Line — French defensive positions along the border with Germany — and moved into the French rear so quickly that it was not expected there and was completely duped. Not even Rommel's staff always knew where he was. Since our forces consist of artillery-supported armored formations with air support from Army aviators, a rapid advance is our greatest strength, especially since we know little about the strength of the enemy formations."

"What do we even know?" asked Nikos.

"We know from the Morphs, whose data is fifty-eight years old in our era, that Species X is divided into several factions that seem to share equally in the mining of this mysterious ore. We know that they do not need this ore themselves, but supply it to the Tears, who take it into orbit via a space elevator a hundred kilometers south of the mine at the planet's equator. We know that an anti-technology field makes the planet untouchable for Morphs and Tears, but it is of utmost strategic importance to both parties in conflict. We know that the natives have no air force, their planet is one and a half times Earth's gravity, and it is a so-called super-Earth. The light spectrum of their sun is about the same as ours, and the average temperature of their home is about eight degrees, much lower than ours."

"You always say *locals*," the reporter cut in again. "Don't you mean the *enemy?*"

"I agree with Nikos on one thing in particular," the soldier replied coolly. "The natives are our adversaries because of a strategic objective important to us. They have not, however, attacked us, nor do we know the slightest thing about them that could serve as a starting point for hostility. We *must* attack this species because our survival is at stake, and we will not succeed without the help of the Morphs. Even the Joint Chiefs have ordered that all units focus exclusively on the strategic target. We will bring an MOAB of the Americans from Ramstein there and far underground, where we suspect is a deep tunnel system, and blow up the mine. After that we will leave again and will try to cause as few casualties as possible."

"What's an MOAB?" The reporter nudged her cameraman, who jolted up as if from a dream and grumbled sullenly. "Watch it, this could be important!"

"MOAB stands for *Massive Ordnance Air Blast*," Sönke said. "The biggest conventional bomb there is. Since the Americans had some stored at Ramstein Air Base, we now have access."

"I wouldn't have put it past our politicians to command a nuclear strike either," Nikos grumbled, trying to bury the image of a massive explosion as first contact with an alien species deep inside himself. It was frustrating.

"That option was never on the table, as far as I know."

"Well, all the same."

"We're in Switzerland now," Schneidfelder stated with a suppressed yawn, as the next moment the ICE plunged into a long tunnel and the windows blackened. The sight of the sudden darkness, made rather more bizarre by the cold LED light of the train compartment, sent a shiver down Nikos' spine. It was as if it was now becoming concrete, as if he was only now understanding that this was all not a dream but was really taking place. They were being swallowed by the Swiss mountains and would soon step through a wormhole and reach an alien planet on the other side of the Milky Way to wage war on it.

At least the two journalists, with whom he had warmed so little despite the long drive, were silent the rest of the way.

They, too, seemed to slowly realize that even their background as war correspondents had not been able to prepare them for what they would encounter in the coming days. Perhaps they too were beginning to realize that this thing was not particularly exciting, but terribly scary and dangerous, highly morally questionable and at the same time without alternative — the worst possible combination of all factors, if you asked him. True, he was merely a former daycare director and involuntarily conscripted Greek who had hated every month of service at arms and spent most of his time working in the kitchen, but he knew when to run away. Only unfortunately, it seemed to become a habit that he kept getting thrown into situations he couldn't get out of without disappointing or leaving anyone hanging.

The ICE went via Winterthur and was diverted to the east, where the mountains rose ever higher beside them and one tunnel replaced another. Many peaks were shrouded in thick clouds, with white masses of snow looming beneath their blanket, making him feel cold even in the heated train. Then at some point an intrusive triad sounded booming through the loudspeakers, and suddenly all the soldiers in their compartment burst into a flurry of activity. When asked what was going on, Sönke replied that it was time to get dressed because they would reach their destination in thirty minutes.

Target in this case meant a secret base of the EU forces, which now included the Swiss units, as far as he knew. It consisted of some tunnels dug during the Second World War to protect themselves from the Nazis. Deep beneath the massive peaks of the three- and four-thousand-meter peaks of the western Alps, something that physicists would have dismissed as unthinkable or even impossible just a few months ago lay dormant in this relic of a dark time. A wormhole that ran right across the Milky Way. To distract himself, he took his prepared bag from the shelf above their heads and slipped into the lined functional clothing before pulling on the rubberized camouflage suit that had tight-fitting rubber rings on the hands, feet, and neck to connect his gloves and shoes, as well as the similarly coated balaclava and helmet to his breathing mask. According to Sönke, the micro-biotic life on the planet was not directly pathogenic, as far as initial medical examinations on the recon teams could tell. Still, Nikos couldn't shake the feeling that he was participating in one of humanity's greatest experiments by exposing himself — or rather, his skin — to this completely alien biosphere. But probably a severe fever would be the least of his worries after this mission, because then at least he would have survived.

I wish Jacek and the team were here, he thought as the train rolled into an underground station teeming with soldiers and came to a stop with squealing brakes. Heavily armed soldiers in combat fatigues and breathing masks were everywhere, hanging under their chins. Partly in chaotic confusion, partly in tight marching lines, they hurried across the narrow railway tracks between the roughly hewn rock walls, from which simple construction lamps hung down.

As they disembarked, Nikos became almost dizzy from the hurricane of sensory impressions that burst upon him. Barked orders, shouts, and conversations assaulted his ears from all directions, mingling with the unreal hall effects of the walls. Veritable crowds pushed to the right and left, but mostly to the right, where the wormhole was presumably located. Sönke steered them in that direction as well, past a platoon of soldiers waiting in line for their superior, and through a large archway at the end of the T-station that led into a massive cavern the size of a football field. There, a wide metal staircase brought them down with a barrage of soldiers shouting in confusion in several national languages. The large hall was already so crowded that

Nikos couldn't imagine how they were going to put one foot in front of the other there. Three rows of heavy Leopard 2 and Leclerc main battle tanks stood front to rear, with tightly packed rows of soldiers with full marching packs between them. Through more archways to the right and left of the cavern, Nikos could spot further approaches, behind which trucks, howitzers, and infantry fighting vehicles waited to be next. Inside their cavern, however, everything faced forward, where a wide, square passageway led into a tunnel so dark, he couldn't make anything out.

"What is that?" he shouted to Sönke over the rumble of heavy diesel engines and the shouts of soldiers. The captain looked at him and followed his gaze, then leaned over and yelled, "That tunnel is where the wormhole is! It's going in twenty minutes; I think we were the last ones because we came with the staff. We'll be the last to go through too!"

Nikos didn't know if he should see that as an advantage or a disadvantage. At least they wouldn't be the first, though he was ashamed of that thought, because it meant that others would have to face that danger instead of him. On the other hand, it meant that he would almost have to wet his pants for even longer at the idea of having to go into that dark tunnel soon.

CHAPTER 6

JACEK

"A FLIGHT TO RUSSIA; at least that's something new," Knut thought out loud with a wry grin, not pausing to pack the huge cargo bag. He was sitting on the wide loading platform of the A400M, which was pushing its way through Kazakhstan's airspace south of the Russian border. Attached to the many loading lugs in the floor were two large pallets of lashed-down mission boxes that his team had already been unpacking and repacking for several hours into the backpacks and bags that would jump out of the plane with them. Knut's cargo bag lay across the latter's lap, a behemoth speckled in winter camouflage colors that he would strap to his stomach before jumping. "Call to Arms" by the American band Manowar played over the speakers in the background, a ritual Uffe had instituted at some point that seemed to help the others focus. He liked it quiet, but he liked his team happy and focused even more, so he tuned out the noise.

"The job never gets boring," Jacek confirmed, taking a fourth magazine for his tactical G36 from the box between them to check each round. When he had done that, he took the next magazine, did the exact same thing, and taped both magazines to each other in reverse with armor tape so he could reload faster in combat. In his mind, he was still pondering the report he had received for his tablet during the last radio transmission. Operation Rolling Thunder — he finally knew what was behind it, and yet he wished he'd never known. The stakes were high, and he didn't want to be in the shoes of the commanding general, that much was certain.

"What do you think is in store for us?" Knut didn't look up from his packing efforts.

"A lot of well-trained guys from the Spetsnaz, I guess. Tough fellows, as you know."

"Yo," his comrade stated succinctly. "At least in the drills. But then, they were always in the desert. I bet they're like little peckers in the snow. Wrinkly and scared."

"Sure," Jacek replied wryly. "I think that's exactly how we should assess the Russians."

"If they do have it in them, then..."

"You kill yourself; I get it."

Knut shrugged. "It's not such a bad idea after all."

"You have nothing but bad ideas, buddy."

"Hey, at least I had the idea of keeping the ET we dragged out of the Congo. Look where it got us that we didn't."

"Um, you said, *He's cute, can I keep him?*"

"Yo." Knut flashed his crazy grin. "So, if you'd just said *yes, Knuterich*, just once, we wouldn't have to fly to the heavily armed shrinky-winkies now, would we?"

"Dude, you guys get left alone *once* and already you're talking about your tyke?" asked Uffe, who had come up beside them. Hands sternly on her hips, she stared down at the two of them like a stern mother. Seemingly disappointed, she shook her head.

"Actually, it was about..." Knut continued to explain, but

Uffe rolled his eyes and choked him off with a throwing away hand gesture.

"Save it, dude. I don't want to hear that you'll kill yourself either if we keep interrupting you." She turned to Jacek. "Plastic: yes or no?"

"Yeah, a little punch couldn't hurt," he replied thoughtfully. True, their escort teams, who were assembling their equipment further back in the turboprop's large cargo cabin, were intended for the very brute parts of the mission, but Jacek would rather have a little too much explosive than a little too little, if in doubt. "Since you ask, let's go over the jump and landing already." He stood up with cracking joints and clasped his hands together to avoid the inevitable shaking. "Guys, come here!"

After waving Pill and Hardy over from the other side of the pallet, they gathered in front of one of the large monitors mounted above the left row of seats that normally displayed the jump order of an entire platoon of paratroopers, along with current wind data and the time remaining until the jump. From his trouser pocket, he pulled out the USB stick with the data Driedler's adjutant had given him, and plugged it into the socket provided. Over his shoulder, he made sure that Uffe, Hardy, Knut, and Pill were standing behind him and had stopped their little squabbles. Only then did he open the prepared map file. It showed a satellite image of Lake Baikal and its surroundings. The northern and southern tips of the lake were free of clouds, as was the rest of the surrounding area, but a huge whirlwind could be seen over the center of the lake, its eye directly over the center of the frozen mass of water. The clouds made a grim contrast to the white surrounding countryside, the plains and mountains of Siberia with their endless forests smothered under the masses of snow.

"We're jumping in uncomfortably cold conditions, so expect a shortened freefall phase. We exit at twelve thousand feet, in three-second intervals. Standard exit; after stabilizing, we track ninety degrees to the jump run for twenty seconds. Got it?" Jacek looked at his comrades, who nodded in turn. "Good, it'll be dark, so keep an eye on each other's position lights. We'll form a loose line; keep contact. If one gets too far away, he'll come back. Minimum pull distance twenty meters. Pull altitude five hundred meters, so I don't want to see any stunts. We're jumping right over the eye of this storm, sixty kilometers from our destination. For the parachute ride, we're going to do left spirals and land on the ice, got it?"

"Sure."

"Yo."

"All right."

"One question, Joss." Knut raised his hand and grinned broadly.

"Yes?"

"Uh, the eye of this storm will surely be the alien wreckage, right? Is it really that smart to land directly on that thing?"

"No, but it's generally not wise to jump into a containment zone, but we have our orders, so the question doesn't arise," Jacek replied.

Knut raised his hand again.

"Yes?"

"But the drop is your call. Why don't we go down much further north, directly over the target area?"

"For two reasons. First, long-range reconnaissance assumes that immediately above the wreckage the Russians' radar coverage is faulty, if it's still working at all over a wide area. Second, we don't know anything about wind speeds in the storm that's raging. If we get into the transition zone between high and low pressure and the chutes pull us into the storm front, we have a very real problem, while we don't know what it's like directly over the wreck," Jacek explained patiently. "The real risk is too great for me. There's a third point: as far as we know, the wrecked spaceship sank in the lake; the thing is really deep. I don't think we should expect any major effects like we had in Athens."

"There's no wind in the eye of the storm," Hardy said, rubbing his broad chin with his worn combat gloves. "Besides, I've never done this before, and I can't say that about myself very often. Sounds good to me."

"Sounds awful," Pill objected sternly, sighing. "But I guess that's what we're going to do. How much time do you plan to spend marching to the finish?"

"With the three buggies?" Jacek looked at the three off-road buggies moored to the ground at the end of the loading dock that KSK Team Four was currently tampering with. "One day. We change drivers every four hours."

"Do you think a round cap will be sufficient to drop the pieces with pinpoint accuracy into the eye of the storm?" Hardy sounded exceedingly doubtful.

"I don't know, but the eye is six kilometers in diameter, so that should be doable if the pilots don't get too carried away with the drop."

"There's one more thing I'm wondering," Uffe spoke up, running her fingers through the longer blonde hair she'd shaved down one side to above her ears. She still looked downright fragile, but also a touch wilder than usual, which suited her character better, he thought. "If the wreck sank into Lake Baikal, why is there still such a freak weather phenomenon as in Athens on the one hand, and radar interference in the vicinity on the other? After all, that would mean that the effects don't differ much between wrecks on the surface or underwater — but that's exactly what remote reconnaissance wants us to believe."

"Yeah," he admitted, nodding reluctantly. "Either way, though, we'd have to land in the containment zone, and we don't know what to expect. That makes it all the more important that we land in one piece, and paradoxically, the quiet center of the storm is the safest place to do that."

"All right," she said with a shrug. "Won't be boring at least, I guess."

"Jump order: Hardy, Pill, Knut, Uffe, me. Check your ammo, check your weapon safeties, and don't forget your buddy check. Not today!"

They nodded and he briefly watched them disperse and get back to their equipment. He picked up his outdoor tablet and checked once more that he had updated all mission, GPS, and map data to the latest version. Once he was sure of that, he glanced again at the map that filled the screen. The storm looked threatening, but the red dot north of the lake gave him more unease. What had the Russians prepared there, and what were they doing with the captured alien? Part of him was angry that the Kremlin had taken something from them that his team and many comrades had suffered and died for. Other parts were curious to see what he would find, glad for the chance to get back at the Russians and do something that seemed nearly impossible one more time. However, it would also be his first time in a containment zone. He'd heard a lot about the military containment zones that crisscrossed the European continent as well, as if someone had dumped a bag of marbles over the map. He'd heard the scariest things from comrades in other units, dismissing most of it as stories of traumatized soldiers, until he'd listened to Nikos and his accounts of the Shard in Athens. The Greek was anything but a blowhard or a busybody, that much was certain. On the contrary, Jacek rather believed he had to take every word the big, bearded man with the soft eyes said times two to get a rough idea of the real horror and intensity on the ground. The fact was that there were the most hair-raising stories about every containment zone he had read about. He'd even heard of one in the south of Sweden where all the trees around were on fire for several hours every day until the fires disappeared as if on cue, and everything was as before. Could something like that really still surprise him after what he had seen in the Congo? He would certainly find out soon enough as they plunged into the center of this storm the size of Saarland. After one last look, he turned away from the monitor and turned it off, taking the USB stick and putting it back in his breast pocket.

He spent the rest of the flight time exchanging ideas with the commanders of the other two teams, discussing with them the satellite images of the former missile silo and a suitable strategy for getting in and later out and onto the opposite side of the lake to board the train in Ulan-Ude. In the end, when they had drawn up a satisfactory plan that didn't deviate too much from what they had discussed with their commanders in Germany, he set about making the final checks on his equipment, checking Uffe and having her inspect him. The plan was a good one that would hold roughly until their parachutes opened and everything changed, but then they would still be able to make adjustments. There were no alternatives to this oldest of soldier experiences anyway. He didn't think much of getting lost in endless possible scenarios, none of which would match the ultimate reality on the ground anyway.

When the ramp was opened a few hours later, the moorings of the buggies were first released and the cargo sledges with their four round-capped parachutes shot into the night with a distinctly audible "flop." The roar of the open ramp was deafening, and the encroaching cold mingled with the drawn-out breathing sounds of his mouthpiece, through which oxygen was supplied, to create that eerie atmosphere which, after so many years, he had already ceased to perceive as such. When it was his team's turn, he took a four-step run-up and covered the nearly four-meter length of the ramp. He jumped with his arms splayed and his legs slightly bent, bending his hips firmly downward so that his center of gravity in the middle of his body quickly brought him level with the ground twelve thousand feet below. The relative wind of the fall tugged at his clothing and equipment, but the sounds were quieter than on the plane, almost blocked out by his full helmet and giving way to his calmly walking breath. After he was perfectly stable as a frog on the relative wind, he tilted his arms, spread like bent wings, to the left and looked up at the brightly shining moon to get his bearings. Then he stopped his rotation until he was ninety degrees to the jump run, the A400M's direction of flight, and put his arms back, twenty inches from his hips. He brought his legs together and stretched them out so that he shot forward and down like an arrow. The digital altimeter gave him the altitudes directly into his ear with soft beeps. Another minute or so. The low density of air at such high altitudes meant the freefall was longer, but not by much than a four-thousand-meter jump, so he couldn't count on long fall times.

Jacek tilted his head to the left and watched his team's flashing red helmet signals fall at even intervals through the night — indistinct shadows, illuminated by the moonlight. He looked down again, and at the massive mountains of clouds from the storm that already enveloped them like a giant drum. In all directions, there was nothing but the rotating maelstrom of dark clouds, as if they were racing to reach the eye of the storm, at the center of which they fell like stones.

"End track," he ordered over the radio and folded his arms back to his sides, spreading his legs and angling them at the knees so that he was lying like a frog on the relative wind all over again. A few hand movements and he was resting stably and without twisting. Again, he checked his position relative to his team and pulled his stomach in slightly to soften his hollow back a bit, reducing his fall rate slightly and bringing him level with the red position lights beside him.

"Two thousand," his altimeter informed him. He gazed at the dark landscape below him, seeing the shimmering dark gray ice surface of Lake Baikal, or rather, a section of it, as the clouds seemed to reach all the way to the bottom. Lightning flashed through the raging gaseous masses of water at the edges of the storm's eye, repeatedly illuminating for a fraction of a second what they were hurtling toward: a structure with dozens of pointed appendages, pitch black but struck again and again by the bolts of lightning that, unlike anything he knew about lightning, forked horizontally from the cloud masses and slammed directly into the towering object. Whenever that happened, the dark surface lit up crimson, from bottom to top, like a pulse beating. Jacek was reminded of what he saw, a bizarre tower that grew more and more pointed toward the top and might have been sculpted by a particularly depressed Gothic artist. All around the broad base of the object, the ice had cracked open, as if it had pierced the frozen ice shell like a dagger.

"Son of a bitch," he muttered into his oxygen mask as he realized that the top of the object had been struck and illuminated by lightning and was only a few hundred feet away from him. All the hairs on his body stood up as the electrical discharge spread as a fine tickle.

"Ninety degrees track left!" he commanded hastily, folding his arms, bringing his feet together, and shooting off to the left, hoping his team would respond as quickly as they had in the countless trainings they had done together.

"Pull height changed: one thousand meters!"

Uffe: "Roger that!"

Hardy: "Copy that!"

Knut: "Roger that!"

Pill: "Copy that!"

Jacek stabilized himself with his bow stance again, and with a balancing motion forward, immediately pulled his hand deploy as the beeping thousand-meter warning sounded in his ear. The auxiliary chute shot out of its sheath with the bridle, pulling first the pin and then his main chute out of the container on his back. The sensation of being pulled upwards was brutal as always, as the cloaked canopy massively slowed his fall. Growling, he noticed that the horizon line in front of him was spinning. At first, he thought it was the clouds rotating around the object in the middle of the lake, but then checking his canopy, he saw that the trap lines had twisted in above him, putting him into an awkward rotation. He reached up into the rear risers, spread them apart, and with violent swings of his legs, spun in the opposite direction. After five attempts, he had spun out and was yanking out the control lines to make a sharp right turn when he realized he was heading straight for a dark boom of the alien artifact and had collided with it like a fly with a flyswatter by a hair. If not for a sudden lightning strike nearby, he might not have even noticed the obstacle.

He let up the steering lines and sped full speed away from the eerie object at his back, farther out onto the shimmering gray ice that glowed white every time one of the many lightning bolts chased through the storm. It was a strange impression to the senses that he was flying through perfect calm and stillness, while two or three miles ahead, the world seemed to be collapsing under a massive storm front. With a steady gaze, he sought the red position lights of his comrades, whose gliders also flashed periodically. Matching their flight directions, he adjusted his by repeatedly pulling the control lines right and left, and as discussed, went into a straight-in approach, as there was no wind at all. A few feet above the ice, he pulled the control lines down to a full brake and landed softly on the snow-covered ice. He removed the glider via the separation cushion on his right shoulder harness after releasing the RSL and immediately ran to join the others who were converging further ahead.

"Shit, what the fuck is that thing?" Uffe wanted to know when he reached them. "Sunk in the lake, my ass!"

"I don't know, maybe there are survivors to fix it or something," Jacek said, breathing heavily and unclipping the large bag from his chest. One by one, he pulled out pistols, his G36 tactical and the ammunition, stowing everything in his combat gear just like the others in eerie silence, throwing away the oxygen device and the bottle. He clamped the thick scarf he had prepared over his mouth and nose and put on the wide flak goggles. A glance at his Battlenav GPS should have shown him the positions of the other teams, but the device wasn't working. He had expected that.

"Come on, it doesn't get any cozier than this!"

CHAPTER 7

NIKOS

EVEN BEFORE THE first units started moving in the huge cavern deep below the peaks of the Glarus Alps, they were picked up by two uniformed men and led through the densely packed masses of soldiers to a small area behind the tanks where they were not pressed so closely together. There stood six people, the front three of whom had not yet put on their breathing masks. They were clearly older than the others and wore conspicuously many insignia on their rubberized camouflage suits.

"Ah, Herr Antoniadis," one of the three major generals greeted him with a German accent. He was another finger's breadth taller than Nikos and possessed a roundish face with a neat gray beard and fastidiously shaved corners. "I am Major General Steutner, commander of Operation Rolling Thunder. To my left, Général de Division Joret, commander of the 7e Brigade Blindée, which will lead the attack alongside our 1st Armored Division." The smaller Frenchman looked considerably more relaxed than his German colleague and even brought an almost carefree smile to his lips. Nikos nodded while Sönke saluted. "To my right," Steutner pointed to a woman with a narrow face and freckles of an upper age, "stands General de Brigada Camacho of the Spanish army units assigned to the French units in the form of a brigade."

"¡Es un placer conocerle!" The Spanish general nodded to him, but seemed rather absent-minded, and at the same moment was already accepting a tablet from her aide-de-camp, who stalked around her like a startled bird.

"Uh, thank you very much," Nikos said, clearing his throat to cover his uncertainty.

"Your presence here," Major General Steutner paused meaningfully, his face as expressionless as a stone, "was not announced. We only learned eight hours ago that we would have war correspondents and a public relations figure from the Commission with us. I guess you were on the train by then."

That would at least clarify what he thinks about me being there, Nikos thought in surprise and had to smile involuntarily, which at least tempted Steutner to raise one of his bushy eyebrows.

"That is correct, General."

"Can you take honesty, Mr. Antoniadis?"

"Nikos, please. And yes. Even though it's a trait more commonly attributed to your countrymen, I've already fought with soldiers from your country and learned my lessons." Nikos' heart grew wistful as he thought of Jacek, Uffe, Hardy, Knut, and Pill, whom he had come to call his friends, even though he hadn't actually seen them for more than six weeks of his life. But he had seen them more intensively than would have been possible under normal circumstances.

Now it was Steutner's turn to be surprised. Apparently, very few military people were actually aware of the KSK's operations. *So now he probably either thinks I'm a blowhard or is angry that I, as a civilian, know something about the military that is hidden from him. Not particularly great options.*

"Good," the general finally said. "I don't want any civilians with me. This mission is probably the riskiest ever undertaken by humans, and I'm also supposed to take care of three civilians and a babysitter so that the populace ends up being served a glossed-over report dripping with pathos and continues to dig in hard. I think the whole thing is a stupid idea from Brussels, so stay in the background, just do as you're told, and don't even think about getting involved in any foolishness. You may want to snap fine pictures and put on a show, like in your war bond commercials, but this is no playground, understand?"

"Sure." Nikos waited to see if the general wanted to say anything else, but he merely jutted his chin sternly and seemed to want to end the conversation. Clearing his throat, the general looked at him without moving his face.

"Anything else?"

"May I speak frankly as well, General?"

"Go ahead." Steutner made a terse hand gesture before crossing his arms behind his back again.

"You're right about everything you said. I'm not here by choice and I think this is a stupid move." Nikos deliberately left it open whether he was referring to the entire Operation Rolling Thunder or his involvement. "I was personally coerced by the Chancellor to be here, nor did I choose my escort. Believe it or not, I hate cameras at least as much as the aliens who reduced my home to rubble. I'm supposed to be supporting you and your staff as an *alien expert,* when I know next to nothing about them, and even if I did, we're dealing with a completely different species and technology here. So, I tend to think you're right and I'm just to be used as an accessible publicity face familiar to ordinary citizens."

Steutner's eyes began to sparkle, and a thin smile played around his thin, bloodless lips. "Well, look at that. Maybe we'll get along after all. Stay here. We'll send the troops through and leave with the staff last." The general glanced at his wristwatch and exchanged brief glances with his colleagues on the right and left, each of whom nodded curtly before he raised his hand and a radio operator came over to hand him a thick field radio with cable.

"This is Major General Steutner speaking. Everyone has their orders. They have been instructed in detail. What we are about to do cannot be prepared for because it has never been done before in the history of mankind. What we are about to encounter you will not understand, it will frighten you and maybe it will kill you. We don't know what to expect, what resistance we'll encounter, what weapons systems we'll have to deal with. We only know one thing: that we are the best our countries could fall back on. Look to your right and look to your left. Look your comrades in the eye. That is what you can be sure of. That each and every one of us is going through the same thing and relying on you. We can only do one thing: our best. For ourselves, for our comrades. Whatever we may face on the other side, never forget that on the other side of the galaxy, we are fighting for the most important cause in human history: the survival of our species. *Nec Aspera Terrent! Victoria pinget!*"

When Steutner took the radio from his mouth and held it out to his radio operator, cheers swelled, gathered under the vaulted cavern ceiling, and echoed down upon them like the thunder of the sky's choirs. It was a maelstrom of shared fears and worries, bursting into a storm of firing into courage and sacrifice — at least that was what Nikos thought he felt. The goosebumps on his arms and neck prickled as if someone had dipped him in an ice bath.

Steutner made a friendly gesture in the direction of the French general, who met it with a tilt of his head and also had a radio given to him. In English, he merely said, "March!" And added in French, "Marche!"

All at once, the chorus of cheers died away and the roar of diesel engines dominated the cavern. Hesitantly at first, then faster, like an accordion effect in a traffic jam, men and machines set to work and everything pushed into the tunnel as if a viscous mass were being forced through a funnel.

"Camera data stable from the other side?" asked Steutner into the headset he had tucked behind his ear. But it was his adjutant with the tablet in his hand who answered him.

"Yes, General. The central star of P3X-888 has just risen, the deployment zone is clear, and our recon teams report no suspicious activity in the immediate area. We also have drone data and can confirm that..."

Nikos stopped listening as it strained him to understand the conversation over the noise of the engines and he couldn't turn away from the masses of soldiers disappearing inch by inch into the dark tunnel as if they had never existed. He felt strangely cold, though he should be sweating under all that food and rubber, even in this place. What if the wormhole swallowed them all and didn't spit them back out? Was it broken down into its component parts during the transition and reassembled on the other side? What if individual molecules of himself didn't make it? What if they did? Would he be a copy of himself?

Suddenly, the cavern, through which a steady influx from the adjoining caverns had just passed, was almost empty, and no one followed.

"Time to move out," someone called, and Nikos blinked to bring himself back to the present.

"Hey, big guy, you okay?" asked Sönke, who had stopped beside him and slipped a pistol into the holster on his belt. Nikos found it to be an uncomfortable dead weight. "Try not to shoot yourself, okay?"

"Yeah, okay," he replied hoarsely.

"Are you alright?" his friend repeated, holding the breathing mask attached to his helmet next to his cheek like a pilot ready to clamp down on his mouthpiece. His eyes looked distorted through the narrow shatterproof goggles, but they still shone with the kindness Nikos so appreciated.

"I'm scared, and I think I've spent the last half hour in a trance," he admitted freely.

"That makes two of us." Sönke sighed and fastened his breathing apparatus, tightening the buckles on the other side of the helmet and helping him do the same after a pat on the shoulder. Once he succeeded, Nikos could hear his breathing as if he were on a dive. Along with the goggles he took off his chest and put on, he felt strangely cut off from the outside world — a state that both worried him, because he felt rapt and helpless, and relaxed him, because it gave him a sense of distance from the horror he was facing. But all that was of no use, because when he looked around, he noticed that the generals with their staff and escort were no longer there. They had already passed halfway through the cavern after the last truck had rolled into the tunnel. Only the two reporters were still behind him. With their uniforms, helmets, and breathing apparatus, they looked like swashbuckling warriors from a science fiction movie, and at the same time like frightened children whose body language expressed nothing but fear and unwillingness.

All at once, he saw the hooded face of a small figure in front of him. Sönke.

"We gotta go," he heard his friend's voice suddenly over the radio in his right ear.

"Okay, it's fine," Nikos replied, wishing he could have kept talking like a waterfall just to delay what he ultimately knew had to happen. So, in a daze, he put one foot in front of the other, striding across the rough cavern floor that he only now recognized as completely paved and littered with chain tracks. The ruts of the tanks formed deep valleys and cracks in the dark grey, where he would have liked to lose himself, for the simple reason that they were here on Earth, which was familiar to him, and he knew that God, Nature, the Universe, or whoever, wanted him on it. Not on the other side of the Milky Way, not on an alien planet, not near a wormhole.

A strong tug on his arm, however, thwarted any attempt to brace himself against the inevitable. For a moment, he wondered if he could turn and run. There were no more soldiers, no more guards, no one. Of course, he knew there still had to be a control center, and of course there had to be soldiers securing the entire complex, but right now, right here, they were the last ones, if you disregarded the general staff that had almost reached the tunnel. Sönke certainly wouldn't shoot at him, that much was certain, and the two journalists didn't possess any weapons. In the end, however, he dismissed the idea again, because forty thousand soldiers had just gone ahead, and he had no right to circumvent what they were about to face.

Why am I so terrified? he thought, shocked at himself. He had gone to the Shard in Athens, had found the strength to still offer comfort and courage to the others even as they experienced the worst horrors a human could endure. He had been in the Congo, between impacting bullets of aliens chasing them, had been injured and betrayed, had lost his wife and child as well as all his friends, and yet he had never experienced such existential fear as he did now. Why, he couldn't say, because his mind left no room for clear thought, but he was sure he would find out.

When they finally reached the passage through which two divisions had disappeared, he noticed that the path, barely twenty meters wide, led downward at an angle, about half a kilometer toward a bright ring that seemed to be spinning.

"Is it?" he stammered.

"Mhm," Sönke indicated and kept walking. Nikos envied his courage, he had to summon all his willpower to keep putting one foot in front of the other and following him. On and on they went, driven by the slightly sloping asphalt, inexorably toward the event horizon. When it was only a few dozen paces away, Nikos finally stopped and stared at the structure with widened eyes. Sönke and the two reporters also stopped, stood next to him and stared fixedly at what was happening in front of them: a pitch-black sphere about 20 meters in diameter, which at first appeared motionless, formed the center of a ring of broken colors and lights, arranged as a glowing accretion disk around the event horizon. At times he thought he saw a tree trunk and leaves; at other times everything was so distorted, he thought it was an optical illusion. Shades of blue, green, and brown dominated the rotating ring, which wafted back and forth yet was firmly defined, like a true thing of impossibility in which every single component was wrong and made his brain scream to turn around immediately and run for the distance.

"This isn't a wormhole after all," he muttered hoarsely, trying in vain to collect enough saliva in his mouth to stop cawing like a dying bird.

"It's a black hole," Sönke confirmed in a surprisingly calm voice. "The wormhole must be in it."

"Are you sure? How do you know?" asked Karin Getzsch nervously.

"Status in scientific report."

"Great, if that's what it said in there, then…" Before she had finished speaking, Sönke started moving and walked quickly toward the jet-black sphere, its edges rotating like a distorted ring. Nikos was about to call after him, when something strange happened: The silhouette of the soldier stretched, became longer and longer. His body stood there as if motionless, frozen in one movement, and yet continued into the middle of the black disk, as if it had been stretched out into infinity and compressed into a two-dimensional point that disappeared into the blackness.

"Holy shit!" the cameraman shouted, stumbling back.

"I guess this is my opportunity to get rid of you two," Nikos said laconically in a fit of gallows humor, swallowing hard as he forced himself to move forward. No, he didn't walk, he ran, ran as fast as he could, trying to escape his racing thoughts that protested in a bright panic.

The transition happened suddenly and infinitely fast and yet felt like an eternity. Its course seemed never-ending, and yet it was as if it were frozen in time. He was dissolving into his constituent parts, was nothing more than pure energy, broken down into its basic components. He knew it, observed it, and yet he could not see it. All he saw was his field of vision endlessly curving and dissolving into bizarre shapes. Then it all came back together, rotating light that stopped for a moment as if it had never moved, turned to blackness, but disappeared again instantly.

Then it brightened and he bounced staggeringly against an obstacle, which momentarily gave way and then caught him. He blinked and shook his head to clear it, only to find that it wasn't he who was shaking his head. Sönke was holding his head and turning it back and forth.

"Hey, big guy! It's all right, you're on the other side. It's all good!"

"Who, me? What are you saying?" Nikos snapped his eyes open and looked around. He was standing in the middle of a huge clearing, teeming with tanks, trucks, and armored jeeps. Soldiers ran around in columns, disappearing between the more distant rows of trees. Helicopters were loaded with mobile cranes from trucks, which in turn were quickly filled with heavily armed soldiers before roaring off, leaving deep furrows in the muddy ground.

"Yes, you! We're on Planet X. You're here and still whole as far as I can tell," the German confirmed, and Nikos' breathing calmed a little at the familiar voice. A heavy lump lifted from his heart and gave way to a deep relief. He would have loved to laugh like a madman, but his mouth was too parched.

"We're really here?"

"Yes. We just traveled from our local arm across the Sagittarius Arm to the other side of the Milky Way into the Perseus Arm. About 50,000 light years from Earth," Sönke summarized, now holding him by the shoulders. They gazed into each other's eyes, almost glasses to glasses, if it hadn't been for the size difference between them. It was a look they were both glued to, as if to make sure it was all real and they weren't dreaming.

"Okay, I think I'm okay. Where are the others?" asked Nikos, turning around. The reporter and the cameraman were just stumbling through the event horizon, the black sphere with the rotating ring of distorted light. The sight horrified him, but he did what he did best. Reluctantly, he took a step toward her and thus toward the black hole, grabbing the journalist by the arms to pull her with him. Away from the strange entity.

"You're alright, you hear? You did it!"

He hoped that was true for all of them as he stumbled on with the older woman in his arms, like a foreign body among the soldiers milling about. A glance upward showed him a billowing, poisonously radiant cloud cover of muddy ochre in which the blocked-out light of the central star looked dirty and poisonous. They were not only alien here, they were unwelcome, and the farther he looked, the more clearly that impression solidified.

CHAPTER 8

JACEK

THEY HAD to find the other teams. That was the priority. On the other hand, Jacek wanted nothing more than to put as much distance between himself and the object at his back as quickly as possible. But in his job, you just couldn't go by what you wanted or what felt like the safer route. So he pulled out his compass and frowned at the needle. It was spinning in circles so fast that the needle became a disk of semi-transparent shadow.

"Well," he muttered through his protective scarf and stopped. "We'll have to hope they have their position markers on their helmets turned on like we do. Get out the binoculars and scan the perimeter. We'll fan out, fifty meters apart, then we can increase the angle to the object in case Four and Six are on the other side of that thing. Look for the buggies while you're at it."

"Roger that," his team confirmed in turn over the radio. Their voices cracked and crackled, but he could hear them, so at least that was something. Through the thick snow and shattered goggles, he saw Uffe and Pill running north and Knut and Hardy running south. He stopped and took a moment to examine the object closely. It stood exactly in the center of the storm, forming the central point of the eye several kilometers across, which rotated like an upturned laundry drum. The pitch-black clouds began a few hundred meters above the ground and spiraled upward for many miles in an endless maelstrom. Lightning flashed through the circling wall every second, overlapping each other so that the entire scene was almost continuously illuminated. The ice of the lake was a flat expanse, reaching far below the clouds where it was too dark to see the mountains that surrounded the third largest freshwater reservoir on Earth. He had visited this place several times in his life, both in winter and summer, and had been fascinated by the lake, which was over a kilometer and a half deep — if you left out the sand that had slid in over time, it was even close to nine thousand meters. The Russians who had lived here had always been very friendly and sociable, except for the many vodka corpses. Jacek had experienced a lot of good things here and had used his visits to seek refuge from the stress of his soldiering on the former Shaman Island of Olkhon. He wondered what might have happened to all the good people he had met. Were they still alive and hiding from the horror that had befallen their lake? Had they all died in the impact of the shipwreck that had sent large chunks of the waters spilling over the mountains in a huge tsunami? Probably not.

His gaze remained fixed on the object that seemed to have broken through the ice sheet from below. A total of a dozen elongated tower structures, standing close together and forming a single, bizarre shape, stretched up through the cracked and churned ice sheet into the sky, several hundred feet tall and framed by lightning bolts that struck the tallest, central tower every second. Whenever it happened, the pitch-black structures glowed crimson and shimmering lapis lazuli. The object reminded Jacek of an organ, except those didn't usually scare him. This thing, however, terrified him. Fear of the sort that dried out his mouth. His tongue felt like someone had wiped it with an old dusty rag. The most disconcerting thing about the eerie sight, though, was that it was framed by oppressive silence. Not the slightest breath of air blew in the eye of the storm; everything happened in absolute silence, as if time had been stopped. Whatever had happened to the wreck, which according to JEMCOM was supposed to have sunk into the depths of Lake Baikal, it was alive. There was no other way he could describe what he saw before him. Even the most negative forecasts of military reconnaissance had interpreted the impact in Lake Baikal to mean that a third of the water mass, as much water as the Nile carried, after all, might have sloshed over the edges. Even that would still have meant over a kilometer of depth through which the debris would have to rise again. How could that be done?

"I found the buggies," Hardy reported over the radio after a few moments of crackling and popping in Jacek's ear.

"And I found the other teams. They're coming at us from the southeast and they've signaled that they see us. I can't get them on the radio yet." The voice, though distorted almost beyond recognition by static, had to belong to Uffe.

"Understood," Jacek replied. "We'll meet up at Hardy's. Keep an eye on our teams."

He wasn't sure what he was trying to say, but in this environment, and with just a kilometer separating them from the alien thing, he thought every horror imaginable. He shouldered his assault rifle and ran south with quick strides, where he could see not only the red lights of the helmet markers that belonged to Hardy and Knut, but also their dark silhouettes that showed against the white ice sheet in the glare of the forked lightning. By the time he reached them, Hardy and Knut were standing together and had removed their goggles so they could take the electronically assisted binoculars before their eyes.

"All right, where are they?" he asked, pulling his glasses

down so they dangled in front of his thickly wrapped neck. The cold immediately groped at his exposed skin as if poking at it with a thousand needles.

"One o'clock," Hardy answered, without taking off his binoculars.

Jacek raised his binoculars to his eyes and looked at the broad base of the alien object, where chunks of ice many meters thick were piled high where it had broken through the ice cover. Then he turned his head a little to the right and saw three red lights flashing. Using the zoom buttons, he brought them closer and suppressed a curse as he made out the outlines of the buggies. One had obviously crashed into the object with its four cargo parachutes and was lying half-destroyed on the crest of one of the towers, which was clearly poking out of the ice more minimally than the others. The other two were upright, half-buried under several of the round-capped parachutes, but they were on the mounded ice wall that surrounded the alien object like a white bulge.

"Hey, where are those things?" asked Uffe breathlessly, coming up beside them at that moment with Pill in tow, blinking in the direction they were all staring.

"By the object. Right by the object," Jacek replied, chewing on his teeth so hard, his jaw cracked. "One's down."

"Oh," the sniper said. "I've got the big gun and I'll cover you."

"Figures," Knut snorted, trading binoculars for snow goggles. "Can I still retrain, Joss?"

"Yeah, to the buggy driver," Jacek grumbled, not taking his eyes off the organ-like alien artifact as he also put his glasses back on. His eyes were still cold, but it helped a little against the chilling air.

"If I have to be a buggy driver..."

"If you argue with me, *I'll* kill myself," Jacek cut him off, pointing at Hardy. "You take charge, Pill and I will go and recover the two buggies. We'll leave our luggage here and take only the climbing gear. Uffe, you cover us. The distance shouldn't be a problem without wind. Hardy, you coordinate with the other teams, get them ready to go. If we can get both buggies recovered, they'll drive those things, and we'll clamp on to the outside."

"All right." Hardy nodded, gripping his assault rifle a little tighter as he looked to the rapidly approaching figures approaching from the southeast. Their silhouettes, peeled from the darkness by lightning bolts, reminded him of distorted nightmare figures.

"And one more thing," Jacek added. "Radio communication only seems to work at very short range. Be prepared to lose contact and radio the other teams as they approach so we can get an approximate range."

Uffe said nothing, sliding the sling of her submachine gun onto her back and unpacking her huge M82 sniper rifle. As she began to unfold the tripod and take out her resting mat, Jacek gave a wave to Pill, who nodded curtly and joined him in a light continuous run.

"Any idea how this could have happened?" the young sergeant asked with his radio on mute. His voice was slightly distorted by the scarf in front of his mouth and nose and sounded a little deeper than usual.

"Do you mean the buggy or the object?"

"The object. I thought the recon data was good. Surely the satellite imagery should have picked it out at least in the eye of the storm. That thing is what, half a kilometer high?"

"Could be getting there."

"Does it swim? Is it still a mile deep and anchored in the sandy bottom of the lake? This thing stinks."

"Everything about alien tech stinks," Jacek countered,

enjoying the quick but easy run because the moderate exertion cleared his head. Any physical activity also kept his hands steady.

"I still don't feel good about approaching this thing instead of following my instincts and getting the hell out of there as fast as I can," Pill insisted.

"This is what every one of our missions looks like. It was like this in the Congo, it's like this here, and we don't know how it's going to turn out in the end." Jacek felt he needed to talk some courage into his youngest team member. He didn't fear that Pill would actually turn around and disobey his orders; he was too much of a professional for that and no one survived the KSK tests who wasn't absolutely solidified and brave enough to tackle even the worst crises head on. But they were still human beings, and as such, sentient and thinking beings, not machines as many officials in the Ministry of Defense thought. "Remember the first time we saw that anti-tech sphere? That thing was really scary."

"Yes, it was."

"In the end, it saved us. If it weren't for those spheres, the Tears' battle drone would have turned us into a splattering blood mist."

"You've got a point there." Pill hesitated as the object in front of them grew closer and the flashes grew more glaring. "This thing is different somehow, though. I don't know what it is, but it clearly scares me more than anything I've seen before. It's almost as if I can sense that it's..."

"*Evil?*" Jacek helped him up, nodding when he felt his comrade's surprised sideways glance. "Feels the same to me. But a feeling like that won't help us. We need the buggies if we're going to stay on schedule."

"True."

"So let's focus."

They were silent the rest of the way, and a few minutes later arrived at the heaped-up ice shield that enveloped the base of the alien ship — or what had been created from it. Like a protective wall, it rose a good ten meters in the form of thick chunks that had tumbled wildly over each other. For the last fifty meters before it, the ice cover of the lake was covered by larger and smaller pieces that had been small enough to be flung away when the object broke through. Some were as large as a man, others as small as buckets, and their shapes possessed the most bizarre outlines. The buggies were in a small depression in the ice pile and were right next to each other, which at first he thought was an unlikely coincidence. Then, however, he saw the limp parachutes between them, their trap lines twisted into each other. It was tantamount to a miracle that both vehicles looked relatively unscathed. There was also the fortunate coincidence that parts of the ice wall in the immediate vicinity formed something like a ramp in a frozen avalanche. With a little luck, they were able to take advantage of this circumstance to lower the buggies. The crash cages were extremely sturdy, but he would rather not test them in a ten-meter fall.

"Are you that sick all of a sudden too?" asked Pill as they looked around with assault rifles holstered and kept looking up at the buggies, their position beacons flashing bright red.

"A little," Jacek admitted. The feeling of nausea in his stomach had already started during the last hundred meters they had covered and felt as if he had eaten something rotten. Mild dizziness was also setting in, which he found extremely uncomfortable. He was about to say something else, when the radio crackled and whooshed in his ear, but he couldn't hear a voice. "Can you get that in?"

"Yeah, glitch." They looked at each other for a moment and then turned around but were unable to establish a clear field of view due to some awkwardly placed chunks of ice.

"Anyway, let's get on with it. Let's hurry. With the crampons and the catching gloves, we should be able to make it to the top. If we take the hooks from the winches on the front bumpers and wrap them around one of the larger ice monoliths out here, we should be able to use the hydraulics to turn the buggies and pull them down."

"Sounds good; let's get going," Pill said, pulling his backpack off his back. Jacek did the same, putting on his climbing gear. When he had just put on his outer gloves with the metallic barbs, he startled.

"What is it?" his comrade wanted to know.

"I heard something," he muttered back, resting his cheek against the butt of his G36 to scan the immediate area. Chunk after chunk of ice appeared in front of his field of vision, always momentarily in darkness, but mostly illuminated by the nearby lightning strikes that slammed into the alien artifact's central tower far above them.

"What? I didn't hear anything." Pill raised his rifle as well and began to cover the other flank. If someone saw something, or even thought they heard or smelled something, you always took it seriously as a good commando soldier. A hundred false alarms were better than a single missed one.

"Sounded like..." Jacek thought and shook his head. The combination of fear, nausea, and proximity to the object was probably playing tricks on his senses. Even if it wasn't, he couldn't see any danger in the immediate vicinity, and it wasn't worth freaking out about. "Anyway. Let's get going."

Pill climbed the avalanche-like ramp first, which was more like a wildly fallen pile of ice chunks, while Jacek covered him and continued to scan the area. Again, there was a rustling in his earpiece and a noise that sounded distantly like an ethereal voice mingled with the radio drifts. It sounded like a ghostly echo from beyond, unreal and fragile.

"If anyone calls us, we can't hear anything. We're only getting static in." He turned and watched Pill climb the not inconsiderable incline on all fours with the rifle on his back.

"How does it look? Is the grip okay?"

"Yeah, I'm fine," the young sergeant gasped. "I'm just pretty dizzy."

"Me too," Jacek returned. "Could be due to the magnetic field distortions the object is emitting. At the very least, there must be some such effect when I look at my compass." He looked at the small box hanging from his backpack strap, its needle bouncing and spinning completely wildly. "I think strong magnetic fields can trigger something like that."

"Never mind, I'll be with the buggies in a minute. The last part is a bit steep."

"Wait there and cover me and I'll come after you. We can't be too careful."

"Understood."

Jacek let the muzzle of his assault rifle wander a few more times. The rubble landscape of ice lay just as still and ghostly as before. When he looked to his comrade, he was leaning back against the last ledge, barely two meters high, where the vehicles stood, flashing red as if calling for help in panic. Once Pill had his rifle in hand, Jacek shouldered his and began to climb up the steeply rising ramp as well. As soon as a crampon caught in the ice, he grabbed a groove or ledge with his barbed gloves and pulled himself further up.

When he was about halfway through the short distance, he heard Pill scream.

"Shit, Jessy, we got something coming!"

"What?" asked Jacek, turning his head over his shoulder, not daring to take his feet or hands off the ice lest he lose his footing and slide down in the worst-case scenario. Even the slightest injury would be a death sentence out here. He looked out into the unreal icy landscape that seemed to flicker from the constant lightning. "I don't see anything."

Just as he spoke, he saw it: a huge shadow appeared between two ice monoliths and disappeared again. Pill's assault rifle rattled off, missing it — whatever it was — by a hair's breadth. The 7.62mm rounds shredded the top of a chunk of ice, sending spattering crystals into the night.

"What was that?" cried Jacek hoarsely.

"I don't know, but it was pretty big. An alien? Maybe we got the attention of the landlords of this haunted castle?"

"I'm coming up," he replied as a mighty roar sounded and made him tremble. His left hand lost its grip, and he slipped half a meter. While his heart leaped from the rush of adrenaline, he jerked his hand back up and managed to stop his fall.

"Jessy!" shouted Pill, sounding frighteningly upset. He looked over his shoulder again, and this time, the shadow had come much closer. A huge monster ran toward the ramp at ludicrous speed and leaped upward onto the lowest pedestal of the frozen ice avalanche. Because of its unhealthily turned head and its combat helmet restricting it, Jacek didn't realize what he was dealing with, but it was at least the size of a small elephant, had its mouth wide open, and thick brown fur. Black blood spurted from its flank, where thick bumps opened up, twitching back and forth as if they possessed a life of their own.

The monster roared out, wrenching its mighty fanged mouth open even wider as it slobbered and climbed ever closer, closing the distance to Jacek.

"Hurry up!" roared Pill, sending down another burst of fire, but the bullets were already whizzing worryingly close to his head. "I don't have a clear field of fire anymore!"

"Already noticed," Jacek muttered, making a decision. With his pulse pounding madly in his ears, he disengaged his hands from the ice and immediately began to slide down, heading straight for the monster's open mouth. Swiftly, he turned on his back, and in one fluid motion, drew his pistol from his thigh holster. Now that he was close to the monster's teeth, he saw the small dark eyes gleaming maliciously in the flashing light, craving his death. He jerked the pistol up and fired round after round at the monstrosity's head, but it wasn't enough. As his feet reached the mouth, his jaws snapped shut and he gritted his teeth in anticipation of the pain as a loud bang sounded and the monster's torso exploded just below his head, the entire body sliding limply downward. Jacek slid involuntarily after it, landing on the carcass and rolling groaning on the ice below.

As he stood again, the lifeless head of a mighty bear slapped at his feet, its mouth frozen in a plaintive cry and its eyes broken.

"That's a damn bear," he called out to Pill, but as he examined the carcass more closely, he suddenly felt even colder. The carcass was too big, and the fur was surrounded by tumor-like bumps that looked hard like concrete and shone unhealthily. "What the hell?"

CHAPTER 9

THE DEPLOYMENT TO PLANET X, or P3X-888 as it was officially called, and which the generals insisted upon, unlike the soldiers, was surprisingly swift and organized. The armored columns rolled their way through the woods, flattening everything between them and the objective. One hundred and fifty kilometers away, this objective was located in a horseshoe-shaped valley. Nikos had seen a map to that effect in the General Staff's mobile command post, which was set up on a converted truck and looked more like a computer center, with soldiers constantly talking into headsets and hacking away on their keyboards. As it turned out, there were many photos and videos of the reconnaissance teams, which had surprisingly only suffered twenty percent casualties. Those hadn't been from possible enemy contact, though, he'd been assured. So far, they had gone undetected, but it wouldn't be that way for long. Even if the locals did indeed lack aerial reconnaissance or satellites, two divisions of over forty thousand motorized soldiers could hardly be concealed.

After the first twelve hours, during which all the logistics had to adjust to the new, greatly increased fuel consumption due to the planet's higher gravity, Nikos left the command truck for the first time and joined the two French soldiers in the driver's cabin, which fortunately still had a bench seat behind the front seats. Sönke stayed in the armored truck bed, apparently enjoying the proximity to the center of power that his status as the civilian's overseer brought him, even though he kept insisting that Nikos had been a soldier himself. This delight for the surprisingly boring work of a combat staff unfortunately seemed to excite the two journalists less, so they followed him every step of the way here as well and so he found himself sitting on the bench behind the drivers, squeezed between the cameraman and the reporter.

If he leaned forward a little, he could see the bizarre forest passing by through the thick bulletproof glass windows. The huge mushrooms, twenty to thirty feet tall, were the most impressive. They looked like the mushrooms on Earth with somewhat thin stems, but they still had the diameter of a tank, and white stuff resembling snow was constantly trickling from the lamellae under their caps. So wherever many of these mushrooms grew, they gave the impression of passing through a snowy landscape. The ground was fortunately dry, it had apparently not rained for a while, which was not only good for men and material, but would have been a disaster in the worst case: due to the heaviness of their vehicles, even the tracked tanks would have problems if it got slushy, as their weight increased by one and a half times in this strong gravity sink, causing them to sink deeper. If both divisions got stuck, the entire operation would be in jeopardy.

But it wasn't just the mushrooms that were exciting — they might not have been mushrooms at all but reminded him most of the earthly counterpart his brain knew. The trees, too, looked familiar but equally alien enough to make him frown as he kept noticing details he'd never seen before. There were yellow creepers, for instance, with fingers as thick as his arms, pressing against the moss-covered trunks and pulsing in a steady rhythm as if they possessed a heartbeat of their own.

It was also interesting that the vegetation seemed less dense to him than on Earth, but this didn't seem to be because they were artificial forestry plants, but because the individual trees demanded more space. For one thing, their trunks were noticeably thicker and lower than back home, which he also attributed to the planet's greater gravitational pull. For another, their branches and serrated leaves, which were more shades of yellow and brown, formed shadowy areas on the ground where no other trees grew. Instead, there was only knotty grass and poisonous-looking moss there. The longer he looked through the windows, the more haunting the feeling of traveling through a picturesque horror landscape of cool but unhealthy pastel colors. The sooty tanks and trucks driving to their right and left, leaving a swath of ruined vegetation in their wake, didn't do much to weaken that impression. Everything was dull and depressing, as if the planet was crying over what was to come.

"Are you okay?" the reporter wanted to know. Her voice sounded slightly mumbled through the breathing apparatus and it was disconcerting to see only her eyes and no movement of her mouth hidden behind the insect-like structure.

"Yes, miss," he said, and sighed.

"Why don't you call me Karin," she offered, and when he looked at her sideways in surprise, she shrugged. "I think I may have made a bad impression and I'd like to apologize."

"It's okay," he said, yet feeling grateful for her little charm offensive, because he couldn't read any cynicism or sarcasm in her eyes.

"No, no, I'm serious. I think I should explain," she objected, shaking her head and pointing at the cameraman to his right. "Rooney and I have been on the road together for a few years.

We've reported from Yemen, where the Huthi rebels and Saudi Arabia are fighting, we were in Afghanistan for the Good Friday skirmish, and in the murky tangle in Syria. If there's one thing you learn there, it's not to get too involved with those you're supposed to be accompanying with camera and microphone."

"Because they're dying?" asked Nikos in a strained voice.

"Yes. At some point, you're either going to have to establish a healthy distance and switch to a mode that works purely professionally, or the job will put you in the grave or rehab." Karin paused, peering through the windshield as if she'd spotted something far away that demanded her full attention. Possibly that was even the case, except it was something separated from her by the veil of memory. When she took a deep breath and turned back to him, her eyes were noticeably softer than before. "This is the mode we sort of automatically slipped into when we got the assignment to work with you. I'm allowed to say, *you*, right?"

"Absolutely, please."

"Thanks. So, we know you from TV, of course, and you're a really nice guy too, but none of this has made it any easier for us. On top of the personal level, there's a lot of pressure from above to make sure everything goes well and we don't make any mistakes."

"That was before we went through that scary black hole," Rooney interjected. The young man exhaled in a hiss and shook his head. "That's some really freaky shit, man."

"What Rooney is saying is that we can't work here with the tools we used back home. This isn't our country, and nothing is normal or comparable to anything except maybe the soldiers," Karin explained, holding out a hand to him. "If we could start over, I would feel significantly better."

Nikos looked at her dainty hand and grasped it.

"It's okay," he assured her. "You don't want to be here any

more than I do, I get that. Let's make the best of it. I'd like to survive." He thought for a moment. "I have friends back home I'd like to see again."

"Me too, a husband and two kids," she returned, and he swallowed hard.

"I'm sorry about that. I didn't know that..."

"Oh." She wiped away his objection with a gruff gesture. "We've all left someone behind, haven't we? It's no different for anyone. We live in times where everyone has to do their part."

"Like mobile infantry," Rooney grumbled from the right. Karin seemed to overhear.

"No one can afford to sit at home anymore because he or she doesn't want to risk their children growing up without a mother or father. No," she said firmly. "It's up to all of us. No one has special rights anymore, not since those damned aliens showed up over our skies."

"You're probably right." Nikos looked at the rear of the Leopard 2 tank in front of them, its tracks flinging reams of dirt against their hood. After twelve hours of driving in a rocking truck, something akin to boredom set in. He had expected to enter an inferno of violence as they passed through the wormhole. In his mind, explosions had flared, soldiers had screamed, and mud had splattered everywhere. Instead, however, all was quiet, and their convoy pushed along at a sedate thirty kilometers per hour, through an alien yet somehow familiar landscape. Nothing seemed even remotely as if they were at war or in an approaching battle. "Don't you think that's strange?"

"What?"

"That it's so quiet. We've come with nearly two thousand tanks, as many transports, tankers and supply trucks and howitzers, and we're driving through the countryside with diesel engines roaring, but no one is stopping us. It's almost as if we're here alone."

"Maybe they haven't spotted us yet. After all, without air support or a settlement nearby to report us, there's no way they'd notice us," the reporter tried to explain. "It's fine with me, anyway."

"I'm kind of uncomfortable with that."

"Don't worry about it. The long-range recon is good. We've got Harfang drones with us, I think, teams on the flanks, front and rear, and helicopters launching as soon as we start fireworks. They should see pretty much everything that's going on around us..." Nikos stopped listening to her when he saw something through the window that didn't want to fit into the leisurely passing monotony of green-brown-yellow vegetation.

"We have to stop!" he shouted, tapping the driver on the shoulder. "Uh, arrêter! Arrêter!"

The French soldier looked back at him and frowned in confusion, but the excitement on Nikos' face seemed to unnerve him and he began speaking a torrent of French into his headset. Shortly after, the entire convoy came to a halt, as far as he could see, as the vehicles around them stopped as well. Without listening to Karin or Rooney's questions, he squeezed past the cameraman and checked the fit of his goggles and breathing apparatus before opening the door and leaping outside. The impact, though only a foot and a half, felt like he'd fallen from twice his height onto a concrete wall. Gravity seemed to just yank him down on its own, and every single step felt like he was lugging a giant backpack.

"Hey! What's going on?" Karin called after him, but he was already trudging through the soft moss toward the truck bed. The body was made of armored composite material and looked like an angular greenhouse covered with an ugly camouflage tarp so it wouldn't stand out from the other trucks. Before he could even climb the stepladder and open the door to the command room, it was pushed open and two soldiers with assault rifles jumped out, followed by Major General Steutner and his French colleague. He recognized them by their different heights, as they too wore helmets, goggles, and breathing apparatuses.

"Mr. Antoniadis," Steutner grumbled, jumping onto the moss behind the wagon, surprisingly catlike for his age. "Can you tell me why we just had two divisions stop?"

"Presumably because you think I must have a valid reason as your so-called *alien expert*?" Nikos asked in an air of petulance that puzzled himself. Surprisingly, the general snorted, but sounded more amused than incensed.

"You're lucky we would have stopped to refuel in five minutes anyway. Besides, only twenty kilometers separate us from our destination. We're making good time. So, what's got you so worried?"

"I saw one of the anti-technology spheres we had also encountered in the Congo. I think you've received reports to that effect?" asked Nikos breathlessly, pointing into the forest.

"Yes, we're familiar with those, and we were briefed that these would be available. They look identical to the ones you found. What are you getting at? We knew about this sphere that keeps the Morphs from dropping in themselves. We also knew about the spheres thanks to our reconnaissance teams who sent photos to that effect," the general explained impatiently. "Don't tell me you haven't read a single report and are surprised now."

"No, General, it's not that."

"Then what is it?"

"If it's alright with you, I'd like to show it to you in person," Nikos asked, gesturing in the direction of the black orb he'd seen to the east.

"Alright, you're the alien expert and I'm the last person who doesn't take every single clue seriously. Lieutenant," he snapped at a soldier standing next to him with a tablet wrapped in plastic. "Start refueling and positioning the artillery. We should be in range now, despite the increased gravity. Have the remaining units take up defensive positions."

"Roger that, General!" the soldier mumbled into his respirator and ran back into the van.

"So, *alien expert,* be an *alien expert,*" Steutner prompted him, gesturing toward the forest with an outstretched arm.

"Shouldn't we take an escort or something?"

"Escort? I'm a general and I make my living doing honest work," the officer snorted. "This isn't a Hollywood movie. There are no enemy formations in the perimeter. We've got aerial recon and reconnaissance teams on the ground, just like plenty of smaller rotor drones in the woods. So don't get your knickers in a twist."

"I'm not, I just..." Seeing one of the general's bushy eyebrows shoot up behind his glasses, Nikos nodded and led the way. As they rounded the Puma infantry fighting vehicle that had driven to their right, the tarps of the trucks were already being pulled up behind them and soldiers were swarming everywhere, giving orders with hoarse shouts. He and the general were accompanied by a few soldiers from the command post.

Nikos led them past the tank and across the short grassy area into the deciduous forest. The trunks were at least ten or twelve feet apart here too, so there was no difficulty in staying together and seeing the black sphere that looked almost identical to the one in the Congo. Seeing it brought with it an uneasy familiarity and a tingling sensation that continued from his fingers down his arms and into his scalp. It didn't take long, as they only had to take fifty steps into the forest to stop not even a vehicle's length from the sphere. The perfect sphere of pure blackness hovered barely a meter above the ground between four trees with yellow bark covered by pulsating creepers. The black of the alien structure was so impenetrable and lacking contours that the sphere could have rotated and they wouldn't have noticed. It floated as if it didn't care about mundane basic physical constants like gravity.

"Really strange, these things," the general mumbled. Nikos hadn't even noticed that the one next to him had stepped up. The soldiers accompanying them formed a semicircle and pointed their assault rifles at the sphere. "Put your weapons down! Those things are the only thing saving us from being turned into biowaste by the Tears, who must be dwelling in orbit." Barely louder than a whisper, he added, "Not that you could even scratch it."

"They are, sir."

"Do they look the same as in Africa? Or are there differences?"

Nikos looked at the object, which looked like a mistake in reality, and considered. "It's possibly a little bigger. Maybe one and a half times that size?"

"Then the size is probably related to the gravity of his surroundings," Steutner speculated. "Is it normal to have a beeping in my ears and feel dizzy?"

"Yes, sir," Nikos confirmed curtly. "It was the same in the Congo. If we get too close, we'll be thrown back or pass out."

"Nice views," the general replied succinctly. "So why are we looking at this?"

Nikos swallowed and pointed to the ground beneath the sphere. "See that forest floor there?"

"Yes. I'm old, but I'm not defective in sight. Looks normal."

"That's just it, sir. It was different in the Congo. The spheres there built themselves from the raw material of their surroundings. They were tiny at first, and dug themselves into the earth, where rock, ore, and wood loosened and bonded with them. They then grew and grew until they floated out of the resulting hole and remained above it. Here, however, the ground looks perfectly normal, just as you said."

"So, this sphere was either ready when it was installed here, or it was fed resources that were on hand. If the Tears did indeed use this new technology to put the native species under their protection in return for resources, that tells us they probably made a deal and knew about it."

"Yes, sir, and it also tells us that the Tears must have acted peacefully toward the locals; otherwise, they would have just taken the ore, don't you think?"

"Yes, otherwise, it wouldn't be a trade. But that could be for a thousand different reasons. Maybe only the locals can mine the ore for some unknown reason. Satan, I've seen giant mushrooms and yellow clouds," rumbled the tall general.

"Sir, what did the experts say about the cities and habitats of the natives?" asked Nikos, turning so that he was standing directly in front of the general rather than next to him. It was time now to get to the point of why the sight of the sphere had so shocked him.

"Habitats? Do you mean cities and settlements?"

"Yes."

"I'd best not even ask you what you're getting at?" Steutner paused and sighed when Nikos didn't answer anything. "All right, then. I hope your little guessing game is leading to something and not solely wasting my time. The analysts assume that the native species either live under domes that effectively keep out acid rain and have filtration systems that purify the water for their agriculture, just like the air they breathe. Or, that they live in houses with specially coated roofs. After all, they wear these suits all the time to protect themselves from the toxic atmosphere."

"But we haven't found any cities, not even individual buildings in the entire area between the wormhole and the mine, and the drones haven't picked up anything on radar directly around it either. They've only seen the orbital elevator as a thin line on the horizon from far away."

"That is correct. However, you are not the first to have noticed this. The analysts have also concluded that the mine most likely emits toxic mining waste products, and therefore there are no settlements for miles around. And you're wrong: there are structures in the mine area that don't have windows, but do have walls and roofs, if you were expecting highly alien structures," Steutner explained, and it was clear from his voice that his patience was wearing thin.

"What if the native species doesn't build cities at all?" Nikos wanted to know.

"What are you talking about?"

"What if they're wearing these fully sealed suits because they need them to protect themselves from the toxic air, the corrosive rain, and the light conditions entirely?"

Steutner considered for a moment, looking at him steadfastly. Finally, he crossed his long arms in front of his chest. "Are you suggesting that we haven't seen any cities or settlements because the aliens live underground?"

"Yes. Think about it: if on Earth the rain became so corrosive that it permanently destroyed roofs, clothing, and vehicles, would it be cheaper to build huge domes or coat houses one by one, possibly on a regular basis, or dig tunnels and let the planet's upper crust do the protecting?"

"Hmm," the general stated. "That option was discussed but discarded due to the planet's high gravity and the higher expected density of the rock as a result."

"For all we know, the alliance with the Tears could have been in place for a long time. Maybe they gave them the technology? Or possibly they did it all on their own — necessity is the mother of invention, as we all know." Nikos stepped closer to the Expeditionary Force commander until only a hand-breadth of toxic air separated them. "Sir, what if we haven't been attacked yet, but the locals have long known we were there? Should I be right, and they really do live underground..."

"...Then they'd almost certainly be using seismic sensors to know what's happening on their surface," Steutner finished his sentence, exhaling audibly. "If you're right, kid, then they'd know where we are all along, and I'm sure they'd just be waiting to hit us in the exact spot that's best for them."

"Yes," was all Nikos replied.

"I hate being rushed into a battle," the general grunted, turning on his heel. "Lieutenant! Return to the command post, high alert for the entire force! Order the helicopter squadrons here, and I want to see an overview map as soon as I get back, but hurry!"

Nikos had to hurry to keep up with the soldiers, but they hadn't reached the first row of tanks when the first thunderclaps sounded.

"THIS IS REALLY SICK," Pill radioed as they sped across the icy plain in the buggies, trailing long clouds of swirling snow behind them. Freeing the vehicles had technically been fairly simple: Disconnect parachutes, extend the winches, wrap and hook them around the largest chunks of ice, then pull them down. Gravity had done the rest for them. The buggies had tumbled down so brutally that they had feared they had destroyed them, but they could still be turned on and driven, so apparently, the reinforced crash cages had delivered what they had promised. They had barely glanced at the disfigured bear, for what good would that have done? There were already enough question marks in their eyes, and they hadn't been particularly eager to see it either; this place was disturbing enough. They hadn't mentioned it again and had vigilantly prepared the buggies. Now only a few hundred meters separated them from their teams, which stood as a long chain of silhouettes on the ice.

"Any of it?" asked Jacek laconically.

"Everything. This object seems to change everything. The environment, the weather, the animals..."

"And us." He voiced what had been on his mind for some time.

"Yes. The nausea is gone and so is the dizziness."

"Mmm."

"I can't wait to put a lot more distance between us and this thing."

"I feel the same way. Even if we cling to the cages, we should have enough fuel to reach the finish and then Ulan-Ude."

"Two days buggy-riding through the Siberian wilderness near this thing, probably pursued by Russian Spetznaz units." Pill snorted. "I've rarely been so uncomfortable with the supposedly positive outcome of a mission."

"Nothing comes as bad as we make out in our fears," replied Pill, slowing his buggy when they reached their comrades. He grabbed the big roll bar with one hand and pulled himself out of the low bucket seat. "Good shot, Uffe. Don't take so much time next time."

"If you hadn't been about to crash into that thing, I wouldn't have had to take so much time aiming," she replied, mumbling through her scarf. She had already stowed the rifle back in the sack on her shoulder. Two tall figures, one a little leaner, the other a little broader, approached him and held out their gloved hands.

"Tom, Ulli," he greeted the two sergeant majors leading Teams Four and Six.

"Gee, Jessy, what was that thing?" asked Tom, who had pulled a broad fur hood over his battle helmet.

"A bear, but it was *changed* somehow."

"Changed?" Ulli inquired.

"Yes, morbid. I don't know. Didn't look like a normal bear and was pretty aggressive. The closer we got to the object, the dizzier and more nauseous we got. We'd better get out of here."

Not wanting any further conversation to ensue, he waved the other soldiers over and pointed to his buggy. "Tom, you and your team take this one, Ulli, you take the other. We'll clamp on to the crash cages two at a time, or three at a time, and let you take us."

"All right," Ulli said, turning toward the seemingly endless expanse of ice that led to the lake's tapered north shore. "Should be pretty quick across the ice."

"The pioneers assured me that with a full load we should be able to do forty kilometers an hour. Since we landed quite centrally on the lake, we have about three hundred kilometers to the north shore. So we should allow eight hours, including refueling." Jacek slapped the palm of his hand on the large gas tank strapped to the back of the buggy. "We're not taking any breaks until we get back to normal ground. I don't know what the aliens are hatching under the ice, but I don't want to find out either. It's about fifty kilometers from the north shore to the finish point, so we'll rest there somewhere. All right?"

"Sure," Tom said and Ulli nodded as well. Uffe and Hardy joined him and stowed their backpacks on the small loading area behind the back seat. Pill and Knut went to the other buggy and did the same there.

Less than ten minutes later, each vehicle was loaded with seven or eight soldiers. Two sat in front, three behind, and Jacek and his team split between the two, clinging to the metal bars of the crash cages. They barely spoke as the open military vehicles swept over the ice. At forty kilometers per hour, the speed wasn't particularly high compared to a car ride, and yet it seemed very fast to Jacek, as there were no reference points for a sense of speed, except for the white expanse of ice all around.

Things got bad when they left the eye of the storm and plunged into the real thing. As if on cue, the wind tugged and tore at them, whistling and howling like an angry animal. It grew abruptly dark, as the lightning apparently occurred for the most part in the immediate vicinity of the object in view, so that all they could see was what fell in the broad cones of the buggy lights: mainly snowdrifts and powerful whirlwinds that raged like angry tornadoes across the snowpack on the thick ice. Whenever the drivers couldn't avoid them, the whirlwinds tore at them so violently that Jacek couldn't just hang on anymore but had to hook his arms behind the metal bars.

It was like driving through a disaster movie that kept flashing horror elements out of nowhere. At one point, they saw a dark area further ahead, which their driver fortunately judged to be a danger soon enough and steered them around to the right. As it turned out, the ice had melted there in an exact circle of perhaps thirty or forty yards, and the whipped-up surface of the fundamentally frozen lake raged there, apparently unimpressed by the bone-chilling cold. The latter was so relentless, especially in the gale-force winds, that even the functional underwear with its military-grade polar rating couldn't entirely protect them from freezing. Jacek's limbs were shaking from the start and his hands and feet were becoming visibly numb, making it harder and harder for him to hold on to the metal bars. Even the great effort this took over the hours no longer sent enough warmth into his limbs to keep out the Siberian cold.

After about half the distance, they had to take a break, as it was no longer possible. Pill was the first to overcome the commando's pride, admitting with a curt radio message that he might lose his footing at any moment. Jacek then ordered them to stop immediately, and they brought the buggies to a parallel halt. Between them, they spread a thermal pad and set up two polar tents, anchoring them in the ice with heavy-duty pegs. Taking turns, four soldiers per tent warmed themselves by wrapping themselves in thermal blankets and heating water with gas stoves. The other seven kept watch in the storm, making sure no phenomenon or monster surprised them.

Jacek felt it was his duty to be the first to take a watch, since he could still move his fingers and toes, and stared into the darkness fifteen minutes later. A narrow night vision device was now clamped on his eyes, bathing the surroundings in shades of green and gray that were similar to the white noise on a television, confusing the eyes as the snow fell so thickly and thudded in on the ground, driven by the storm. Uffe stood beside him, also looking intently at the endless expanse of ice.

"I'd like to be back in the Congo," she said, her voice trembling slightly.

"Anytime," he agreed with her, clearing his throat to hide the tremor in his voice.

"See that up ahead?"

Jacek narrowed his eyes and followed her gesture. A few hundred yards — the distance was hard to gauge — to the west, the snow did not fall with the same intensity, but seemed to float. "What is it?"

"I don't know, looks like one of those anomalies Nikos told me about once," she replied.

"Gravity anomaly?"

"Yes, that."

"This is not good."

"None of this is good," Uffe grunted.

"I mean, for it to occur so far away from the alien wreckage. That's not good."

"Do you think the destination could still be within this thing's sphere of influence?"

"Right now, I think anything's possible," he admitted, rubbing his hands together, which didn't do much with his thick gloves on.

"I wonder where Nikos is right now?" the sniper wondered aloud.

"Probably at some war rally or TV appearance."

Uffe looked at him from the side. "He's just doing his job. I don't think he's doing it voluntarily."

"Yes, he does, but he doesn't like it."

"What do you mean?"

"He'll be sick of it, but he'll do it anyway because he thinks it's the right thing to do and one just has to do it," Jacek explained, shrugging his shoulders. "That's just the way he is."

"Yeah, that's him."

"You've got a crush on him, haven't you?"

"I think he's hot."

"Sharp?" he asked, surprised.

"Sure. He may not be very pretty, except for his bald head, which is really strong, but he's hot."

Jacek raised a brow under his night vision and chuckled — a sound amplified by the shivering of his limbs that almost happened of its own accord.

"He's really sharp because of his character. Rarely seen such a strong-willed civilian doing the right thing with absolute conviction. Sucked at first because it pissed me off. But then I realized it pissed me off because I'd like to be like that myself but have too much hate for the human condition. We see a lot of shit, you and I, and eventually, you stop believing in the good in people and just see the shit oozing out of your fellow man's brains." She paused and clicked her tongue. "Not Nikos, though. He always sees the good and does the right thing — and that's after the shit life has dumped buckets of, in his face. Without him, there'd only be people like you and me, and we need less of that, not more."

"The perfect world would be one where we were unemployed." Jacek repeated the words of his instructor at the time, Company Sergeant Major Teckelmann, and nodded.

"Maybe if there are more Nikoses, it won't be a utopia anymore. And if there are, I don't care, I'll keep killing people, and envy Nikos his positive outlook on life."

"Nikosse?"

"Niken would hardly be the correct plural."

"Maybe the name doesn't have a plural. You don't say Wolfgänge or Manfrede."

"You could say Knuten, though," she replied seriously, and after a moment, they both giggled.

"We should go warm up. I think we're starting to show signs of hypothermia," Jacek said, tapping her on the shoulder.

"No objection, your honor."

The break lasted an hour, and then they were on their way again, exposing themselves to the fierce squalls that tore and tugged at them as if someone or something wanted to tear them from the buggies and make them disappear into the darkness. Their world consisted only of the perpetual snowfall that played out in the broad cones of light from the vehicle's headlights, giving the impression of frantic movement due to the speed at which they were traveling. The length of the drive would have seemed interminable to any normal person, because unlike on the highway or on a train, they couldn't pass the time, but even though the drive was monotonous and long, the time passed quickly. That was probably because Jacek was constantly scanning the ice surface backwards and sideways with his night vision, looking for danger. Without knowing what he was looking for at all, since the alien object seemed to have a habit of constantly throwing around new anomalies or occurrences, his brain was on maximum power the whole time, not allowing him a moment's boredom. The sight, while monotonous with the ever-changing snowdrifts between ice and racing cloud cover, was also hazy enough to make him expect something coming toward or following them at any moment. He found it harder not to keep looking ahead, worried that the others were missing one of those inexplicable melting holes in the ice. The thick snowflakes made it difficult to see much further than a few dozen yards due to reflection and density of the snowfall, and if they were to fall into the floodwaters, there would be no help. It would mean the end; it was as simple as that.

Four hours later, he knew that this fate would at least no longer befall them, for they finally reached the northern shore of Lake Baikal. In the last few hours, the storm had cooled down noticeably, still blew violently, but no longer in the form of strong gusts, and the howling had also decreased to a level where one could at least talk loudly even without a radio.

"That's a problem," Hardy noted. They stood lined up in the headlights of the buggies, fifteen KSK soldiers with hooded faces and angled assault rifles. Morning was already dawning enough to show them the mighty silhouette of a mountain range they now faced. The slopes were bare and rugged and looked alien, as if they were standing on another planet.

"If the water level should have dropped by a third, that's a good five hundred meters that was under water before. So that's the mountain that was underwater and is now open," Jacek said, feeling like he was talking to himself by saying what he was thinking.

"Doesn't look like a gently rising coastline anyway," Uffe found. "More like a fucking cliff."

"Yes." He tried to recall a trekking trip he had taken many years ago. "I think it's flatter to the west. We could go see if it looks any better."

"How long are the steel cables on the winches?" asked Knut.

"I think just under a hundred yards. That's already the long version."

"If we have to, we'll just have to have some guys climb up and hook them on somewhere."

"It's all iced over." Jacek shook his head, eyeing the mountain range ahead of them. "The north coast isn't more than thirty or forty kilometers wide. We should be pretty far to the east if the silhouette doesn't fool me, so we'll head west and see where we can find better access. The breaking daylight should help us, and the storm's weakened enough to let some brightness through."

Following his orders, they headed west, close along the exposed rock massifs that had once been home to particularly hardy algae and micro-animals and now formed an icy, polished wall that was sometimes smooth, sometimes spotty and craggy, an insurmountable barrier. Further to the west, it improved, as the mountain there rose more gently, but the gradient was still far too steep to ride a buggy.

"This isn't going to work," he finally decided as he stood with Tom and Ulli staring at a map that they had to hold with four hands to keep the storm from snatching it from them. "We should be about here." He lowered his right index finger to a spot in the far northwest of the lake, then tapped the red-marked target point that seemed to be in close proximity, according to the map's scale.

"Shall we leave the buggies?" asked Tom, his voice sounding at once reluctant and insightful. There was no other solution, but sometimes it was hard to accept something as fact when the only alternative was a big problem.

"Yes. We'll tie her down as best we can, take only the most necessary gear, and climb the rest." Jacek looked up the rock that led smoothly but endlessly upwards. "With the crampons, we'll be fine. We'll have to march the rest to the silo. Don't forget your snowshoes."

"That sets our schedule back a bit," Ulli indicated.

"Yes, but we have no alternative. I guess we'll have to be extra quick with our access. Then we'll come back and drive back across the lake in the buggies."

Tom rubbed the thick nose that was tucked under his scarf. "Back through the storm and past the artifact?"

"Yes," Jacek repeated in a firm voice, tracing a line with his finger from the north point of the lake to the south. Over Ulan-Ude, one of the southernmost cities in Russia, a little east of the lower third from the lake, he paused. "We are making much faster progress on the lake than through the wilderness east of it, especially as we know nothing of the nature of the countryside since the waters of the Baikal spilled over the mountains. The calculations for travel time were very conservatively estimated at four days. Over the ice of the lake, we could make it in a day or two."

"Unless an anomaly kills us, we fall into one of those melting circles, or mutant bears attack us," Ulli grumbled.

"Right." Jacek wasn't in the mood for a discussion. He hated discussing unavoidable things and thought it was a waste of time. "Get ready; take only what you need and check each other out. What we forget now, we can't go back for, got it?"

"Understood," Tom confirmed, and Jacek looked questioningly at Ulli, who finally nodded as well. "Aye, aye."

"Good."

After they had packed everything they needed, they divided into the three teams. Team Four started, followed by Jacek, Uffe, Hardy, Knut, and Pill, and Team Six behind them. The climb was relatively gentle and just enough that they didn't have to scramble on all fours. Still, it took a lot of concentration to set the crampons properly, because the icy rock was slippery and had some pitfalls. In some places, the ice was so thin that the tips of their irons cut through it and slid ineffectively against the rock below. Thus, Uffe once nearly fell and slid several hundred feet into the depths. A protruding piece of ice would have been enough to slash her body open. Fortunately, Hardy had been able to catch her, and since then, they had made good progress.

Jacek wondered what surprise would befall them next once they entered the land beyond Baikal.

CHAPTER 11
NIKOS

NIKOS INVOLUNTARILY DUCKED his head as the first thunderclaps sounded. Even the soldiers, who somehow served as the general's escort after all, flinched and reflexively crouched with assault rifles strapped to their shoulders.

But when no explosions were heard, they looked around in irritation like a pack of startled weasels.

"Was that the Artillery already?" shouted Steutner angrily, but one of his soldiers shook his head.

"No, General, the artillery reported ready to fire in ten minutes."

"Back to the command post. Go!" barked Steutner in response, and Nikos had to hurry to keep up with the old warhorse, who proved to be surprisingly fast and nimble. As soon as they reached the outer row of escort tanks, he already saw soldiers at the mounted gun turrets securing to the sides. He couldn't shake the feeling that someone — or something — was after him, as if he were about to flee from an unseen danger. It was only when he passed the first platoons of soldiers, nervously aiming their battered rifles into the forest, that he calmed down a bit amidst the armored steel colossi.

Again and again, it thundered, and the echo of each thunderclap continued between the composite armor of the mighty hulls.

"I want to know who the fuck is shooting!" hissed Steutner before disappearing through the back door into the command truck. Nikos, meanwhile, stopped at a group of soldiers who looked like surreal figures from myths and legends with their fully hooded faces and breathing masks that resembled the mouthparts of insects. None of them said anything, nor did any of the thousands of soldiers who knelt between the tanks to the north and south, their huge smoothbore and machine guns sweeping sideways into the forest, waiting for the approaching threat.

But it didn't come.

When there was another thunder, as if an artillery position had opened fire nearby, he winced again and searched the forest like everyone else. Nothing. No movement, not the slightest change. Following more of an impulse than a hunch, Nikos craned his neck and stared upward into the thick cloud cover. It hung low, as thick and impenetrable as concrete, and glowed yellowish, as if someone had lit a light within them. Then suddenly, there was a flash, like a discharge. Then again and again, until all at once the color of the clouds changed. The dusky, yellowish glow of gray turned to a lighter hue, and shortly thereafter, it began to rain. Single drops at first, then more and more slapped on his glasses and the army around him.

The soldiers grew restless, casting uncertain glances at each other. Nikos knew that every drop was corrosive. Not that he was going to dissolve anytime soon, but at least enough that he'd get a mean rash if he got any on his skin — and worse if it happened for a long time. The scientists back home had pointed out that the soldiers' suits should be able to withstand the strain for a few days, but now that they were standing in the middle of a thick downpour, he didn't feel sure of that. True, the rain looked normal, but that apparent normality only made its sight more eerie in contrast to what he knew about the translucent drops.

Nikos shook his head and began rubbing his rubberized gloves over his glasses to wipe away the sulfuric acid water as he turned on his heel and ran to the guarded door of the command post. The two soldiers seemed to recognize him and let him through as the door opened simultaneously and Sönke peered out searchingly. Nikos recognized him by his slender stature and the notch in his helmet.

"Come on, get in here!" he heard his friend say over the radio, and took the latter's helping hand to be pulled up. Inside the wide booth, the three generals stood with three other soldiers among the dozen men and women who operated the screens and keyboards on the walls. It was cramped and gloomy, with only the light from the monitors illuminating the scene. The claustrophobic atmosphere was now joined by the relentless patter of thick raindrops.

"Did they strafe the clouds?" asked Nikos breathlessly.

"Looks like it; probably something like silver iodide," Sönke replied. "They want us to get stuck."

"Where are they shooting from anyway?"

"The drone squadrons spotted heat sources in multiple locations that came out of nowhere."

"More like from the ground," Nikos said hoarsely.

"Huh?"

"It's okay. What happens now?"

Instead of answering, Sönke pointed at the three generals standing in front of a monitor, talking in a hushed tone. Without asking, Nikos moved closer to hear what they were discussing. General Joret seemed to be explaining the situation as Steutner had joined them later. He pointed to a topographical map on the soldier's huge monitor in front of them, which used blue symbols and different number identifiers to indicate their own units. Six flashing red locations to the west crowded the observer's attention.

"From the looks of it," the Frenchman explained, "the shots were fired from there. The drones sent the evaluations of the infrared data before the second salvo was fired. We had the projectiles on screen, so they must have been pretty damn big. From the looks of it, they detonated in the lower cloud layers. They're firing at clear intervals, so it looks like they're not finished yet."

"Send in the helicopters. Tell them to cover everything with their Hellfire; otherwise, we'll soon suffocate in the mud!" ordered Steutner.

"But, sir," Joret objected cautiously. "We don't know anything about their air defense capabilities, and the helicopters are an important part of our attack strategy on the fortified mine complex."

"I'm aware of that, Jean, but since the enemy has no air force, he won't have any anti-aircraft defenses. If he should manage to bring our birds down with other weapons, that's a problem, but not as big a problem as us being stuck here and getting shot to pieces."

"May I make a suggestion, sir?" the Frenchman asked politely. He sounded tense.

"Always, but hurry."

"We could realign the artillery and destroy their positions, then we still have the helicopters as an ace in the hole."

"No," Steutner objected with surprising clarity for the mask in front of his mouth, shaking his head. "The artillery is already aligned with the mine. That's our ace. We'll incise the complex and advance on two lines. One swerves to the west, and we fake attack their gun emplacements. Your division will lead this fake attack and veer north before enemy contact to join the assault on the mine, while my division will head straight for it and try to take what they've most certainly prepared for us."

"Sir, they knew we were coming," interjected General Camacho, the Spaniard. "How did they know?"

"I don't know, Sara, but they clearly knew. That means we're walking into a trap because there's no logical target other than the mine in the perimeter. They may also be getting sensor data fed to them from orbit by their cursed Tear allies, but that doesn't change the situation. We have one advantage, and that's that they don't know anything about us or our capabilities."

"That goes the other way too," she returned in a heavy, rolling accent.

"Maybe so. But we have no choice. We go into the trap, but open-eyed, and we keep moving." Steutner paused. "I suggest we let half the artillery fire on the mine as planned. Have the other half level the last fifteen kilometers of the trail ahead of us, then we'll know what they've prepared there. Let's send the launcher batteries ahead. Have them immediately strafe anything that moves on radar. Agreed?"

"Oui, sir." The Frenchman nodded and the Spanish woman also confirmed briskly.

"All right, let's go." Steutner raised his voice. "Artillery on batteries one through ten with primary target, fire at will! Eleven through twenty, realign. Overlapping fire. Calculate a corridor ten kilometers wide to the mine. Clear five kilometers ahead." The general turned around as the other generals also started moving, talking down to more soldiers. "Divisions will be split up. The First Panzer division continued according to plan! Tell the men to stay outside and not get in, the danger of direct fire is too great. Tell them to leave their marching packs on the trucks."

"General!" a young female soldier — at least she sounded young — called from a seat just outside the entrance.

"What?" he blubbered.

"Remote air reconnaissance reports a massive and increasing number of heat signatures to the north, directly in front of the mine, extending to the east and west."

"Show me!" the general shouted and ran to her. Since Nikos was in the way, he roughly pushed him aside and stared at the monitor, where Nikos could only make out a lot of red dots. "The fuckers have prepared a cauldron. Alright. Realign howitzer positions eleven through twenty to the eastern arm of the cauldron. I don't want to see anything else on my flank there." Steutner turned and tried to pass Nikos again. "You!" he barked at Sönke. "Get our civilians out of here and into one of the Pumas. Go!"

"Come with me," his friend said immediately, pulling him back by the sleeve. Nikos didn't need to be told twice and stumbled toward the door behind the smaller soldier. Gravity still felt relentless, but its depressing weight seemed to have increased – or his knees were softening. Now he was in the midst of an igniting battle.

Together with Sönke, he stormed down the stairs and pushed the door shut behind him. There was apparent chaos around them: soldiers were running around and spread out on the tanks to the right and left of the long line of trucks in the middle. Many climbed through the tiny hatches of the armored personnel carriers at the rear, but most climbed onto the hulls and clung to the outside because there wasn't enough room for everyone. Sönke stopped toward the next Puma infantry fighting vehicle, which was on their left and whose rear hatch was just being closed.

"Wait, Private!" shouted Sönke, giving a quick wave to the soldier who had the lever of the hatch in his hand. When they reached him, he shooed him away and pulled open the armored door. "You two, out!" he ordered into the interior, without Nikos being able to tell who he was talking to. In any case, a moment later, two figures in combat fatigues came out, ducked through the narrow opening, and saluted obediently. "Come on, Nikos, come on!"

Reluctantly, Nikos went ahead, gave the two soldiers who were losing their place in relative safety because of him an apologetic look that they couldn't see anyway with his hooded face, and climbed into the tank. There were five folding seats there, with the seats directly on the floor. Four soldiers waited here with G36 assault rifles pressed to their chests, looking at him through their flak goggles like the foreign body he was. But there was nothing to do but sit down, facing Sönke. Their legs touched. As massive as the tank had looked from the outside, it seemed tiny from the inside.

"Close the fucking hatch," someone yelled from the front, perhaps the driver, and Sönke, though certainly of higher rank, hurried to comply. As soon as he had jammed the heavy lever into its socket, the forty-ton vehicle roared to life and the chains began to move. It sounded almost as if God himself was grinding down a mountain with an iron chain. In addition, the roar of the diesel engines was deafeningly loud, even penetrating his helmet, which went over his ears.

No one said anything as it wobbled and jerked like they were on a roller coaster gone wild, except everything went back and forth more leisurely and harder for it.

"Are we in battle yet?" Nikos wanted to know, feeling richly stupid at the question. He had never been in one before, let alone a battle or anything even comparable. Well, there had been the Congo thing, but he hadn't really perceived that engagement like a battle, since he hadn't done much besides carry a wounded man a few hundred yards and get shot at. It had all been so surreal and had taken place in such intense pain that he barely remembered the details. Sitting here now, with five others crammed in between the driver and gunner, who seemed to be fused to the steel further forward, part of an intricate piecemeal of armor parts, cables, and cladding, was a whole new experience. He felt like he was squeezed into a sardine can that could be cut open at any moment without him being able to do a thing about it. Added to this was a sense of isolation, as he couldn't even glimpse faces that looked at least familiarly human. Instead, he saw only motionless breathing masks under gloomy glasses that reflected the flickering cabin light. He might as well have been sitting among a handful of aliens, they looked so unhuman.

"No. We're going full speed into the cauldron now and hope that the Ari softens the right flank properly; otherwise, it's going to get very uncomfortable soon," Sönke replied. His friend sounded downright calm, but also very serious, which was always a sign that something wasn't going according to plan. The last time he had seen the German without any mischievousness in his voice was when he had been suffering from a stomach flu while Nikos had to play a gig in Frankfurt.

"The general's plan, is he... is it..."

"Is he any good?"

"Yeah, something like that."

"I think it's the best we can do in this situation. We have two aces up our sleeves, well, three actually: the MOAB bomb, the air superiority from the helicopters, and the artillery. The Leos shoot a good five kilometers effectively, the artillery has nearly sixty kilometers range with V-LAP ammo and some serious bang. If we're going to go to war on an alien planet, let's do it with the First Armored Division," Sönke explained, and to Niko's ears, he sounded more hopeful than convinced.

"We don't know what we're going to be up against yet."

"No, but the greatest advances we humans have made have been when we reached out to orbit. Just by running the space race in the sixties, we produced so many new developments and research results that it borders on miraculous. This species here has never seen their planet from above, and perhaps never developed as much innovative pressure as we have."

"They have an orbital elevator," Nikos countered. "How do we know they haven't already colonized their entire system with the help of the Tears?"

"That's what the Morphs would have told us."

"You have too much faith."

"And you, too little," returned Sönke.

"We'll see," Nikos sighed, pulling his knees closer to him. He was so drenched in sweat by now that his functional clothing felt like a second skin. Pulling his lips from his left, he pulled the small drinking tube up against the suspension and drank from his four-liter supply that was in the small backpack on his back. It was stuffy in here and the little skin between his goggles and balaclava itched terribly, but he couldn't scratch it as he would only have made it worse with his wet gloves. Shortly after, mobile artillery fire began. Each rumble of a Panzerhaubitze 2000 sent a 155mm artillery shell toward the enemy at the speed of sound. Six times each howitzer fired, resulting in a dull staccato that announced the beginning of the war. Using the MRSI method, the six shells per howitzer hit simultaneously, which they could still hear as an overlapping boom that just barely reached Nikos' ears over the roar of the diesel engine, despite the impacts being thirty kilometers away.

The real battle began fifteen minutes later in the form of radio calls that resounded tinnily through the cramped interior of the Puma. Excited voices that appeared as if from an otherworld and announced the most diverse things with excited cries.

Sometimes someone yelled "Contact!" followed by relaying positional data, and among lots of unintelligible hissing and shouting, Nikos also heard clear, almost sleepily calm commands reverberating through the ether. The excitement lasted only a few moments, then radio discipline was restored and the calm, monotonous instructions from someone, presumably in command, were a sharp contrast to the impressions of before. Nikos had expected it to start with explosions, screams, and the rattle of the machine gun on their roof, but instead, everything settled down to cool radio transmissions and muffled responses from the Puma crew. Driver and gunner talked so quietly into their headsets that he couldn't hear it through his helmet, and the instructions that came in through the speakers didn't raise their voices either. The excitement of the beginning had given way to cool professionalism unlike anything he'd imagined.

"What's happening?" he asked over the radio to Sönke, who was being rocked back and forth across from him as their Puma raced over hill and dale.

"The tanks are now in effective engagement range of the enemy and have initiated battle. So the enemy formations are under five kilometers away," Sönke explained so calmly that Nikos became even more nervous. "Our Puma's machine gun has a maximum range of three thousand meters. It's simply not our turn yet."

"You're in the command channel, aren't you?"

"Yes, but only as a silent listener in case I receive instructions to transfer you."

"What are they saying? Do we know anything about the defenders yet?"

"Except that they have mechanized troops. Smaller and larger vehicles and large infantry units. Apparently, you were right, they must have reached the surface via a tunnel system.

However, their formations are spreading slowly, probably because the tunnel systems create bottlenecks."

"Where are Karin and Rooney?" it flashed through Nikos' mind and as soon as he uttered the words his pulse skyrocketed.

"They've been moved to the Puma right behind us," Sönke tried to reassure him. "Don't worry."

"We are in a battle."

"Good, but at least they don't have to sit on the outside of the tanks like a lot of our comrades, huh?"

"Yes," Nikos breathed, lowering his helmet backwards against a steel bracket. He tried to steady himself, though the feeling of claustrophobia crept through his bones.

CHAPTER 12
JACEK

IT TOOK them three hours to climb the mountains created by the impact of the debris into Lake Baikal. What had once been underwater formed a steeply rising ice ramp in the north of the lake that eventually led to the former shore. What had once been a beach had been swept away by the tsunami after the impact. Even the range of hills through whose forests he'd hiked a decade ago, he barely recognized. The wave must have milled away all the trees like a giant grinding machine. It didn't pose a direct problem, as they made good progress due to the slight inclines and aisles between the hills, but the surroundings were eerie enough to add a fair amount of discomfort to the bone-chilling cold, making it even harder for Jacek to warm up his body. While they had been climbing and marching for a very long time, which should have warmed him by means of muscular activity, he hadn't eaten in a long time and the energy deficit was making itself felt more and more urgently through lack of heat regulation.

Finally, he ordered them to rest after they had brought the first hill range between them and the lake. There was only a short rest for Tom, Ulli, and their two teams, because they had been sitting and resting during the whole trip across the lake, while Jacek and his team had been holding on to the crash cages with a huge effort. Another eight hours of marching should be no problem for them. The goodbyes took place in relative silence and consisted of silently shaking hands in the twilight of a morning that would see no sun, only the dirty gray foothills of the storm.

They pitched the two tents in the lee of one of the hills, which, depending on how you looked at it, was the last hill of the first chain or the first of the second. The ground was littered with tree stumps that had been torn off just above the ground. The ice had covered the gross injuries to the trees like a transparent band-aid on the battered vegetation. It was a kind of ice that didn't belong here, showing that it was lake water that must have flowed back after the tsunami. Sporadically, as they hammered down the pegs, they could see fish and crustaceans trapped in the layer of ice about six inches deep, their mouths agape in disbelief. Some had dorsal fins or parts of the body sticking out of the ice, frozen as hard as stone.

Jacek let Pill talk him into going to sleep first and was actually too tired to protest or play the strong leader, the last to fall back on the few comforts of a commando soldier. So, he lay down on a sleeping pad in full battle gear and covered himself with one of the thermal blankets. He couldn't even count to ten before he was asleep. In his dreams, he saw distorted images and impressions of disfigured bears and bizarre icy landscapes battered by storms. These brought with them insane and terrifying faces, taller than skyscrapers and darker than night. But the nightmares soon subsided, as his body seemed to understand that he was too tired to actively dream.

When he first awoke, he was cold, and his muscles ached from his toes to his neck. His wrists cracked in protest as he looked at the clock. Five hours of sleep, that was pretty solid for a combat mission behind enemy lines. Beside him, Uffe and Pill lay under shiny thermofoils that they had placed over their thermal blankets, and apparently his as well. They looked a bit like tinfoil-wrapped dolls, as you could barely make out any of their faces. Just like him, they had learned to sleep in gear, including with their helmets on their heads. Their instructor had once said that the real strength a commando soldier needed to develop over regular soldiers was the ability to sleep anywhere, in any conditions, and take whatever regeneration he or she needed.

Today, he understood why that was such an advantage. With outstretched arms, he roused his comrades, who silently opened their eyes and nodded when they caught sight of him. As dumbly as they had awakened, they greeted Hardy and Knut, who after a few minutes had come running from the hills surrounding them, barely recognizable because of their white camouflage clothing. Jacek wanted to scold them for not waking him to take a watch, but he was too cold and the surroundings too uncomfortable to speak up. They each ate an EPA ration and silently packed up their gear. Twenty minutes later, they were marching north again. With both the hills and the washed away woods, which were now nothing more than tree grave-yards with the many tree stumps representing their gravestones, and everything else under an uneven sheet of ice, they made quick progress. With snowshoes, each route required about three times as much time as with normal shoes, so the strange environment had its advantages. Of course, that didn't outweigh the fact that there was no cover or visual protection left at all, but it was still an encouraging point. The encouragement ended, however, when they passed the second range of hills and entered the plain, which stretched northeast as a plateau to the snow-capped mountains, merging into the upper Angara Moun-tains a few miles to the west. The pinnacles of the massive mountain range were stuck in the cloud cover, which at the same time formed the edges of the storm.

The wind was still tugging at their winter fatigues and rustling unpleasantly at the edges of their helmets, but that wasn't what made Jacek uncomfortable and gave them pause as a team: it was the peculiar figures they faced. At first, he thought they were illusions in the twilight of the fading daylight: ice figures that represented waves, frozen in the middle of a breaking motion. Sometimes they were as tall as a man, sometimes like a house and elongated like a freight train. It got worse as they moved carefully among the formations, where the Angara River fed smaller lakes that were here and now unrecognizable under the layer of ice and snow. After a few hours, they encountered the first cars and ships, first some fishing trawlers, held at an angle or lying on their sides by the ice like exhibits of the catastrophe that had struck this place. But they also passed a large car ferry, lopsided to the north, half encased in a frozen wave. The silhouettes of the crew on the bridge deck were frozen in place, as were the many vehicles preserved by the ice on the far north side — some still with passengers inside. They sat at the wheel, holding babies in their arms, or had their eyes open behind the windows in eternal terror. Now all they had left was the silence of this mass grave in the heart of Siberia.

"They look like wax figures," Uffe said as they arrived at the last car washed off the ferry and looked in affected silence at the family that had been shock-frozen inside the Lada bus.

"They look like fucking scared people," Hardy corrected her sullenly. "Can anyone tell since when a giant tsunami freezes in a very short period of time?"

"Or splits into lots of little waves before it does?" Pill pointed at one of the congealed wave formations that made their way north a constant back and forth.

"Doesn't matter." Jacek interrupted the rising conversation, giving it over to the whisper of the cold wind for a few moments before continuing. "This containment zone makes me want nothing more than to run for the hills, but that's not what I'm paid to do. We've been living in a world since the beginning of the year where we have to accept new facts, and for better or worse, that includes the old ones no longer applying."

"No more bears, after all," Pill muttered at the edge of audibility.

"See?" Knut nudged his comrade in the side with the butt of his rifle. "That's why I like you so much, kid. You're always so positive, always seeing the best."

"Until I see you."

"Ice cold, man, ice cold. Do you want me to ice like those Russians?" Knut snorted emphatically. "Once I'm dead, I'm sure you'll miss me."

"Sure, you and your psychopath grin," Uffe grumbled. "Then they'll mill you out of here and put you on display at Madame Tussaud's to scare little kids."

"They're wax figures," Hardy corrected her.

"All you have to do is thaw him out and he'll be one again."

"Are you guys done?" asked Jacek, rolling his eyes. "You guys really need to find a new outlet for your anxiety."

That hit home. Knut and Uffe turned to him and said simultaneously, "We're not scared shitless." As soon as the words had faded away, they looked at each other.

"Well, you see, I like that much unity in my team." Jacek reached into his fanny pack and pulled out the detailed map of the target taped in foil. He placed it on the frozen hood of the Lada and waved his comrades over. With one finger, he tapped the missile silo on the southeastern slopes of the Angara Mountains. "That's about twenty kilometers to go. I still haven't been able to establish radio contact with Teams Four and Six, but there's a settlement southeast of our target – at least there used to be. It was called Kichera. I remember they had a huge radio tower; maybe it survived the wave. If so, one of us could climb up there and see if we can get a connection, if we don't have it by then anyway. It's only a few more miles from there to the silo."

"Hmm," Hardy said, pulling the scarf from his mouth and looking north before shaking his head. "I don't think the tower's that high."

"You mean because of the frozen water?" Jacek nodded. "That could be. There must be twenty or thirty meters of ice. However, the settlement was a little higher than the surrounding countryside because it was in a river delta. We might get lucky and the tower is still sticking out far enough from the new facts to give us an advantage with the radio."

"What if we can't connect?" asked Uffe, stroking her M82, which hung in front of her chest and was almost as long as she was.

"Tom and Ulli have orders to wait for our launch signal. If we can't establish radio contact, they have orders to respond to improvised signals. We've agreed on a shot from the flare gun."

"You got it." Uffe seemed pleased. "Then we should check out your hamlet. It can't get any creepier than this snot."

"You didn't see the zombie bear either," Pill grumbled.

"Okay, that's it, we're moving out. When we get to the target, you can go back to shooting people if that makes you feel better." No one said anything in response as Jacek folded up the map and stowed it back in his pocket.

Silently, they walked on, fanning out a short distance apart and roaming the bizarre landscape of unnatural ice formations and preserved flora and fauna, frozen and smothered dozens of meters deep. When summer came – if it ever did, under the influence of the alien object many hundreds of miles to the south – there would be floods here that would change the map forever. He found this idea sad, knowing full well what a place of raw beauty lay buried beneath his feet.

It got even worse when they reached the former Kichera after six hours. There, the top of the radio tower was actually poking through the ice — a good ten meters high. It seemed the gigantic tsunami must have already lost so much of its power by the time they got here that it didn't destroy everything. He could still accept that and make sense of it. That didn't apply to two other things, though: for one thing, there was a rectangular shack made of corrugated metal right next to the radio tower remnant that made no sense unless it had been put up after the disaster. For another, there was no snow here and the icy surface beneath their feet was exposed. They could see between their feet the half-destroyed houses in the depths, held in place by the ice. The houses of wood and brick had solidified into shapes that looked as if they had been torn apart by a hurricane and then preserved in time. As if that wasn't strange enough, there was light down there — which was probably why they could see the remains of Kichera at all; they were several dozen meters down, after all. Where the light came from, Jacek could neither see nor explain.

"Good, now that's really fucked up," Uffe found himself puffing laconically.

"It is," Jacek agreed with her, pointing to the small building made of gray corrugated metal. "That one worries me more, though. That must be what the unit stationed in the silo put up." He pointed at the radio tower. "That can only mean they're using the last bit of the tower to keep in contact with the Kremlin or whoever."

"Blasting?" asked Knut, and Jacek nodded.

"It's best to do it now. If they've already noticed us or are about to notice us, radio out immediately and we'll have a problem."

"But then they'll know we're coming and the element of surprise will be gone," Hardy mused thoughtfully.

"We'd rather bite our way through a threat we know about than a backup we don't," Jacek decided.

"Speaking of reinforcements." Uffe, who had raised her rifle and was peering through the telescope, pointed west with a nod. "Looks like a snowmobile. Five kilometers."

"Knut, you climb the tower and plant an explosive charge. Uffe, you find a point to the south where you have a clear view of the target; we'll hide behind the house. Cut the engine as soon as I tell you. Stay close enough for the radio."

The sniper nodded, shouldered her long rifle, and headed off in a southerly direction while Knut climbed the first metal rungs of the upper radio tower.

The snowmobile turned out to be a Lada bus converted for the military with snow chains on the wide tires. Jacek stood with his back to the corner of the house facing away from the vehicle and, raising his hand, told Hardy, the returned Knut, and Pill to wait. Only when the Lada turned the corner did he signal Uffe, and a thunderous shot echoed across the plain. The screech of glass shattering under the force of a cigar-sized, armor-piercing bullet mingled with the echo of the shot as it ripped through the entire driver's compartment. Blood splattered like dark oil against the windows and Jacek charged forward. Four steps separated him from the driver's door; after two steps it was opened and a figure stumbled out. He shot it twice in the head. A butterfly of blood arose behind it on the car, while the lifeless body crashed to the ice with its head pulled back. More short bursts of fire rang out, then silence fell.

Jacek walked past the man who had been killed, who was in thick winter clothing that was white and gray patch camouflage. The driver's cab was empty, the other door also open. Two bodies without heads sat on the seats, the bench seat behind them empty. Four combatants.

"Secured," Hardy said over the radio.

"Environment calm," Uffe announced.

Jacek nodded as if to himself and examined the man he had killed in detail. It was a young man in his late twenties, whose face was covered with acne scars. He had a set of keys on him and a pistol, nothing else.

"Hey, Joss?" called Knut over the radio. He sounded neither amused nor absent-minded, which made Jacek queasy. "You should come to the tailgate."

As he rounded the boxy vehicle, Knut and Pill stood there in front of the open double doors, staring into the interior. Jacek made sure Hardy was in front of the car and walked over to them to face what they were seeing. As soon as he did, his eyes widened in shock: there were countless corpses stacked on the open cargo area of the interior. They wore the white surgical gowns of hospital patients and were stacked in a checkerboard pattern all the way to the ceiling. His first thought was soldiers, but then he realized that women and men of all ages were among the victims. They had dark hair, light hair, but also gray hair, soft and wrinkled skin, and the only thing they had in common was that they were dead.

"Give me a hand," he grumbled and began to pull the first corpse — an old lady with long grey hair and a narrow mouth — out of the Lada. One by one, they laid a total of sixteen bodies side by side on the ice and went over them step by step. One young man with a shaved skull and large feet was missing a hand, where someone had apparently tried to attach a metal object. It looked like a three-headed top hat and had been screwed into the deceased's forearm via buckles. Next to it lay a middle-aged woman with red hair and freckles, her face covered in green pustules. The skin on her hands and feet looked like that of a leper, and seemed to have dissolved to the flesh. Another man possessed neither hair nor scalp, but a dark gray grid of plastic that extended from his forehead down his neck. Gray brain matter was visible in some transparent places.

"What kind of sick shit is this?" asked Uffe as she breathlessly arrived at their house and caught sight of the depressing collection of disfigured corpses.

"Looks like they've got more than one alien trapped in that silo," Pill replied with a bitter expression.

"They're experimenting on alien tech," Jacek said quietly, only now realizing he had clenched his hands into fists. He picked up the two grips of his rifle again and grasped them tightly. "Apparently, they need locals for this."

"Anyway, they don't seem to have much regard for ethical concerns like the eggheads at EUSFOR. I was beginning to think those guys were allowed too much." Pill turned to the west, where somewhere at the base of the mountains was the silo. "Would like to know if they're doing tests on the captured Tear or bunkering parts of the wreckage in Lake Baikal in there."

"That could be a problem," Uffe noted.

"What exactly?"

The sniper pointed at Jacek, who noticed it out of the corner of her eye and looked at her. "Well, the face of Joss. I know that look, and it means our engagement targets just expanded and the body count is going to go up." Uffe pointed at the disfigured civilians next. "The second problem is that we don't know if these disposed bodies are the beginning of a failed batch or dead witnesses to the first successful attempts to recreate or use some of the alien tech."

"We'll find out very soon," Jacek growled, pointing to the open minibus. "We'll drive the rest of the way."

CHAPTER 13

NIKOS

NIKOS KEPT a tight grip on his knees as their armored personnel carrier was shaken several times.

"What's going on?" he yelled over the din. Across from him, Sönke tapped his outstretched finger against the spot on his helmet where his right ear was located. When Nikos understood, he said more quietly, "Sorry."

"Probably dodging something."

"Hang on, guys!" one of the crew members yelled from the front. The smell of heavy diesel and heated cables permeated his nose through the respirator. "Something's coming at us!"

"What?" asked Nikos, irritated. "What do you mean, something's coming..." That was as far as he got, as there was a crash outside and the entire floor of the vehicle vibrated like a vibratory plate. There was a clang and crackle against the wall of the tank behind Sönke and then the entire world dissolved into chaos: Up became down, left became right. Arms and legs of the strapped soldiers jerked first in one direction, then in another. Everything was spinning, rolling over. Smaller objects that appeared too briefly before Nikos' eyes to identify flew back and forth between them, hit, rose again, and hit somewhere else. His helmet was slammed violently against the ceramic paneling behind him — so hard that a brutal gong sounded in his ears, and he blacked out for a moment. The direction of the relentless gravity changed a few times, shifting toward the seated people across from him, who suddenly became the new "down." Nikos' arms and legs were pulled in Sönke's direction, then there was a crash that drowned out even the noise of the diesel, and all movement stopped. For a moment, it remained quiet, except for the howling engine, which his brain was already tuning out. After two breaths, he opened his eyes, which he had unknowingly squeezed shut, only to close them again as a volley of bullets rattled through the Puma's armor like hail.

"Got hit!" shouted someone from the crew further forward in the tangle of the infantry fighting vehicle.

"Negative!" another voice bellowed over the engine noise.

"Hannes, get us the fuck out of here. We're sitting on a fucking platter!"

"Controls are down!"

"Son of a bitch."

"What's going on?" asked Nikos into his radio for what felt like the tenth time.

"I don't know, but doing nothing is bad."

"We've got to get out of here or we'll get barbecued!" someone shouted, and this time, it wasn't anyone from the crew, but one of the four soldiers who sat with them on the three folding seats on each side. He peeled himself out of the straps and crawled to the hatch at the stern — disregarding the legs of Nikos and Sönke that were in the way.

"Hey!" he protested, but the other three soldiers had also already unbuckled their seat belts and were pushing him from behind with the force of approaching panic.

"Keep that damn hatch closed!" someone from the tank crew yelled, but the order was lost in the general shouting of the soldiers, who sought their salvation by fleeing outside. Nikos could understand them, would probably have gotten up as well and run outside in a blind panic, but the men or women between him and Sönke filled every cubic centimeter of space and pushed him back into the seat. He heard Sönke shout something too, but a moment later, the first soldier had already opened the hatch, and a gush of cold air rushed to them. But the toxic air of the alien planet wasn't the only thing waiting for them outside.

Nikos was just trying to fend off the hands of the men and women who were trying to squeeze past him side by side to get out as quickly as possible, when red paint suddenly splashed onto his glasses. Before he could wipe it away, panic-stricken screams rang out, which immediately died away. Through a free spot in front of his left eye, he saw the bodies of the soldiers in front of him twitching as if they were electrified. Blood sprayed in all directions, sparks flew back and forth in the cabin. Further forward in the vehicle, someone yelled wildly, but their voice was also replaced by silence shortly after.

"Nikos!" gasped Sönke over the radio. "We're taking fire from outside. You... argh... are you hit?"

"N-no, I don't think so," he stammered back, trying to push the tangle of lifeless bodies away from him.

"We need to close the hatch as soon as we can!"

"I'm stuck!"

"Me too!"

"Panagía mou! Skatá!" scolded Nikos, pressing an animalistic growl over his lips as he activated all reserves of strength to free himself. His left arm, with its barely half-healed biceps tendon, protested with a pulling pain that continued into his shoulder. But he'd given himself a little wiggle room — enough to undo the clasp on his straps, which in turn gave him more options. These he used to grab the lifeless body in front of him and carry it out through the open hatch. Now he could see Sönke, who at that moment jerked his head back, slamming his helmet against the vehicle wall as a volley of bullets whizzed through the open hatch, producing the hollow clang of metal on metal somewhere.

"Shit!"

"I'll get to it," Nikos promised. He knew what had to be done, and without further thought, he set himself in motion: Crawling on his knees through the blood and over one of the two corpses lying intertwined in the narrow center aisle, he reached out with his right hand for the metal wheel of the hatch. As he did so, his left hand slipped in the blood — at just the right moment, as the alien fire immediately resumed. One volley coated the hatch with sparks, another hissed just past his ear. It resounded deafeningly loud twice in his helmet, then he had stretched far enough to get his hands on the wheel and pull it toward him with a jerk. Before the composite armor had even touched the rubberized frame, more bullets struck from the outside and he hastily turned to his left until the bolt clicked into place.

"Nikos? Nikos!"

"What?" It took him a moment to realize he was being addressed, and another to realize that Sönke had unbuckled his seatbelt and had just wiped the blood from his glasses. There was a ringing in his left ear so loud, he almost didn't hear his friend.

"Are you hurt?" His friend sounded concerned. There was a loud clang somewhere.

"I don't think so," Nikos replied lamely. Then something occurred to him. "No, no, that's not my blood."

"Your helmet's been hit!"

"My helmet?" He felt his helmet and found some indentations on the left side near his ear. "Oh."

"Can you breathe normally? How many fingers am I holding up?"

"Four. I'm not stupid."

"Good. Listen to me. We're trapped. We can't get out, but we can't stay here either until they bring in guns that can cut this tin can open, you understand?"

"Yeah, I guess so."

"I believe the crew has been killed. The first thing we need to do is get an overview with the sensors, you hear me? Now, to do that, we're going to have to move forward and pull the bodies back to make room. It's very tight there."

"All right," Nikos replied hoarsely, following Sönke forward on all fours, past the two riddled soldiers in front of him.

You do what you have to do to survive, and for your friends to survive, he admonished himself as he felt nauseous at the sight of an obvious neck puncture. So, he averted his eyes and kept them upward. The cabin was splattered all over with blood and there was smoke in several places, but that was still more abstract than facing direct death.

The tank crew consisted of three people, he now found out. Sönke made his way between the panels and cables in front of him, first pulling the commander from an elevated seat at the very front, only to hand him over to Nikos with a groan. He dragged him to the front of the door and deposited the gravity-increased weight in front of the hatch. The gunner and driver followed next, just as faceless dead meat as the rest in their fully-veiled faces. In Niko's memory, they were just blathering orders, but now all was dead and lost.

"Nikos! Come here," Sönke urged him and climbed under a canister that looked like a gas cylinder strapped down, until finally only his legs were visible.

"I'm here."

"Climb forward over this ledge and stand so you can look through the periscope."

"All right." As if in a dream, Nikos scrambled over the bloody corpses, swallowed his nausea several times, and climbed under a wiring harness and a vertical armor plate onto a downward-framed seat. Sönke was already talking into his radio, but he couldn't hear the exact words over the roar of the engine. He stood and had to slouch slightly because he was too tall. A rubber socket for the eyes was right in front of him, so he pressed his face against it and instinctively grasped the two control levers underneath, which reminded him of pictures of a submarine.

"Can you see anything?" asked Sönke.

"Yes." Nikos blinked a few times and swung the periscope back and forth. The image was obviously not a direct image through a mirror and lens, but electronically processed through several sensor systems. The right handle he could turn to zoom. They stood on sloping ground. In front of them stood, and lay, dozens of other tanks, most of them flat, squat Pumas with their predator-like turret attachments, but also a few main battle tanks, one of which was slewing its turret and firing straight. The huge muzzle blast blinded him for a moment. The vehicles looked like they had been shaken in a dice cup and dumped out randomly. Soldiers ran among the tanks, taking cover behind them. Their rifles spat hundreds of bursts of fire toward a patch of woods about twenty yards to the right. The ground was muddy and uneven like a field after a storm surge, and to the left was a freshly torn slope.

"What do you see, Nikos? The computer system has been damaged; I can't see the sensor data on my end!" Sönke demanded impatiently.

"I think they fired down the slope, which then tore off in a landslide with our section of the column, throwing us right into their arms. MALAKA!" he interrupted himself as something came flying at lightning speed and the Leopard 2 that had just fired exploded. After Nikos blinked once, the tank was still there, albeit slightly dented and sooty. He fired again but was hit two more times in a row and finally burned to a crisp. Some soldiers who hadn't scattered in time and had taken cover behind the tank before it caught fire and ran back and forth with arms flailing. "They've got heavy guns." Nikos licked his lips and turned the turret to the right toward the woods, oversteering too much, and the image spun so that he felt sick until he finally managed to stabilize it. Back at the forest, he saw muzzle flashes near the ground and some indistinct figures. He looked forward again, then back, only to find that they were one of the few infantry fighting vehicles that had come to a stop upright. The one directly behind them was even upside down on the turret, half obscured by an avalanche of mud and debris.

Karin and Rooney! he thought in horror.

"Nikos!"

"Yes?"

"I need a target; I don't see anything here."

"Okay, okay, swing the turret ninety degrees to the right," he instructed his friend. "Good, now fire!"

The Puma's MK 30-2 machine gun came rattling to life, spewing seven-hundred-thirty-millimeter rounds per minute into the forest. The automatic fire was set too high and sawed horizontally through the trees and giant mushrooms, shredding flesh, wood, and leaves, and covering everything in a thick shower.

"Further down!" shouted Nikos excitedly into his headset, and the hurricane of destruction shifted downward, plowing through the undergrowth like a scythe. Earth and rock splashed up in high fountains, where the cigar-sized projectiles turned life into death. Enemy muzzle flash was no longer visible.

"Nikos! Talk to me!"

"Looks good; if you keep swinging back and forth like that, you should hit something. I'm going to get Karin and Rooney!"

"What?" asked Sönke in horror, but Nikos was already climbing back into the bloody cabin of the tank, slipping twice and finally reaching the macabre pile of corpses in front of the hatch. Accompanying him were his friend's warning shouts of protest, but since he could still hear the gun rattling, he knew Sönke was still in place and wouldn't stop him. Placing both hands on the wheel of the lock, he took a deep breath and then turned it to the right until he felt resistance in his fingers and pushed the hatch outward.

With a leap, he jumped out, got caught in the bodies, and tumbled into the mud behind the stern. He hurt himself in several places where he hit rocks, propelled by the relentless force of gravity, but ignored his sensory input to pick himself up. After a quick look around, he stopped toward the Puma directly in front of him, the one his friend said the two journalists had ridden in. On the right side, the tank that had crashed on its head was covered by part of the avalanche, so he ran around to the left. Each step sent burning lactic acid into his muscles, which acknowledged his unaccustomed weight with protest. Shots whizzed past him as the roar of the machine gun died away, but he didn't turn, kept running toward the rear of the crashed Puma with his head down until he reached the hatch and held the wheel in his hand. At the same moment, as shots struck just above his hands, and sparking blasts ricocheted off the armor, Sönke's machine gun kicked in again, plowing through the forest floor once more. Nikos' attention was drawn by movement from the other direction, however, and his gaze jerked instinctively around: tanks were gradually appearing on the crest of the brute-force torn slope that dropped steeply toward them. At first, his brain thought they must be the aliens, but they were leopard tanks, stopped on the crest; there had to be at least a hundred of them, lined up there, and the next moment accelerating with their tracks – straight down the slope. Even as they toppled forward, their powerful smoothbore guns fired across the forest at targets he couldn't see. He ran two steps to the right and looked past the tank to the front, then to the rear. Everywhere, surviving soldiers rushed from their cover toward the forest, firing blindly. At first, he thought they were joining the attack of the tanks, which were racing to them, but then he understood that they would be in the worst position imaginable when the tanks reached their position, for surely they would not brake in the mud. Sönke's machine gun fell silent, presumably to avoid hitting his own soldiers.

"Damn it!" Nikos turned back around and went to pull open the hatch, but it was already open and soldiers were pouring out. Ignoring him, they rushed past him and joined the storm — or flight — into the forest.

"Karin! Rooney?" he yelled questioningly into the brief but insistent surge of bodies in camouflage clothing.

"Nikos?" A small figure stopped in front of him, a second also, but both were run over by a trailing soldier and had to pick themselves up. They were not armed.

"Thank God. Are you hurt?"

"I don't think so," Karin yelled over the renewed thunder of the guns, wincing involuntarily as if someone had punched her in the neck.

"We've got to get out of here before they get down here," he yelled back, pointing at the battle tanks that were racing down the slope in irregular rows like a force of nature — straight at them.

"Oh you..." That was as far as she got, because Nikos was already yanking her along hoping Rooney was following them.

In the confusion of running soldiers who all looked alike, it was hard to spot anyone.

"Sönke!" he shouted. "Sönke!"

"I'm out. Nine o'clock!"

Nikos looked around, not stopping running toward the forest. A figure waved roughly in his direction and he waved back. With Karin and Rooney in tow, he hurried over the first logs felled by the machine gun, thick as Litfass columns. When they reached each other, they quickly grabbed hands and ducked into the mud under hissing enemy fire.

"They're going to roll over us!" yowled Karin, barely audible in the din of battle.

"We need to get further into the forest," Sönke said over the radio. He held an assault rifle in his hand and gestured for them to follow him. Nikos didn't need to be told twice and shooed Rooney and Karin after his friend to bring up the rear.

Through the ruins of what had once been a forest, they followed the charging soldiers, some of whom kept getting hit left and right and going down, charging into the arms of the enemy with their backs tucked in front so as not to be pulverized by their own troops. Then, for the first time, Nikos saw with his own eyes the aliens who had attacked them: four figures at an alien yet remotely familiar device that resembled a cannon barrel with cone-shaped tanks around its rear base. The structure was perched on a square hull, which in turn was mounted on wheels. The aliens were smaller than humans, with bulky torsos and short limbs. In their hands, they held guns that looked like elongated boxes and spat out garish flowers of fire. The aliens' heads were in helmets with oval visors that were mirrored yellow. Nikos was transfixed by the sight, which was at once mundane and disturbing because his mind could not come to terms with the fact that these were actually life forms from the other side of the Milky Way. They too possessed arms and legs and a head. Almost certainly they also possessed intelligence and a sentient consciousness, and the first thing they did was kill each other.

Just as he was about to stop, paralyzed by the sight, a tank shell crashed into the aliens' gun, destroying it in a blinding explosion. Smoke and fire enveloped everything, mingling with splattered earth. Nikos turned to see the tanks rolling between and over the damaged vehicles at the base of the avalanche. The first soldiers were already running back, escaping in small groups into the clear lanes between each tank. Sönke turned around as well, but Nikos had spotted something else: enemy vehicles, large box-like structures, like giant beetles with shimmering armor, that appeared out of nowhere not a hundred meters away.

"We can't make it!" he cried as an idea occurred to him. The turret that had just been destroyed had had wheels, but no traction engine.

Ignoring Sönke's words of warning, he charged past his friend, hoping that he and the journalists would follow. He ran twenty meters to the destroyed position, where secondary fires ate through the undergrowth, and jumped over a half-eaten alien corpse. Something hissed over his head and he winced so hard, he fell — right in front of what he'd been looking for: a half-open hatch leading down. Dim and eerie, it unfolded vertically into the depths.

CHAPTER 14

JACEK

"TEAM One to Teams Four and Six, stand by for access," Jacek called into the mouthpiece of his headset. Hardy sat at the wheel of their Lada, deftly steering the minibus over the ice in front of the narrow aisle in the foothills of the Angara Mountains that towered before them like a colossus of stone and snow, hiding its pinnacles in the low-hanging clouds.

"Team Four, Leader, copy that," came the curt reply from Tom, followed by a similar confirmation from Ulli. The teams lay in wait, each to the right and left of the aisle, on the finger-like mounds that rose ever more steeply to the west. Although the tsunami had also shaved away the lower parts of the hillsides after the impact, unlike further down, nothing had iced over there, but the water had sloshed back down into the valley. That didn't bring back the cover of the trees, but plenty of fallen logs and ripped open holes in the earth for their escort teams to use — with the simultaneous advantage that there were fewer obstacles blocking their view into the small valley.

The opening of the valley was still about two hundred meters away and was marked by two inconspicuous wooden posts, which Jacek had spotted with his binoculars rather by chance. He guessed that there must have been a path there in the past, but it must have been washed away or covered by the tsunami. The new water level reached quite far in front of the hangar building and the box structure next to it, which was why they were heading straight for it now. He was under no illusions: for sure they had been noticed long ago and were in the crosshairs of some sniper Tom and Ulli hadn't spotted yet. They had caught one on the right ridge, but he didn't believe the Russians had only one hidden. As always, the question at this point was whether the enemy knew about them and was laying low to set a trap himself and fight the battle on his terms. Or he didn't know anything, and the ball was in their court. Either way, they would soon be in the picture. Hardy and he had slit open the jackets of the two riders who had been shot and placed them in front of their chests like blankets to fit over their gear. It might be enough for the view through the dirty windowpane.

When they reached a high barbed-wire fence, its roll-up gate closed and lined with cameras, the large shortwave radio jammed above the control lever buzzed. Splashes of blood obscured the display, which came to life at that moment. A torrent of Russian gurgled from the speaker. Jacek looked questioningly at Knut, who was squatting on the bench in the back between Uffe and Pill, grinning as he took the radio that was held out to him.

"He wants to know why we're back so soon."

"Now we'll see if your Russian sucks," Uffe interjected spitefully.

"I've got an Irkutsk dialect on it, so I can cover up any accent!"

"Come on now," Jacek hissed impatiently.

"Vse proshlo bystro," said Knut in Russian, shrugging his

shoulders. "Eto bylo ne slozhno!" His comrade took his thumb off the *send* button and waited. It buzzed a few times, then a short reply rang out.

"Wants to know what's up with our discs."

"Then think of something!"

"Eto moya vina, izvinite. Ya trachu odin!" Knut gave a short laugh and then released the button again. This time, there was a very short reply, and the gate rolled aside.

"Well, what did he say?" asked Uffe curiously.

"That he'd bust my ass for it. And that I was a useless Siberian bastard. Something like that." Knut's crazy grin widened a bit. "I'm looking forward to meeting him, seems like a cool guy."

"We'll have a chance to do that in a minute," Jacek grumbled, gesturing curtly for Hardy to head for the boxy building next to the hangar. "Uffe? Ready?"

"I was born ready, Jessy boy."

He rolled his eyes and focused on the approaching building, behind which the mountains rose steeply, forming a sort of notch into which the small complex ducked. The main building was single-story and constructed of plain concrete, with only a squat window at the front. Below that, there was only a wide door with a slot in the middle. Only now did he spot a wide snow camouflage net in front of the right wall of the building, fluttering slightly in the wind. Beneath it were a couple of skids, presumably from snowmobiles.

"Drive right up to the door, Hardy."

"Will do, Joss." The telecommunicator drove a wide arc that brought them parallel to the door, about five meters apart. Before they had even slowed, the two massive door panels slid aside and two soldiers in snow-white uniforms with equally white steel helmets came running out with AK-74s strapped to their backs. One gestured wildly and shouted something at them that sounded so angry and threatening that he didn't need a translation to understand there was a problem.

"Knut?"

"Oh, he meant something about the hangar and the next batch and that he was about to grill our sausages."

"He said that?"

"No, but that sounds nicer."

One of the soldiers came to the window and froze as he looked into the muzzle of Jacek's pistol. The other — standing slightly off-center toward the open door — jerked his Kalashnikov up, but Uffe had already leaned forward from the back seat and was grinning, aiming the short grenade launcher outside.

"Hiya, Popeye," she gurgled, and the grenade launcher went "whoop" as Jacek simultaneously shot the soldier in the face. The grenade hit the area behind the door and the explosion hurled the second soldier in its direction. Jacek hit him before he had even touched the ground and the blast wave shook the car, sending heat into his face.

"Move in!" he barked, pushing open the hot door and running toward the smoking entrance of the missile silo with his pistol extended in front of him. Behind him, the Lada's side door was yanked open and his team followed in quick strides. The entryway smelled of burnt cables and dust and was so dark that he switched to his assault rifle and turned on the flashlight. Gunshots rang out behind him, but they were farther away and possessed the typical reverberation of a valley.

"Four ECs down outside the hangar," Tom reported tonelessly over the radio.

"Copy that. Team Six, you find the generators and take them out. We'll take care of extracting the package."

"Affirmative."

Jacek turned to the left, where an elevator shaft led down, then to the right, where there was a small door with a glowing emergency exit sign in Cyrillic letters. Hardy was already on the spot and tried to open it but shook his head.

"Electronically locked."

"Fine, we'll take the elevator." He gave a wave and Pill and Knut positioned themselves to the left and right of the metal double doors. Along with Uffe, Jacek slid his combat knife between the halves of the door and began to pry open a crack where they could stick their fingers and pull. Neck straining with effort, he tugged as hard as he could, and they managed to clear a passage wide enough to let one person through at a time. A hydraulic whir sounded and the steel cables in the center of the shaft began to jingle.

Carefully, he pushed his head through the opening and looked down. At a depth of about fifty meters, the elevator car was just starting to move — upwards.

"C-4, fist," he ordered, holding his open hand back without turning around. A few moments later, he held something the size of a fist in his hands and reached out to release it. The packet of plastic explosives followed gravity into the depths. Jacek pulled back and counted to three in his mind, then gave Knut a wave, and he pressed the trigger. The detonation echoed deep and pierced through the shaft, making the concrete floor beneath them tremble. Dust trickled down from the sooty ceiling onto them.

"I guess we won't take the elevator back," Knut decided with a grin.

"No, we take the stairs. Attach another charge to the door to the stairwell, then we can set up a false trail and maybe have a little more peace down there." Jacek made a beckoning motion behind him and peered into the elevator shaft again after a thick cloud of smoke had pushed its way through the open door. The car had been blown out of its socket and crashed to the bottom of the shaft as a burning wreck with the ceiling ripped open. His face burned with heat and he pulled his scarf a little higher over his nose.

"We'll take the maintenance ladder. Go!" He waited until Hardy and Pill had passed him and followed them ahead of Uffe and Knut. The ladder rungs still felt warm, but quickly lost their heat the longer the descent took. Again and again, Jacek peered into the shaft, past his comrades who were climbing swiftly and nimbly into the depths. Nothing moved. An alarm sounded, which they probably hadn't heard before because the flames were extremely loud under the echo in the shaft, but no one came into it or fired at them. That was a good start. If he hadn't known this was a decommissioned nuclear weapons silo, he would have been worried by the tenth basement at the latest, as there were large radiation warning signs emblazoned on the bare concrete walls on every floor from that on.

"Hey, Joss," Hardy whispered over the radio. "There are two entrances: the last basement and the second to last. The last one's even hotter than here, though."

Sweat was already dripping down Jacek's shoes and he felt like a steak too close to the grill flames, yet there was only one decision as he looked at the tan and the unsteady glow of light below them. "Bottom floor. Prisoners and valuables are always on the lowest floor."

"Then I hope they've got a Coke ready for us down there at three degrees." Hardy climbed on with a groan and unslung a stun grenade from his belt, the cotter pin of which he deftly disengaged with his thumb. With his feet, he hooked into the lower rungs of the ladder and leaned back to toss the grenade into the passage to the lowest floor. Apparently, the door was open.

There was a dull bang and Hardy moved away from the shaft, closely followed by Pill. Jacek followed them quickly, ignoring the heat on his legs as best he could. As he swung through the open door, its edges charred, the cold of a long hallway welcomed him with a pleasant embrace.

With his rifle raised, he secured to the right, where the corridor ended after two doors. Cyrillic letters were printed on the walls, helping the linguist find his way, but Jacek could only read the radiation warning signs. When Uffe and Knut also joined them, their faces flushed and their scarves pulled down, he gave Knut a wave.

"Which way to the radiation shelter?" he hissed.

His comrade narrowed his eyes and read the signs. The alarm sirens urged them to hurry with noise screeching for attention and red warning lights under the ceiling.

"To the left," he finally said, and Jacek motioned for him to go ahead. With Knut and Pill, they formed a kind of wedge and ran through the narrow corridor in a tactical continuous run. It was disconcerting that no one stood in their way. None of the few doors opened, no shots rang out, and not even the loud-speakers jammed in the corners every five paces spat out a sound — apart from the blaring alarm.

"This stinks of a trap," Knut grunted from the front.

No one said anything, for it required no response; their comrade had merely voiced what everyone was thinking.

"This way!" said Knut, stopping in front of a door. It looked massive, had an old combination code lock and a metal wheel for manual locking — and it was open.

"Joss?" asked Pill warningly.

"We're going in!" he ordered. The trap was clear – someone wanted them to go this way. If the power had already gone out, he could still have believed that the electronic lock had failed and someone had forgotten to operate the manual one, but that wasn't the case, and no one was leaving the door to their best-kept package open. There was no arguing: Knut yanked the door open and Pill charged forward, G36 at the ready. Jacek followed him, slightly staggered so they had a clear field of fire in the new corridor. Another door stood open, revealing a short flight of stairs leading to another door. It was solid and had a thick rubber coating around the edges. This one wasn't open, but it opened easily with a quick jerk. Jacek jumped in with Knut and Pill. Uffe and Hardy stayed in the hallway and secured the way back.

Since the room was pitch black, he turned on his flashlight and shone it on the walls first, looking for any entrances or windows, but saw only smooth concrete in all directions. They were standing in a rectangular hall the size of a small dormitory. Old beds were lined up everywhere, sometimes separated by heavy-duty shelving. The cones of light from their flashlights hastily skimmed everything until all three paused at the same time on something strange in the far-left corner.

"Grenade!" yelled Uffe from the corridor, and a heartbeat later, he and Hardy charged through the door to the bomb shelter. Jacek reacted immediately, throwing himself against the inward-opening door as his comrades came rushing through. At the same moment that the locks clicked, they heard a muffled sound from the other side and the metal of the door grew warm.

"Shit, that was close!" cursed Uffe. "Came out of nowhere!"

"Team One to Team Six. If you can turn off the power, now would be a good time!" growled Jacek into his headset, but he only got static in response. That was what he was afraid of. He tried to open the door again, but it was locked, electronically and from a central location, he'd bet.

"So now the rabbit is trapped," grunted Uffe.

"Uh, guys?" The voice belonged to Hardy and had moved away slightly. Jacek searched for him with his flashlight and found him as a glaring silhouette next to a heavy-duty shelf that obscured the view of the back left corner where the outline of the strange object shone through.

"Hardy, you guard the door. Pill, you search the right half of the room. Look for any ventilation openings and hidden doors. I don't want them sending gas in on us." With that, he turned away and followed the narrow corridor between the beds with Uffe on his heels. When he had rounded the heavy-duty shelf with a lot of futuristic and old-fashioned machinery, he gasped.

Before them lay the Tear they had dragged from its spaceship wreckage and brought to Europa-or at least an identical being in a pure white suit. The figure, humanoid but somewhat elongated in appearance, was stuck on some sort of torture chair, tilted at forty-five degrees so that he was half-sitting, half-lying. The contour-less helmet part of the suit, which seemed to be made of one piece, was fixed to his thick neck on the couch — with heavy steel straps; the same ones also held his arms and legs. Rolling tables with all sorts of small and large machines stood all around, looking as if they had been hastily left behind. Behind the alien's head was a large magnetic resonance tomograph. But there was also far less high-tech equipment. He brushed his hands over a circular saw with a diamond-coated blade. It was worn and dull.

"They clearly couldn't get through the tank with that," Uffe commented on her find. Standing between him and the alien, she had placed a hand on the white suit and was eyeing the tall figure thoughtfully. "Didn't even get stains on it. Like it was fresh out of the washing machine."

"At least now we know why they let us get through to the package on purpose," Hardy opined, tapping an angled index finger against the alien. "What could we do to their prisoner that they haven't already tried for themselves?"

"Do you think he's hurt?" Uffe sounded downright concerned.

"I assume so, or he or she or it would not have allowed itself to be dragged here voluntarily."

"Or it's very well-armored but doesn't have superhuman strength. After all, there's bound to be suits like this and suits like that, and this one looks pretty narrow, not exactly like a battle suit or anything."

"Don't know, won't find out," Jacek intervened, baring his teeth. Team Six would have to hurry, or every passing minute down here would play into the hands of their unwilling hosts. A distress call had surely already gone out to the nearest military base.

"They've really tried everything," Hardy said, and when Jacek looked up, he saw the telecommunications technician standing in front of the heavy-duty shelf, examining the equipment. "This all looks like run-down Soviet stuff, but I can tell you they've got some of the finest technology on the shelf. Voltage transformers, a BAE Systems EMP prototype, and a high energy laser." He pointed to a tapered apparatus at the end of the shelf, the rest of which was apparently behind it. "You can't say they didn't try to get the suit open or shine a light through it."

"You can't assure me they wouldn't have collected artifacts either," Uffe spoke up. As Jacek glared at her, she stood on the other side of the motionless alien behind a wide rolling table, holding an alien yet remotely familiar-looking weapon. It reminded him of a cross between a bazooka and a machine gun, with a grip that was a little too long and a sort of glowing bubble where the shoulder rest should have been. In Uffe's hands, the alien weapon looked huge. "Fuck the wall, that's either the latest Russian shit Putin's sick scientists have cooked up, or an alien weapon like anyone would love to get their hands on."

"Can you activate it?" asked Jacek.

"Nope." The sniper shook her head and he looked back at the alien. The pure white figure with slender, long limbs ending in six fingers lay like a foreign body of ethereal purity amid the intricate-looking equipment and objects, bound yet menacing.

"Maybe they were trying to use the Tear to activate the weapon," Hardy speculated. "That's probably how I'd do it."

"We're here to save him. The last thing we need is to torture an alien and have his people incinerate the entire planet in revenge," Jacek countered, examining the restraints that held the prisoner in place. As far as he could tell, they appeared to be a composite of steel and composite that would withstand even a flex for a while.

"Rescue? This one looks pretty dead." Uffe let go of the gun and approached the alien. "Annoying, I kind of like him. After all, we lost a lot of people to drag him out of the Congo and negotiate with him, or at least chat."

"What if he's just hurt?" asked Hardy.

"Then I'd be happy to patch him up, but I didn't get my medical license in alien medicine." The words came out of Pill's mouth, who had just come running around the shelf. Addressing Jacek, he continued, "Scoured the place and found a vent. Stuffed that up with some old blankets for now."

"Very good."

"Maybe we need to reanimate it," Uffe continued to speculate, as if nothing had happened. "Every complex living system has a cardiovascular system, right?"

"On Earth, yes," Jacek objected.

"We have to do something!"

"They've already tried a defibrillator," Hardy interjected, raising two contact patches for clarity. Before he'd even lowered his hands again, there was movement and Jacek's assault rifle automatically jerked its flashlight toward the alien. Two areas about the size of a hand below the suit's chest had turned black and slightly sunken in.

"Guys, I think it knows we're here."

CHAPTER 15

NIKOS

THE HOLE in the forest floor had been hard to see at first and, had Nikos not expected the gun he'd seen to have been brought very quickly, he probably would have missed it. But now that he looked for it, the crescent-shaped opening was clear and distinct from the green-brown forest floor. Moreover, the impact of the shell had formed a crater from which the edge of the hatch stood out. This was round and apparently disturbed by some sort of short circuit, as it jerked back and forth as if it couldn't decide whether to snap shut or open completely.

"We've got to get in there!" he shouted, beckoning his companions to him with frantic movements.

"No, we have to get behind our lines!" objected Sönke as all hell broke loose on them at the same moment. The entire armored front began to fire, and the hissing of their guns was so loud that Nikos' head was spinning. Vaguely, he also noticed the opposite side returning fire, and they found themselves in the middle of it. Initial explosions flared, sending waves of pressure and heat tugging at their uniforms despite the relatively large distances involved. Sönke's protest died immediately, and he ran the last few meters toward the hole. Before Nikos could interject something cautionary, the soldier slid the rest of the distance on his uniform and slid through the wide hole like something sucked up by a sink. Karin and Rooney followed him without comment and leapt into the darkness. At the sight of them, Nikos' heart sank. What if it went far down into the depths? The planet's high gravity turned even low drops into potential death traps. As another volley of projectiles flew around his ears in the next instant and he began to shudder between the pressure waves, he decided to find out and jumped into the blackness.

The fall was very short and launched him onto some sort of platform made of dark, corrugated metal. With the right side of his body, he slammed against something soft, which complained loudly.

"Sorry," he groaned, looking up at the single source of light. The opening of the hatch, twitching in perpetual short circuit, was so close above them that he could reach out for it and reach over the edge. The archaic crash of battle echoed many times over on the platform, which was in a wide, circular shaft, making the scene above them even more menacing.

"Now we're stuck!" complained Rooney before Karin silenced him with a stern "Shhhh." Once everyone was standing, heads just a span below the hatch, they stared upwards as if transfixed, their necks tilted all the way back. Something was approaching. It sounded like an avalanche of huge boulders, full-throated and unstoppable.

"What's that?"

"It's the tanks!" shouted Sönke, and then louder, "Duck!"

Nikos obeyed his friend and went to his knees, when shortly after, the chains of a tank rolled over the hatch and dented it slightly. Dust, mud, and moss debris trickled onto them, and the roar of the diesel engine made his heart vibrate.

"Hey, guys," Rooney yelled, standing next to him. Nikos

removed his arms, which he had above him protectively, from his head, only to see the cameraman standing next to him. He held his smartphone in front of him and shone the flashlight on something that was very obviously a control panel made of bright metal. It had six buttons, four of which were labeled with strange symbols he couldn't read. Two, however, possessed ones he was very familiar with: One arrow pointing up, and one pointing down.

"Is that..." Karin raised her hand to question and Nikos nodded mutely.

"Looks like an elevator control panel," Rooney confirmed, swinging his flashlight right and left until the white cone of light stopped on a hand-sized welt in the smooth-hewn rock that held thick steel cables. Too late, they noticed that Rooney's hand was meanwhile passing over the arrow symbols and he was pressing the arrow down. "Be curious to see if this thing will get us to safety."

A barely perceptible jolt went through the platform and a hydraulic slurp sounded. Looking up, Nikos saw the hatch, one-third open, moving further and further away.

"Are you insane?" asked Sönke unusually sharply, roughly knocking aside the hand of the cameraman who no longer had a camera to press the other arrow key after turning on the mounted flashlight on his assault rifle.

"All hell's going on up there right now. All it would have taken was for something to fall down the shaft and we'd have been history!" justified Rooney in a high-pitched voice that showed how tense he was.

"This thing's not responding," Sönke grumbled, ignoring the younger man. "Nikos? Do you still have your gun?"

"Yeah." Nikos swallowed and put his hand around the firearm at his right hip. With his thumb, he removed the safety bolt and pulled it out.

"There's a flashlight in your fanny pack. I think we're about to need both."

Cursing, he loaded his pistol and rummaged for the flashlight he found in his right belt pouch next to the buckle. Its beam was small and the light ghostly white, but it worked and reliably dispelled the darkness. The fine texture of the smoothly polished walls showed him that the way continued downhill and that the hatch above them had already become very small.

"What do we do now?" wanted Karin to know.

"The only thing we can do, because your careless colleague creates facts before he thinks," Sönke replied calmly. Just as his last word had faded away, there was another short jolt, and the elevator came to a halt. Nikos raised his flashlight, pistol and all, and turned in a circle until he found the exit: a square opening in the rock that led into a wide tunnel that could have accommodated two trucks side by side. The elevator was evidently at the very end of the tunnel section, because barely over a yard to the left was a sheer wall, in front of which stood a huge machine with large canisters behind a cone that looked like a drill. A wide white band at waist height was inscribed with green symbols that glowed in the dark like phosphorescent paint.

"This must be a section of the tunnel system, as I suspected," Nikos whispered into the darkness, spotting more symbols, including arrows in every direction that glowed green even without him having to shine a light on them.

"Maybe we should turn off the flashlights so as not to give ourselves up right away," Karin suggested, and Sönke and Nikos followed her suggestion without hesitation. They then stood in the darkness and waited for their eyes to adjust to the new visibility. It wasn't long before he spotted a ledge at foot level in the green glow of the symbols, also glowing on its own, but quite irregularly placed. Curious, he stepped out of the elevator, fending off Sönke's protest with a raised hand, though he probably couldn't see his gesture. Like a moth to a flame, he was drawn to the strange green band, which he had at first mistaken for a luminous strip of light, similar to those on an airplane during an emergency. When he finally reached it, he knelt down and slid closer. Now that the distance to the light source was so close, it surprised him how brightly it shone. He was even more surprised, however, that it wasn't a strip of light, but luminescent mushrooms. Smaller than a baby's finger, countless stalks lined up. Their inherent glow was greenish and dim, but by sheer mass, running the length of the tunnel wall in a meticulously milled indentation the size of a man's fist, they provided a surprising amount of light.

"Have you gone mad?" hissed Sönke over the radio, but he could hear him standing behind him as well.

"Look, these are mushrooms, obviously planted, or at least only growing in this gutter," Nikos replied unapologetically.

"Whatever it is, we have to look to get back up there."

"But shouldn't we look around first? This could be..."

"Look around?" asked Sönke so quietly that he almost squeaked. "Look to your right!"

Nikos followed his friend's request and turned to the right, toward the open side of the huge tunnel. At a distance, he couldn't possibly gauge due to the darkness, the tunnel was brightly lit. Lamps on the ceiling set a stage for his eyes to see something that made Nikos gasp in fright. Countless figures and vehicles bustled about there in a jumble of bodies and machines that gradually disappeared into the walls.

"That must be a deployment area. That's where they're bringing supplies from to the front," Sönke commented on the scene. "We should leave as soon as possible and inform the division command before they discover us."

"They would have by now if they'd had a chance," Nikos objected, surprised that he didn't want to seize the prospect of immediate escape without comment. This place intrigued him. Sure, he was so scared his knees shook and his pulse maltreated his veins at unhealthy levels, but something here was different from the Sklithra in Athens. There, everything had felt threatening and so foreign that his brain had felt lost in an incessant creepy cabinet of oddities and abnormalities. Here, however, it was different. He might as well have been standing in a mine tunnel in Austria, with a few exceptions like these mushrooms as a substitute for light. "Besides," he added, "cameras are useless down here in this light, if it's infrared or seismic sensors that recorded our arrival. But this is the end of a tunnel. You can tell by the drill. So they're either not going to have sensors installed yet, or they're going to think we're the team from above that came back."

"That sounds like a lot of wishful thinking," Sönke grumbled, unusually scowling.

"Um, guys?" asked Karin, and they turned to her at the same time. In the green glow of the mushrooms, she looked like a ghostly insect. "Can we get out of here? This place is really creeping me out."

Sönke turned to Nikos and, even without being able to see his face, he knew his expression would say something like, "See? So can we go now?"

"We can send up a radio with the elevator and call in what we've found," Nikos suggested. "I'm willing to bet that this tunnel system leads to the mine."

He was about to make another comment when the floor beneath their feet began to shake like an earthquake. A low growl reached their ears from the elevator shaft, sounding as if a giant had coughed, and Rooney, who was still the only one standing in the elevator, came running in their direction in a panic.

"RUN!" he yelled, and the next moment was buried by an

avalanche of debris that smashed through the shaft onto the elevator floor, blowing a cloud of splinters and dust that seemed to glow green in the mushroom light, like poison gas, in their direction. When the noise and dust had settled, they scrambled back to their feet and looked stunned at the wall of dirt and rock where the entrance to the elevator had been a moment ago – and Rooney Schneidfelder.

"Shit," Karin crowed. "Shit! He... such a shit!"

Nikos grabbed the journalist by the shoulders and gave her a sympathetic squeeze. For a while, they were silent, without anyone daring to say anything. He merely glanced to the side now and then to watch the mass of aliens and machines thinning out at the far other end of the tunnel until it was finally completely empty. That was good for them, but bad for the troops on the surface, from whom they were now completely cut off.

"Karin," he said softly. "We need to get out of here and find an exit."

"Yeah," she sniffed, clearing her throat. "Yeah, we should."

"Where the enemies went up, we should be able to get up."

Nikos looked at Sönke questioningly. "But there are the aliens too."

"Quite possibly, but I'd rather put my money on our people winning upstairs than wandering around down here. Because here we know for a fact that there are plenty of aliens and no humans."

"I guess you're right." Nikos weighed the pistol in his hand, examining its presence, and nodded to himself. "So, let's try our luck. You probably can't get a radio connection?"

"No, not since we came down in the elevator."

"Crap. Can you remember our last position? In the Puma, I mean?"

Sönke was silent for a moment. "Just under thirteen kilometers from the mine. That was to the northwest of us, so the division's forward thrust wedge should be much closer. Maybe the main battle even started long ago. Not that it would make any difference to us down here."

"Alright, let's head up front and hope we catch an elevator that doesn't make us look directly into the guns of a couple of aliens."

"So that's how good our chances are." Sönke sighed but got moving and brought his assault rifle to bear. He led him and Karin along the left side of the tunnel wall, close to the strip of light and close enough that they could actually see the wall rather than it being a shapeless nothingness that instinctively gave them the creeps. The further they got, the wetter the ground became beneath their boots and the clammier the air, which could be felt even through their breathing masks. It smelled musty half the time and plastic the other, which Nikos attributed to the filtering system on his breathing apparatus. The painted strip at chest level featured glowing green symbols at regular intervals that bore some resemblance, if any, to Arabic or Farsi letters, curved as they looked. Sometimes he saw arrows as he passed, so he guessed they were signposts.

They walked on and on, cautious and deliberate as the ground, while not invisible, was still difficult to see in detail, but the illuminated part where they had seen the aliens did not seem to be getting any closer. Apparently, the distance had been much greater than they had expected.

"You know what's funny?" asked Karin quietly, but loud enough that Nikos flinched involuntarily after the long silence.

"Huh?" asked Sönke without slowing down.

"If this ore we're being asked to sabotage is so valuable, why do the Morphs want us to destroy it, and not bring it back to them through the wormhole? We could set up a colony here, unmolested by the Tears, since their own anti-technology field keeps them out and quite obviously, yes, protects them from orbital bombardment, or the Morphs would surely have shown up here and not over Earth."

"Surely only the Tears can do anything with it," Sönke speculated, not sounding as if he was particularly excited by this discussion. "After all, their technology is probably very different. Maybe it's based on different raw materials."

"Or," the reporter countered, "the Morphs have an entirely different reason for sending us here. Maybe the ore will power the orbital elevator and the colony will lose its access to space. Or maybe the locals are originally Tears and not a third species, and this planet is something like their ancient home, which they're protecting with their latest technology, and we're the Morphs' Trojan."

"That sounds richly theoretical," Sönke countered.

"Those aren't Tears," Nikos objected.

"So? Why not?" the reporter wanted to know. Her voice quivered slightly, but not because she sounded angry. She was probably trying to distract herself from thoughts of her colleague who had just died by talking. Nikos would have done it that way.

"Because I've already seen a Tear."

"You *what?*" she asked, half amazed, half horrified.

"Pssst!" Sönke hissed from the front.

"You *what?*" she repeated, this time so quietly that he barely understood her through the mask.

"I've held a Tear before. He was a little taller than me, with long limbs, not short and squat like the locals here. His armor looked quite different too."

"But what if that was a robot or something? Or did you see his face?"

"No, the suit was impenetrable to us," Nikos replied quietly. "But I don't think if these were Tears, they'd be attacking us with tanks and soldiers to contend with. These aren't Tears, I'm sure of it."

"There's still the matter of the ore, though," Karin persisted. "Why shouldn't we do the mining?"

"The scientists suspect that the ore might have something to do with the climate catastrophe on this planet. Besides, you never know how an ecosystem will react if you bring something from a completely alien biosphere," Sönke explained. "The risk is too great."

"So you think the Tears, who unleashed a battle in our orbit, and accepted the extinction of our species as collateral damage, are particularly interested in what we do to our biosphere?" Karin's snort clearly showed what she thought of that idea.

"Wait!" Sönke spoke fast enough that Nikos and Karin froze in place, expecting danger.

"What is it?" hissed Nikos.

"There's water here. We should turn on our lights until we get across."

Nikos didn't wait, but immediately turned on his flashlight as if his hands had only been waiting for him to throw caution overboard to dispel the creeping primal fear of darkness by dancing photons. As soon as he had flicked on the lamp and pinned his left hand under his outstretched pistol, his eyes widened so much that his eyelids ached.

In front of them, an underground river flowed along a wide stretch where the ground must have been torn away. The water was about three meters wide and the edges on both sides were broken and jagged. A makeshift bridge made of two metal rails with raised sides was anchored in the ground with thick bolts. They were at most as wide as a car tire and there was nothing between them that would have been suitable for pedestrians.

"You're not going to balance over there, are you?" asked Karin, horrified.

"We have no choice." Nikos shone his light into the tunnel behind them. The light from his lamp didn't reach far enough to reach the drill. "There's nothing behind us."

"We could wait until they find us."

"Until we die of thirst? If anyone even comes looking for us."

"We have water," she objected.

"With foreign microbes and bacteria, possibly toxic," Sönke indicated. "Let's go. That's wide enough. We'll go slow and careful and leave the lights on."

Karin yelped something incomprehensible when the soldier stepped onto the metal bridge and put one foot in front of the other in the rail with deliberate movements. They balanced in a row — Sönke in front, followed by Karin and Nikos behind — over the raging underground river, which swept along beneath them with such power that its roar drowned out even the blood in his ears.

Disaster struck when Nikos thought he saw movement in the water and instinctively moved his flashlight in the appropriate direction. Karin flinched and stepped with her left foot on the raised bead on the side of the rail and slipped off. As if in slow motion, she rowed her arms as her body toppled to the side. She tried to grab Sönke, who scooted to the side and snatched at her, but he had no grip of his own that could have counterbalanced the leverage of her body, plunging him with her into the floodwaters that swallowed and swept them both away instantly.

Horrified, Nikos did the only thing his heart and brain could agree on: he dropped his gun and jumped after them.

CHAPTER 16

JACEK

"IT KNOWS WE'RE HERE?" repeated Uffe, pressing her cheek a little harder against the butt of her submachine gun. Jacek thought he was under an illusion, but when he blinked and looked again at the chest section of the white armor, the two indentations on its chest had disappeared. Frowning, he indicated with a flat hand for the sniper to follow suit and lower her weapon.

"Not only does it know we're here, it can hear and understand us."

"Or see," Hardy objected gloomily.

"Weapons down!" he ordered, looking right and left until Hardy, Uffe, and Pill pointed their barrels toward the ground. Again, he shone a light over the entire armor, looking for any openings, recesses, or anything else that might suggest sensors or even any kind of accessibility or interactivity, but to no avail. The suit had no scratches, no dents, not even the slightest stain. When he touched it, there was no frictional resistance. His hand slid against it.

"I think it wants to be reanimated," Pill said, and immediately, the two wells reappeared. Astonished, their eyes met, and the medic shrugged. Then he pointed to the indentations, which were slightly lower than the human solar plexus and very close together. "For a human, however, such positioning would be quite awkward."

"But then, it's not human, so I guess we don't have to worry about it." Jacek waved Hardy over impatiently, who held the small box and held it out to Pill. The latter took the two pads, connected to the box by thin cables, and hesitantly stuck them to the indentations in the alien's carapace.

"Is this really a good idea?" asked Uffe doubtfully.

"Have you got a better one?" Hardy wanted to know.

"Nope, not at the moment. But giving an energy boost to an Uberalien whose carapace you can't even scratch with a diamond saw isn't particularly high on the smart-idea list for me."

"The Russians have us penned in here, and if the guys and gals of the Fourth and Sixth don't box us out, I figure our chances of escaping are pretty slim before word gets out that someone's trying to get the prisoner out and reinforcements arrive. We may be in the ass end of nowhere, but I can't imagine the Kremlin hasn't made provisions just in case — hideout or not."

"Hardy's right," Jacek found hesitantly. "I don't see a better way either. I think he or she or it wants to get out of here as much as we do, and the general was quite clear. If we don't manage to get the pris... the *guest* back, I don't want the Russians to get it so they can cannibalize it. So, if that thing runs amok and shoots us and all the Russians in the area, at least we've met the second operational priority."

"Great outlook," Uffe said seemingly cheerfully. "Why not come right out with the optimistic reasons for a decision. Now that's what I call a motivational speech!"

From the side came Knut, startled. "Holy shit! What's going

on here?" He looked at the pads and cables in the light of their overlapping cones of light.

"We're shorting an alien, I think," Pill replied, pressing the plus button on the defibrillator box.

"Uffe, you go with Knut to the door and let me know if we get any surprises. Hardy, search the corners again for cameras and black out anything you find," Jacek ordered and waited until he was alone with Pill.

"Shouldn't the others be here if... well..." The medic nodded in the direction of the strange patient between them.

"We have no chance of making any difference with our weapons anyway."

"All right, then. I'll be ready then. Full charge?"

"I guess so. You're the medic."

"Good." Pill licked his lips and lowered his hand to the mushroom-shaped red button. Nothing happened.

"Shouldn't it twitch or something?"

"I don't know, it's not human. Not even a living thing, but a suit, I guess."

"Do it again!"

Pill pressed the button again, and this time, Jacek saw one of Tear's many fingers move. He jerked up an inch or less and froze again.

"Wait a minute." He put a hand on Pill's forearm over the white suit and pointed to the pads. "Take those off."

The medic raised a brow but shrugged and pulled the pads off. The indentations lay open again, black and half an inch deep.

"Um, if you understand us, give us a sign." The hollows disappeared and Jacek looked up, straight into Pill's astonished eyes.

"It really understands us. It doesn't just interpret our intentions; it understands our language."

"Yes," Jacek breathed, his brain not wanting to wrap itself around the significance of the fact that he had just possibly made first contact with the Tears. "So, it's not just the suit, it's the intelligence inside it, the real Tear."

"Unless it's a robot," Pill objected, waiting as Jacek raised a finger in his direction.

"Do you need more power?" The hollows appeared again and once more they looked into each other's eyes.

"Hardy?" shouted Jacek loudly.

"Yes?" came the reply from somewhere out of the darkness.

"Did you black out the cameras?"

"Yeah, I guess so."

"Then come back. We need you."

After a few moments, Hardy came walking around the shelf, announced by the back and forth of his flashlight. "Well, did you resuscitate him?"

Instead of answering directly, Jacek pointed to the MRI behind the headboard of the couch where Tear lay bound. "That thing runs on heavy current, doesn't it?"

"Are you kidding me? This thing runs on enough heavy current for ten homes."

"Good, can you disconnect the cable and connect it to the suit?"

"Uh, no?" The words sounded like a question coming out of Hardy's mouth. "That thing doesn't even have connections!"

"Pull the cable. We'll push the couch over if it's not long enough."

"I'd honestly rather turn off the power first before handling heavy current," Hardy objected. "You haven't seen a fuse box, have you?"

Pill snorted and Jacek shook his head.

"Great," the telecommunicator grumbled. "I'll think of something." He began rummaging through the shelf, going back and forth, taking things out here and there, putting some things away and picking up new ones. Finally, he disappeared behind the MRI and thrumming noises mingled with suppressed curses.

"Are you really in such good spirits about this idea?" asked Pill in a conspiratorial tone, leaning forward a bit. His eyes kept wandering to the motionless alien below them, as if it might startle at any moment like in a horror movie.

"I am of the good opinion that it is the only starting point at the moment," Jacek replied evasively. It was true, but he didn't want to get his hopes up that the alien could be judged by human standards, or even that its actions could be predicted. At the same time, he also didn't think much of worrying about things that weren't worth thinking about because they took place outside his horizon of experience. If you asked him, musings were the great Achilles heel of most people.

"Good, good. Then we'll be surprised."

They waited in silence, checking again with Uffe and Knut to make sure everything was quiet at the door, and prepared the C-4 for the door, though they didn't hold out much hope that it would work. After all, it was a well-secured bomb shelter in a former silo for nuclear missiles. Using too much of the plastic explosive was also out of the question because the pressure created in the enclosed space could injure or kill them. After about fifteen minutes, Hardy returned to the cot where the alien still lay exactly as they had left it. The indentations on the hull were also in the same place. Hardy held a finger-thick cable in one hand, which was stuck in a huge rubber glove. Jacek thought he heard a crackling sound.

"There, that's done. Now what?"

"Come over to the side and hold up the cable," Jacek suggested, and Hardy complied with a furrowed brow. Then what he had expected happened. The two indentations disappeared, and instead, a finger-thick hole formed on the upper right arm of the suit — on the side facing Hardy.

"Yeah, fuck you," he marveled, holding the exposed cable in front of the hole. He looked questioningly at Jacek, who nodded without hesitation. His comrade stuffed the end into the dark hole, which then seemed to actively close around the insulation. After that, nothing happened for a while. Then, just as Pill was about to clear his throat and say something, the suit's fingers began to move as if they were playing invisible piano keys.

"Hello," an androgynous voice rang out, too high for a man and too low for a woman.

Jacek, Pill, and Hardy drove together as if they had been punched.

"Shit! Did that thing just talk to us? In German?" Hardy wanted to ruffle his hair and instead ran his rubber glove over his helmet before getting rid of it and quickly putting his combat gloves back on. Pill said nothing, but was about to yank up his assault rifle, but Jacek put a hand on the barrel quickly enough and pushed that down.

"Hello," he said, gesturing for his soldiers to be silent with a forefinger on his lips. "Who are we talking to?"

"I am the intelligence of this suit and serve my wearer," came the calm reply of the androgynous voice. "Thank you for powering me."

"Are you some kind of AI?"

"I am an artificial intelligence, that is correct. I require more energy to wake my carrier from the stasis I had to put him in."

"I think that's the strongest thing we can find here," Jacek returned, looking at Hardy, who nodded quickly.

"This is suboptimal. Without a stronger power source, I can't initiate the termination of stasis."

"Can you get free without him?"

"Yes."

Pill signaled Jacek and he nodded.

"Are you authorized to free yourself without him?" the medic asked.

"Yes, if it ensures his direct survival."

"Good. How much more energy do you need to get free, and can you get us out of here?" asked Jacek with barely concealed impatience in his voice.

"At the current charge rate, in eleven minutes of your time, I have accumulated a sufficient supply of energy to move this suit for an extended period of time," the AI replied. An accent-free machine voice that simultaneously sounded so natural it could be fooled by the suit's wearer was so startling and simultaneously surreal that Jacek had to force himself to think clearly. It all seemed so unforced in its awesomeness that it almost seemed normal to him.

"However, destroying the deployed restraints would consume a lot of energy," the AI added.

"We'll take care of it."

"You're not going to kill us, are you?" asked Hardy doubtfully, shrugging as Jacek gave him a frown.

"Negative. I am authorized to respond to direct threats. You have supported the survival of my carrier. Your survival is in the best interest of my carrier."

"How do you know?" This time, it was Pill who asked the question. "I thought your carrier was currently unconscious?"

"That is correct. I have served my wearer for more than one hundred Earth years and have gathered sufficient data on his behavior to extrapolate an appropriate position," the suit intelligence replied.

"Ah," Pill went silent.

"So, guys, let's try to cut it out of there, shall we?" suggested Jacek. "At least then we can make ourselves useful while its... *battery* or whatever is charging."

The two soldiers nodded, and it was ten minutes before they had gathered enough tools under Hardy's instructions and set to work with grinders, saws, and an oversized bolt cutter to cut through the alien's bonds. It was tedious work, and the only reason Jacek wasn't getting nervous was the fact that every passing minute was charging the AI's suit, which would surely benefit their escape from this place. At the very least, he hoped they could slip out in the slipstream of the white giant. True, the previous encounters of humans and Tears didn't exactly give him reason for hope — after all, their ruthless battles near Earth had claimed hundreds of millions of victims, and he still remembered too well how the aliens' drones and warriors had hunted him down in the Congo — but the prisoner they'd taken was something special. After all, Jacek had watched as his own species had tried to destroy his ship, and as they had sent landing pods of soldiers to finish what the drones couldn't. If he was to learn anything from all this, it was surely that he couldn't be too quick to commit himself as to the motivations and backgrounds of the aliens. There was one thing, at least, that he could count on in a Socratic sense: He knew perfectly well that he knew absolutely nothing, so he didn't need to pretend he did.

After about twenty minutes, the power went out just as they were cutting, or rather sawing, the ankle cuffs and one side of the arm cuffs.

"The power supply has been cut," the AI stated dryly.

"Those were our people from outside," Jacek said truthfully as the ground trembled beneath their feet and he exchanged a look with Hardy. "And that's probably the Russians' reinforcements."

"Then we should leave this place," the suit chimed in, though he couldn't have located where *exactly* the sound was coming from in the first place.

"Wait a minute," Pill said. Deep furrows had formed on his

forehead. "If neither we nor your guards are a threat to you, why do you want to get out of here? Were the Russians about to make a breakthrough?"

"No," the AI objected. "The threat is not from your species."

Jacek considered for a moment, looking into the sparks Hardy's battery-powered Flex sent into the darkness like swarms of short-lived fireflies. "You mean the object in Lake Baikal, don't you?"

"That is correct. It is possible to use the energy cells of this weapon to replenish my storage." The alien's already freed hand — or suit — went up and, without moving its head, pointed at the huge alien weapon leaning against the wall. "I have activated it. Please extract the power cells as per my instructions."

Out of nowhere, Uffe appeared in the darkness and took the alien rifle as if it were a natural extension of her arms. "Pretty intuitive."

"No sooner is there an oversized gun somewhere than Uffe is suddenly there." Hardy sighed. "You heard the suit: out with the power cells."

"Please proceed with extreme caution," the AI calmly advised the sniper as the muffled sound of explosions rang out from the doorway to the hallway. "It would be to your advantage to cut me loose before your fellows kill you. Otherwise, it would be difficult for me to re-establish a suitable power supply."

"Sounds like our new AI friend cares a lot about our well-being."

"Uffe, give them the rifle. When the Spetsnaz comes in, they can take care of them."

As the sniper's face — already pale in the cold light of the flashlights — took on increasingly disappointed features, the AI spoke up again, "Negative. I am not allowed to take or use a functioning weapon."

"Excuse me?" asked Jacek, puzzled. "Why not?"

"This information is not relevant to you. Please continue with the liberation procedure."

The explosions came closer, and the constant bass was now mixed with the drumming of boots on concrete.

"I'll buy you some time," Uffe announced, disappearing with the rifle before Jacek's hissed, "Stay the fuck here," reached them. A moment later, his ears crackled and a flash of light from the direction of the door blinded them enough to make them turn away. When he could see again, there was a hole where the armored door had been before, and Uffe was standing in front of it with the giant alien weapon and running, followed by Knut.

"Hardy, hurry up," Jacek urged his comrade. The high sawing seemed to go on indefinitely. At last, the steel composite gave way, and the alien was free. As if in anticipation of a catastrophe that would have to be virtually simultaneous with the suit's release, he jumped back a step at the same time as Hardy and Pill. At least he was able to resist the impulse to raise the weapon.

The alien rose with a fluid motion that seemed at once unnatural, as if performed by a robot, close to a perfect imitation of a humanoid. When it stood on its feet, it towered over them by at least a head, and the neckless head turned right and left, though the armor — or whatever it was — looked exceedingly stiff and immobile.

"Thank you for your cooperation. My carrier greatly appreciates the service." With that, the mysterious alien being walked in apparent peace of mind toward the door, through which glaring flashes of muzzle flashes and explosions kept lighting up the bunker.

"Wait," Jacek called out, but the alien didn't stop. "Can you get us out of here?"

"This is not among my defined primary or secondary goals. Thank you for your cooperation."

"Hey, at least it didn't turn us into clouds of dust," Pill remarked with a shrug, reloading his assault rifle. Jacek thought about the words and made a decision. Artificial Intelligence would not help them, it had made that clear. But — and here Pill was right — it had also made no move to kill him and his team, which he already chalked up as a success. So, there was nothing to be said against using that circumstance to their advantage. At least he hoped so.

"Uffe, Knut," he called into his headset. "Run as far forward as you can, and make sure you don't point your weapons — even accidentally — at the damn alien, all right? Get as far ahead as you can so it doesn't get to the power cells." He waited for their acknowledgements and turned to Hardy and Pill. "Come on, I've got an idea."

CHAPTER 17

NIKOS

THE WATER WAS EVERYWHERE. Jumping into the floodwaters of the underground river had at first made him feel he was a balloon, since he wasn't going down. His closed clothing, while not sealed like ABC gear, because there hadn't been forty thousand ABC suits, was good enough to keep water from getting to his skin for a few moments. It was only when he struck his upper body against the rock wall under which the water flowed, and which formed a kind of resistance against which the floods piled up, that he felt the gnawing cold in liquid form penetrate to his limbs and back. He began to shiver even before the pressure of the water submerged him and fired through the natural tunnel that had probably carved through the rock over eons. The darkness underwater was absolute and flawless, and yet he thought he could see bubbles of water forming before his goggles, giving the cold a visual equivalent that was by now all-encompassing. Even before he could worry about his breathing, he was freezing all over, feeling the icy wetness on every square millimeter of his skin. It prickled and stung like myriads of tiny needles, as if trying to penetrate to his bones, which were struggling to protect themselves by trembling uncontrollably.

Nikos rolled over, was thrown from left to right, forwards and backwards, like a plaything of the rushing current. At times he thought he was going to be thrown down, hit the rock with his helmet, almost fainted, and yet was dragged back into the now by the cold.

Then the respiratory distress began. In the first few moments of being peppered through the natural underground channel in the darkness, he had still been drawing on the tiny oxygen supply of the breathing mask, but that had only been enough for a few breaths. After that, panic had set in, as he could no longer control his body movements and no longer knew where up and down were. His world was losing its horizon and any traction in the truest sense of the word. But when the air was gone and he realized the fact that he was breathing against a wall, as if someone had sealed his throat with a rubber stopper, the panic increased more and more. The whole thing became even worse when the first drops of water penetrated the membrane filters of the breathing mask and his mouth filled with water. Slowly at first, but then faster and faster, his lungs threatened to cramp and the urge to breathe in became superhuman.

Suffocate or drown, he thought on the brink of madness, a traveler between racing thoughts of death and destruction and a life that played out in the form of unclear images before his inner eye. At that moment when his body made the decision for him and he wanted to give in to the indomitable urge to breathe in, he was spat out along with the floods around him — spat out into nothingness.

No, there was no nothingness, because nothingness certainly didn't glow green. Nikos tried to see what was happening around him, but his field of vision had already shrunk to a narrow tunnel, at the edges of which everything was black and pulsating in time with his racing heartbeat. Reflexively, he ripped the breathing mask from his mouth and inhaled the humid air hoarsely. Masses of water beat down on him from above, and as he greedily struggled for oxygen, more and more water also entered his windpipe, causing him to start coughing. He was falling. He fell faster and faster, staggering violently, and next to the falling floods, he saw craggy rock faces dotted with green glowing lamps.

Then came the impact. Nikos saw the black surface of the water with the white spray of the waterfall spreading across it, then he crashed into the underground lake with such force that it forced all the air he could breathe back out of his lungs. He cried out, but his scream immediately turned into an unhealthy bubbling as he was pushed deep underwater by his own force and the increased gravity. Panicked, he kicked his legs and tried to bring himself up with swimming motions. The effort was inhuman. On Earth, he might have made it, but Planet X's one-and-a-half times gravitational pull tugged at him relentlessly. He was about to reach the surface, which shimmered greenish, when his screeching muscles failed, and he understood that he had lost the battle. It was his left arm, its bicep still too damaged to go to full load, that sealed his death.

Just as the hopelessness of his situation dawned on him, he felt a pinch on his shoulders and a movement upwards. He didn't understand it, it didn't make any sense, but his body took control and activated all his reserves, small as they were, one last time, and forced him to swim weakly.

Miraculously, he poked his head through the surface of the water and looked into Sönke's face. He no longer had his helmet on, and the breathing mask had also disappeared. His face was pale and full of freckles and just the sight of another person, especially his friend, was the greatest relief he had ever felt.

"I got you, buddy," the soldier said over the loud patter of the waterfall, and his soaking wet face parted in a wide smile. "Here, hold on!"

Nikos clutched the improvised buoy that Sönke held out to him. It looked like a small balloon, but he realized on closer inspection that it was a rubber uniform knotted at the arms and legs. The buoyancy was low but allowed them to stay afloat with kicking movements of the legs.

"W-w-where is... K-K-Karin?" Nikos asked, shivering, and let Sönke direct him to the right.

"I'm here, Nikos!" a third voice called. He tried to turn his head in its direction but found it only when he looked up. She was standing on a platform that was about twenty inches above the surface of the water and seemed to be made of a thin layer of metal. Karin was in the process of undressing. Only now did he wonder that he could see her and noticed the many joints in the huge rectangular cavern, with the same bands of green glowing mushrooms running along them as in the tunnel through which they had passed.

"There, the ladder!" exclaimed Sönke, his voice also beginning to quiver slightly. "S-see it?"

Nikos didn't answer as the cold had robbed him of his voice but nodded choppily and reached with shaking hands for the ladder that stretched from the metal platform into the water. His boots found the rungs far too close together to be suitable for an adult human. He almost lacked the strength to pull himself up, but Karin — now in her underwear — came over and grabbed him under the arms to pull him to her.

"Euxaristw," he said, not realizing he had spoken in his native tongue. Reaching the platform, which stretched at least five meters by five meters and had a rippled surface, he lowered himself onto his back and pulled his arms and legs toward each other to ward off the cold. Of course, he did not succeed.

"You need to undress and move," Karin urged him, and began to undo his uniform. At first, he resisted, afraid of the alien germs he had been so forcefully warned about, only to realize that he had long since torn off his respirator. It still hung from the elastic around his neck, but his entire mouth and nose area was exposed, and he was breathing in the air of the alien biosphere. So, he began to help her rid his body of the heavy wet stuff.

Sönke also came up the ladder and threw his dripping uniform, used as a buoy, onto the platform beside him. He was still wearing his functional clothing, which he now took off with trembling limbs and flung off him. By the time he was done, Nikos had also shed his functional underwear and was standing there in his underpants, about to freeze to death.

"H-H-Hampelmanns," Sönke said in a trembling voice and began to do jumping jacks. Nikos didn't wonder at the absurd sight but started to follow his example — just like Karin. With sweeping movements, he spread his legs and brought his hands together above his head and then again from the front. Again and again, first with stiff, half-frozen joints, then with more fluid movements as he grew warmer. His muscles protested at the extreme exertion of being in this place, but he paid no attention. He merely enjoyed the warmth returning to his body, and enjoyed being able to feel his hands and feet again. As he did so, he also used the time to consciously look around. They were standing on a platform that stood in the corner of a rectangular room that was about the size of two tennis courts side by side, and so high that he could only make out the greenish glow of the waterfall about a hundred feet up as a small hole. It looked like they were standing inside a giant monolith. The faint green light from the dozen or so bands of mushrooms made Karin and Sönke look pale, like ghostly imaginings. Only when he looked at them did he glance again at the corner where the platform was enclosed and notice that there was a door and an open passageway.

"Hey, did you guys see that?" he asked breathlessly.

"Yeah, but we had to warm up first," Sönke replied. "Otherwise, we would have frozen to death before we could see where they lead."

Nikos stopped his jumping jacks and looked down at himself. The goosebumps were persistent and his thick arm and chest hair stood up vertically. He felt vulnerable and defenseless, as if he had signed his death warrant with the loss of his suit and breathing mask. His body was now breathing in the alien air — which smelled clear and fresh, if a little damp, but was full of alien microorganisms. Even if they weren't pathogenic germs to the natives, to his immune system, every bacterium and virus in this alien ecosystem was probably a threat, as it was entirely unknown. This would cost him dearly, probably even his life. However, that was no reason to give up, because they were alive and could contribute something to the success of the mission. Even if he thought it was questionable, the very existence of his entire species possibly depended on them being able to form an alliance with the Morphs. He knew absolutely nothing about the aliens, except that they had ever-changing bodies rather than fixed ones, and that they were negotiating with former NATO diplomats in Scotland.

"It's really cold down here," he found, shivering under a chill.

"The water makes it worse," Sönke agreed with him. "The best thing to do is to go into one of the corridors and keep moving, then we might have an hour or more."

"An hour or more for what?" Karin questioned, gathering up her clothes dripping with wetness.

"Before our toes and fingers freeze off."

Nikos searched his friend's face for a hint that he was joking or exaggerating, but Sönke looked very serious and knotted his clothes around his stomach. "Are we going?"

"Wait," Karin kneaded her hands and blew warm air into them. "We're supposed to go into one of those dark corridors now, with no weapons, no breathing gear, and half naked?"

"Do you have a better idea?" asked Nikos in Sönke's place, not even meaning it ironically, but rather hopefully that she really did have a more helpful suggestion ready.

"No," she admitted, slumping her shoulders.

"Anyway, we can only get out through here, and it's much too cold near the waterfall with its splashing water," Sönke explained. "I think this is a water reservoir. If Nikos is right and the aliens live underground, it makes sense that they tap into underground rivers to get fresh water, which is conveniently already pre-filtered. I'm willing to bet that there are pipes running along the bottom to distribute the water, and this platform is a maintenance platform."

"I don't know if that's supposed to be good or bad."

Sönke eyed the reporter. "When we fell into the water, I thought that was our death sentence. We were so lucky..."

"And helmets," Nikos interjected.

"And helmets, yes... that I'm sure I can tickle a little more happiness out of my life."

"Then we should get going."

With that, they walked across the platform, each step a wet smack on the metal. Sönke stopped toward the dark corridor, but Nikos faced the other, which was blocked by a charcoal-grey door. The top edge was about level with his chin and there was a small porthole further down at chest level. Instead of a door handle, there was an indentation on the left with a vertical metal bar that possibly served the same function. Carefully, he placed his hands on the cold metal and leaned forward until his nose touched the slightly bulging porthole. Twice he had to blink, then he could see clearly enough and...

With an involuntary yelp, he jerked back and stumbled backward, nearly falling.

"What's wrong?" asked Sönke excitedly, coming running with Karin from the entrance to the open tunnel.

"Someone's coming!"

"What, from..."

"Yes, someone's coming!" he repeated impatiently, and made a dash for the door. "Your gun! Take your gun!"

Sönke had already reacted and pulled the pistol out of the holster he had slung around his half-naked waist. Nikos didn't know if it still worked after being underwater for a long time, but it felt better to know that his friend had something in his hand. Karin pressed herself next to him against the cold wall, which was smooth and solid as concrete. Sönke stood on the other side, where the handle was.

"How far away were they?" he hissed, but Nikos could only shrug.

"Very close, and I think it was only one," he whispered back, falling silent as there was a metallic clang on the door and an electronic whirring sound.

The door swung open and a figure, a little smaller than Sönke and not even reaching Nikos' chest, came out. Before he could get a proper look at it, the soldier grabbed it and pulled it onto the platform with a powerful jerk. He was beginning to fear that the alien would be hurled into the water, but the figure skidded a foot or two and came to a stop, arms waving. Nikos threw himself against the door and the lock clicked as Sönke pointed his gun at the stranger. This one wore a blue suit with helmet and thick boots, which, just like the gloves, were connected to the rest of the suit by massive rings at the joints, giving the alien the appearance of an archaic diver. This impression was further reinforced by the helmet, which had an oval visor on the front, similar to that of the soldier aliens on the surface, which was heavily mirrored. Small antennae and shells were attached to either side, like sensors on a robot. The arms and legs were thick and knobby, and the torso round and massive.

"Take it easy," Sönke said in a firm voice that trembled just a little, which impressed Nikos as his guts seemed to tighten at the sight of the stranger.

The alien barely stirred, staring at him with the opaque visor and spreading both arms from himself with his hands outstretched. This might have been some kind of gesture of surrender. Nikos noticed the oddity of the hands, which seemed to have webbed fingers between them. They certainly didn't look like the fingers of a human, but more like two large baseball gloves. In one he held a mixture of a basket and a suitcase, which now fell from his hand as if the creature had suddenly lost all power. It clanked loudly and a torrent of tools clattered across the platform. One piece landed splashily in the water.

"Shit, we're looking at a fucking alien," Karin groaned. "So, what now? Should we ask it for directions?"

Sönke did not answer and Nikos was silent as well. Too alien and terrifying was this moment where two intelligent species faced each other and stared at each other like the foreign bodies they were to each other. No one stirred until the alien in the full body suit stepped from one foot to the other and slowly lowered his hands. Nikos noticed that where his belt might have been, he had several hard-to-identify items attached to small eyelets.

"Sönke!"

"Hey!" his friend cried loudly, extending the pistol a little further. The alien put his hands up again.

"Hey-Kolpa!" the alien replied, and the barrage of sound

boomed over the rush of the waterfall so suddenly that Nikos winced.

"Did... did he just speak?" Karin asked croakily.

"I think so." Sönke's gun sank a little before it seemed to catch his eye and he raised it again. The alien's voice had sounded tinny, as if it had come through a speaker.

"Hey-Kolpa! Masma-Cheerup-Tak!" The alien's voice rang out again, and the melody of his sentence was so alien and sounded so guttural that it made Nikos shiver — and not just because he was about to freeze to death.

"He's talking to us!"

"You don't say," Sönke agreed. "I just don't know if I should shoot him now. See if the door opens."

Nikos obeyed and felt with one hand for the vertical handle in the indentation. Then he pulled, and sure enough, he was able to pull the door open. It was hard, but it worked. "Open."

"Alright, so..."

"We can't shoot him!" protested Nikos.

"I know that – the gun probably doesn't even work after all the water it swallowed."

"What if he's been on the radio all this time?" asked Karin anxiously. The alien was still standing in front of them, arms splayed and baseball glove hands open, not moving.

"Radio down here?" Sönke shook his head. "Not a chance!"

"Surely he must have some form of communication!"

"Maybe one of those things in his basket that just fell off?"

"Hey-Kolpa! Masma-Cheerup-Tak!" the alien repeated over the invisible helmet speakers, and then, in an undertone that sounded higher and more hysterical, "Koomla-Hak-Tarma! Hak-Tarma!"

Sönke looked out of the corner of his eye at Nikos, and shrugged. "Sounds like the kid's pretty excited."

CHAPTER 18

JACEK

JACEK, Pill, and Hardy followed the alien in its slipstream to the blasted-open door, through which the noise of rattling automatic weapons and occasional explosions reached them. Thick smoke billowed down the long hallway into the bomb shelter, gathering as dirty soot under the ceiling. In the light of their flashlights, it looked like a living tissue of shadows, which only settled when the suit did something outlandish: it began to glow. From feet to crown, the white figure was suddenly no longer white, but a body of pure light that seemed to seep evenly from every pore. To protect his eyes, Jacek pulled his shatterproof goggles up his nose, which had a self-darkening coating to protect him from snow blindness. Only now could he see the outline of the suit clearly again and see the AI steering the alien body into the long corridor.

"The stairway is to the left. The elevator is destroyed," Jacek said to the alien's back.

"Thank you for sharing," the AI replied calmly, continuing to move toward the main hallway of the lowest floor. The suit's movements were graceful, like those of a feline predator, and at the same time, there was something mechanically heavy about them, probably related to its size.

When it reached the hallway, it turned left, lighting up the large hallway like a small sun. Gunshots rang out from the other side, hammering the alien figure, but the bullets ricocheted ineffectively. They didn't even make noise on impact, seeming to deflect off the armor and eat into the bare concrete walls as ricochets that smelled of mold and dust. Jacek stayed low, gesturing for Pill and Hardy to stay pressed against the wall of the small hallway.

"I hope Uffe climbed through the elevator shaft, because I'm out of radio contact," he murmured to his comrades. "You guys go through the shaft too and climb up. If we're lucky, Tom and Ulli will keep the reinforcements that have arrived busy, so they won't be bothered with the shaft at the moment. As soon as you make contact with Uffe and Knut, tell her to put the rifle in front of the entrance. I don't want that thing to shoot her, understand?"

"Sure," Hardy confirmed, and Pill nodded gravely.

"Good. If this thing needs more power to reanimate its wearer, we should give it the power and not get in the way."

"Otherwise, we're fodder."

Jacek looked at Hardy and nodded. "But we might also get the unique chance to talk to a Tear face to face."

"Aren't they our enemies if we ally with the Morphs?"

"We might find out then."

"Since when do we act beyond our orders?" Hardy wanted to know, sounding more curious than critical.

"The aliens have chosen our planet as a battlefield. There must be a reason for that." He peeked around the corner and saw that the alien had passed the elevator shaft and was currently working its way through a group of Russian soldiers. It swiped at the attackers with short, precise movements, killing them in a matter of seconds.

"Let's go!" he shouted, running after the running sun with his assault rifle carefully angled.

The footsteps of Hardy and Pill behind him were loud at first, then swallowed by a hellish crash as the alien stepped through the security door at the end of the corridor as if it were paper. The emergency exit sign above his head flickered briefly, as if trying to fend off the glare of the figure from outer space — and went out. As Jacek passed the stairwell, Hardy and Pill turned, and their footsteps were no longer heard.

Then he reached the dead Russian Spetsnaz soldiers, their knife emblems splattered with blood on their shoulders. They wore bullet proof vests and simple uniforms with knee and elbow pads and lay with twisted limbs to the right and left of the aisle. He counted six. A wild confusion of Russian shouts and explosions could be heard from the radios on their shoulder straps, breaking off and resounding again and again. Jacek left them behind and climbed over the off-hinge door into the stairwell, which spiraled upward with wide concrete steps. The alien, whose glow he could see through the banisters, climbed the steps with a composed speed, as if it knew no exhaustion. He had to scramble to stay in sight – always half a floor behind it. The defenders seemed to understand what they were up against and yet left no stone unturned to stop their alien prisoner, for which he respected them. It was sad respect that made him oscillate between pity for his fellow aliens and lack of pity for his enemies, who had brought on this situation in the first place. After five floors, four soldiers with heavy shields were waiting for them, firing grenade launchers at the alien, nearly destroying the entire stairwell. They too were killed with precisely calculated blows. Still further up, a sniper was apparently waiting, hitting the suit with a well-aimed shot through the clear center column — seemingly with anti-vehicle ammunition — that didn't even faze the alien. It marched stoically on upwards while Jacek pressed close to the torn open walls of the stairwell out of an abundance of caution. And so it went for twenty-two floors: again, and again, he had to step over corpses with broken eyes that had tried in vain to stop their prisoner, whom Jacek had freed instead of taking with him in inert form. He was tempted several times to open one of the doors leading off each floor, even though he knew most of the entrances were for the maintenance engineers to the missile bays, but he managed to keep his curiosity in check and forced himself to follow the alien at a short safe distance. Whatever the Russians were cooking up or exploring in this secret facility would prob-ably remain a secret forever.

As the glowing alien reached the ground floor exit Knut had blasted before her descent, the glow abruptly stopped and there stood the white, oversized figure again. It paused for a split second and stepped into the entryway. Jacek followed the alien cautiously, and as he stepped around the corner into the open, he paused in amazement. There were burning pieces of debris and bodies in the snow everywhere. Columns of smoke rose into the grey cloudy sky in dozens of places. To the left, behind some half-shattered snowmobiles, Tom and his Team Four crouched with two injured men being tended to, and on the ridge to the right, he saw the silhouettes of Team Six waving at them from a distance. Directly between the field of destruction and the alien that had paused, Uffe stood in front of the extraterrestrial rifle lying on the ground while Hardy, Knut, and Pill knelt near them, aiming toward the exit of the small valley, looking for new threats.

"Uh, the power cells, you said?" the sniper asked, pointing to the rifle. "I've already prepared it."

"Press with a fingernail into the small indentation behind

the grooved area above the trigger, please," the AI replied after a moment's hesitation, and Jacek's heart dropped so big, it felt like an avalanche. He had expected it to wipe out Uffe and his team without further ado. But that risk had apparently paid off as well.

The sniper followed her instructions and pulled a splint the size of a forearm from the rifle, its underside glowing red. The alien took a step forward and Uffe immediately stiffened, but it placed a hand on the splint and took it to unceremoniously press the energy cells — at least that was what Jacek guessed they were — against its chest. The cells were engulfed by the white of the suit like a viscous liquid and were gone.

"Thank you for your cooperation," the AI announced, continuing on her way toward the valley exit. With Uffe standing in the way, she jumped aside before she could pass through them and glared after the white giant, who almost blended in with the snowy surroundings, had it not been for the background of burning and smoking debris.

"What happened here?" asked Jacek, nodding toward the field of destruction.

"I used this weapon," Uffe replied, eyes blazing, lifting the monstrous thing off the ground like a fragile infant.

"The Russians had to have a quickly deployable unit nearby or still have forces at a short distance because of the object in Baikal. Have arrived with armored cars and a lot of soldiers," added Knut. "This weapon spat out little blue dots that flew on their own toward anything that came our way. The whole fight didn't last more than a few seconds, then everything was destroyed or dead."

"It was dreamy." Uffe sounded downright gushy.

"Uh, Jessy?" spoke up Hardy.

"Yes?"

"The alien's away. What do we do now?"

"I'd say we follow him."

"But that's not our mission objective," protested Pill.

"No, but our operational goal is to get the prisoner to Ulan-Ude, which is southeast of Lake Baikal. From there, he is to be taken by train to Ulan Bator. We can't take him; he proved that on the way out of here. But if I understand it correctly, the AI sees the object in Lake Baikal as a threat to its carrier and will probably go right there to eliminate the threat. Also, it now has enough power to reanimate its carrier. I have no idea when that will happen or how we'll know, but we won't know by turning away now. If it marches south, that's on the way for now anyway." Jacek glanced after the white giant, who was marching in a straight line through the debris field and had almost reached the edge of the ice patch that formed the new valley floor. "Just make sure you don't pose a threat."

"Team Four hit it hard, one down and one badly injured." Tom delivered the bad news. He had come over from the snow-mobiles and was anxiously pointing a thumb behind him where his team was tending to the wounded.

"I see. Take the wounded back to the buggies. We'll walk and stay in sight of the alien. If you put the wounded in the back seats, those who are still healthy can hang on to the crash cages on the outside. That should be enough room," Jacek ordered, and Tom nodded. "Proceed with the extraction plan; we will either meet you in Ulan-Ude, or you report back on my actions and we will see."

"You got it. Take care of yourselves, alright?" Tom said goodbye with the typical ghetto fist of soldiers and returned to his team.

"How does that work, looking out for us when we're chasing an invincible alien controlled by an AI?" asked Uffe. Instead of answering, Jacek motioned for her to shoulder the alien weapon. "This thing is really heavy!"

"You've fallen in love with your new toy, haven't you? For better or worse, remember?" sneered Knut, and she gave him a dirty look.

"Easy now!" hissed Jacek. "We stay in sight, fifty meters away at least. No one aims at it, not even by accident. Understand?"

After making sure everyone nodded, he gave them a wave and they retrieved their marching packs from the half-destroyed Lada, which was still in front of the door and seemed to have taken quite a beating. At least their things were still intact.

As soon as they had left the small valley, the alien turned off to the south and increased its speed so much that they had to go into a light continuous run in order not to be left behind. After all, every meter they lost ran the risk of them not being able to see where it was going, as its pure white form quickly blended in with the snow and ice landscape.

"Do you think that thing will give us a break?" asked Uffe, not sounding particularly hopeful.

"It's a computer controlling a suit. Why would it pause?" grumbled Hardy. As the wind picked up again the further south they got, they had hooded up again and were communicating with each other by radio.

"But then we'll get a problem soon. Forty kilometers of endurance running, okay, fifty, also okay if I'm allowed to puke in between, but then we'll eventually realize that we're not machines."

"Let's deal with it when the time comes," Jacek suggested, though he had been thinking the same thoughts and hadn't found a solution yet. "Do you also have the impression that the storm has gotten worse?"

"Yeah," Knut murmured. "When we came, this part was still outside the storm foothills; now we're already inside and it's getting really drafty."

Jacek eyed the many frozen wave formations on the ice, growing large and small out of the cold, as if someone had frozen the image of a wild ocean — with the difference being that, on an ocean, there would not have been completely smooth surfaces between the waves. But what else was here the way it should be?

After a few hours, the alien stopped abruptly. It happened so suddenly that they ran a few more meters before they noticed it. But there was no doubt about it: the white silhouette, which was now more clearly visible as the sky was already becoming ominously gloomy and grey again, stood there as if rooted to the spot and then turned around.

"Shit!" cursed Uffe.

"Is it going to shoot us now after all?" Knut's crazy grin was almost audible in his voice. "Maybe it's tired of chasers."

"I'll find out. You stay here." Jacek gripped his rifle a little tighter and forced himself to keep the barrel pointed toward the icy ground. Cautiously, he walked ahead and toward the tall white figure. When only a few feet separated them and he looked into the shapeless face of the alien standing there as if frozen in place, he pulled the scarf from his mouth.

"Hello."

"Hello," the androgynous voice of the AI replied. "I am detecting approaching flying objects from the west. I've initiated the reanimation process, depleting large portions of my energy reserves and preventing me from using some functions to conceal my presence."

"You want us to make sure you're not seen?" asked Jacek.

"That is correct."

"But nothing on this planet can touch you."

"That assumption is not correct. There are hostile entities on Earth that you call *Morphs*. I can register the approaching objects, but I cannot identify them."

Jacek thought and held a hand in front of the mouthpiece of his headset. "Come here and unpack the camouflage net; our position is under approach by flying objects."

It took less than a minute, then they were under a thick white tarp, sitting on the folded edges so as not to give the wind a chance to carry them away. After what felt like an eternity, helicopters thundered in the sky, recognizable by the roaring rotor sounds. While they weren't flying directly overhead — it wasn't loud enough for that — they couldn't have been very far away either.

"The objects are moving away in the direction of the place we left," the AI announced, standing up.

"I hope Tom and Ulli can manage," Jacek said, trying again to reach them by radio — to no avail. They packed up the tarp again and stowed it hastily in Uffe's backpack so as not to lose contact with the AI, who was steering the suit south again without any regard for them. This time, however, he decided they could stay right with it, since it was obvious the AI had no interest in killing him. At least not as long as they didn't get in its way.

"Is your carrier an important person to your species?" asked Hardy of the AI after another hour of silent marching through the increasing howl of the storm. The telecommunicator already had to speak very loudly to be understood.

"Yes," came the monotone reply.

"Which one? Like a leader?"

"Something like that. I am not authorized to divulge details of the person of my bearer."

"So, he's a person? Flesh and blood?"

"Yes."

"Did the resuscitation work?" Jacek wanted to know, as he had been wondering for a while about the AI wanting to start the resuscitation process — whatever that was — and expend a lot of its energy, but nothing else had happened. Still, they were talking to the AI and not a real alien. Why?

"The resuscitation was successful. My wearer will soon be stabilized and regain consciousness," the suit confirmed, circling a particularly large wave of ice that towered over everyone many times over.

"I hope you'll put in a good word for us, then," Uffe interjected. "And I want to keep the gun, preferably with new power cells, please!"

"I fear that will not be necessary. Regarding your assistance in freeing my carrier, I will of course report the facts to inform him what has happened since his capture by you."

Uffe fell silent and exchanged a glance with Jacek, who had already feared something along those lines. A snake coiled in his stomach.

"Uh, there was something," the sniper admitted. "It wasn't personal, really. Besides, we made sure your carrier wasn't reduced to rubble by his own people, so that has to count for something."

"That will be up to my carrier."

"You said *he*," Hardy stated. With one hand, he held the scarf in front of his mouth against the increasing wind, making his voice sound muffled and slurred. "So, your wearer is male?"

"That assumption is correct."

"So, there's men and women in the Tears."

"Among other things."

"What do you mean by that?" asked Hardy in amazement. "Are there more than two sexes?"

"Yes." The AI stopped suddenly and turned around, as if something had occurred to it. Jacek was startled.

"What is it?"

No answer.

"Uh, guys, this is new," Uffe found, tapping the white suit

with one hand. There was no response at all. Then, after endless minutes of growing more and more restless and standing like bent figures in a storm, movement came to the suit. The hands made grasping motions and the shoulders circled back and forth.

"Hello, Earthlings. I am T'Chall," a deep, soft voice sounded from the suit. It sounded neither androgynous nor remotely alien like that of the AI, but melodic and accented at the same time. "I am the wearer of this suit."

CHAPTER 19

NIKOS

"HEY-KOLPA! MASMA-CHEERUP-TAK!" the alien boomed throatily from its helmet over and over again.

"I think he's trying to tell us something," Nikos remarked unnecessarily, carefully placing a hand on Sönke's outstretched arm, at the end of which the pistol was pointed at the native. Still, he was afraid that the gun might go off after all. After so much luck he had already enjoyed, he didn't want to push it.

"You don't say," Sönke grumbled. "I just don't speak Planet-X, unfortunately."

"But he speaks. Or she." Nikos thought the deep, rolling voice had more of a masculine sound, but they didn't know at all if this species had two sexes or three or even just one, as was quite common in the animal kingdom.

"Of course he does. Probably something like, *don't shoot!*"

"He speaks," Nikos insisted. "So we have something in common. He has arms and legs like us, a head and feet. At least if he's not a robot. And he must have a mouth to speak."

"That's enough for you?" asked Karin. "What if he takes off his suit and looks like a xenomorph? They had arms, legs, and a head too."

"Xenomorph?"

"Well, the aliens from *Alien*!"

"Does that look like a monster to you?" Nikos pointed at the alien with the blue suit that looked like it had been pumped up and whose surface was spotty and uneven. There was something sinister about the mirrored surface of the visor, as if there was a deep void behind it. "Alright, maybe that was the wrong question. Still!" He pressed Sönke's gun down further and watched as the alien slowly lowered his splayed arms but continued to stand in place — until he suddenly raised one of his fish-skin hands and pointed toward the door. Immediately, Sönke had the gun pointed at him again, and the alien defensively pulled both hands up and in front of his torso.

"Hey-Kolpa! Hey-Kolpa!" rolled out of the suit.

"Yeah, *don't shoot,* I get it," Sönke growled. "Then keep your hands where I can see them."

"Wait, he wanted to show us something!" Nikos took a step forward and stood in front of his friend's gun.

"Are you crazy?"

"No. I just don't think it's going to do us any good to stand in front of each other indecisively for hours. We're lost down here, one way or another."

"I don't feel like getting captured by these aliens without a fight, though," the soldier muttered.

"Hey-Kolpa," Nikos tried what was probably a rather poor imitation of the alien standing before him like an overweight hobbit, craning his small, broad head back. The movement reminded him of a child looking up, even if the mirrored oval visor sent a shiver down his spine. "Uh... Kolpa, Kolpa, what do you mean? Door? Did you point to the door?"

The alien regarded him for a while, following his outstretched finger toward the door. Finally, his shoulders twitched twice, as if he wanted to shake himself.

"I think he's headed for the door."

"Of course he is," Sönke snorted. "That's his escape route, man!"

"Why don't we just go with it?"

"Are you insane?"

"Does he look violent or dangerous to you?" countered Nikos. He knew that was the worst possible argument, since he couldn't even see the true nature behind the full-body suit, and even if he could, he probably couldn't interpret the slightest movement correctly.

"Big guy, what would you do, please, if aliens were attacking Earth, you were making your rounds as a sewer worker, and you found three of them naked with a gun?"

"I don't know, pee my pants."

"See?"

"Because they're aiming at me and they're nervous!" added Nikos, demonstratively turning around so he could look his friend in the eye and turn his back on the alien. The gun was now pointed at his chest.

You've gone completely insane, he thought, slowly putting his hand back on the gun to push it down.

"We're toast!" wailed Karin beside them. "We are toast."

"Then it doesn't matter," Nikos said, carefully taking the gun from Sönke's hand, "if we take a chance. Whether we get lost or starve to death, get shot by aliens or freeze, our chances are slim down here. So," he turned back around and handed the gun to the alien, causing horrified sounds from his companions, "we go all out."

The alien tilted his massive head forward a little and contemplated the proffered gift before taking it with a slow motion and holding it in front of his visor like a goldsmith trying to assess the value of a material with a magnifying glass. Nikos was aware that his fish-skinned counterpart could never have triggered the pistol even if it had worked. Still, the gesture was an attempt that would probably end badly, but no risk, no gain, and risk was probably the only thing that could still save them from their predicament.

"Are you crazy?" asked Sönke. Nikos did not turn around.

"No. The gun doesn't work anymore, remember? Were you going to stand here until we froze and he walked out?"

"I don't know. Damn it, I don't know."

"Exactly." Nikos took a step to the side, giving way to the door. The alien — or rather, the visor — focused first on him, then on the door. Finally, the small but exceedingly broad figure started moving and took jagged short steps to the door, grabbing the vertical bar in the recess and pulling it open far more effortlessly than Nikos had before. He, Sönke, and Karin formed a loose semicircle and watched him until he turned in the doorway, half standing in the open hallway beyond, lit by bands of fluorescent green mushrooms.

"Hey-Kolpa!" the creature shouted, and then it made a gesture they all immediately understood: a wave of its finned hand.

"I think he wants us to follow him," Nikos spoke what everyone was thinking.

"And I think I'm going to have a fucking heart attack," Karin boomed, shuddering.

"We don't have a choice now anyway." Sönke took a step forward and Nikos also followed the alien, who turned his back on them and ran into the hallway. His steps were short but quick, so they could keep up well with normal gait of their much longer legs.

He's turning his back on us, Nikos thought as they walked through the semi-darkness. He had to keep his head tucked in and arch his back slightly or he would have hit the low ceiling. His legs protested at the exertion, but the movement at least brought a semblance of warmth back to his limbs. On and on they walked, accompanied by the muffled echoing footsteps of their boots and something he hadn't even heard before, probably because of the volume of the waterfall: breathing sounds. The alien was clearly breathing through an air filter as well — which had been expected. The breath was quite fast and sounded like the alien was whistling, as if the device was defective. At one point, Nikos tried to reattach his breathing mask in front of his mouth, only to find that he no longer had a helmet on his head where the attachment points were.

At some point, they came to a staircase with too-short, shallow steps that led further into the depths. The light here was also provided by a single band of fluorescent mushrooms, with their perpetual poison green that gave the impression of suffering from color blindness or looking through a night vision device. Then they reached a fork in the road. A path led downwards, from where distant conversations in a strange language could be heard. Snatches of it flew through the darkness, eerie and reason enough for him, Sönke, and Karin to freeze. The alien turned to them, and his head bobbed back and forth before he finally led them down the other corridor, away from the voices, in whose direction the light was clearly intensifying.

"Do you feel like it's gotten warmer too?" asked Karin in a whisper behind him.

"No, I still have the feeling that my feet no longer belong to my body," Sönke replied, and Nikos inwardly wanted to agree with him, but had to realize that it had actually gotten a little warmer. Unless it was an effect of the approaching death from cold and his brain was fooling him one last time into thinking he was warm.

Before Karin could retort anything, the alien stopped so suddenly that they almost collided. Nikos swerved to the left, an instinctive fear shooting through his limbs that contact with the alien might somehow cost him his life.

"Kolpa! Kolpa!" the alien murmured in a deep voice, cutting off his slurping breaths. He had stopped in front of another door, which looked identical to the one by the waterfall except for the slightly lighter coloring from several scratches and wear marks in the metal. The finned hand grabbed the door handle and pulled back again. This time, he didn't pull on it, but it moved up automatically, accompanied by a hydraulic hiss. The alien waved at them and trudged with powerful steps through the opening into a room as pure white as cherry blossoms. Floor, walls, and ceiling formed a perfect cube of nearly ten feet on each side, leading toward a second door, before which the alien stopped. With a hiss, the doorway closed behind Nikos, and he flinched involuntarily.

A torrent of rolling sounds came from the alien's helmet and a lamp on the ceiling, which he hadn't seen until it began to glow brownish-blue like an alarm siren, came to life. Uncertainly, he turned in a circle with Sönke and Karin, surveying the strange room that contrasted so starkly with the darkness outside that he felt like Alice in Wonderland.

"What is this place?" breathed Karin, shrieking in surprise as several fountains of white steam hissed at her from the ceiling like the breath of a dragon.

"Cover your mouths!" shouted Sönke, and Karin jumped to the side, away from the cloud that had enveloped her. She yanked the uniform off her hips and pressed the soaking wet fabric in front of her mouth. Nikos, on the other hand, did nothing of the sort, for the entire room was already filled. He did have his breathing mask in his hand and pulled forward so that the rubber cut painfully into the back of his neck, but he lowered it again as he looked at the alien trotting toward him through one of the clouds and raised his hands demonstratively.

"I don't have any weapons," Nikos said, coughing against the steam that hit his lungs and tickled them. He tasted something that reminded him of ozone and solvents.

His counterpart tilted his helmet in the same manner he had done several times before, then aimed his mirrored visor at the pistol he held awkwardly in his finned hand. The creature knelt down and placed the weapon on the white ground before rising again and looking directly at him — at least Nikos thought he did.

Sönke and Karin were coughing, kneeling on the floor with their eyes closed. Sönke pressed his breathing apparatus in front of his mouth.

"The steam isn't corrosive," Nikos said over the hiss of the valves as it was suddenly silent. He looked up and saw no more steam shooting from the ceiling. The blue lamp was also no longer visible. Instead, the door behind the alien now slid open, revealing a room lit by warm yellow light. The small figure walked through and disappeared. Nikos followed him with uncertain steps, not waiting for the others.

Stepping out of the white surroundings was like stepping out of the sun into the shade. The walls here were longer and hewn from rough rock, the room rectangular with a low ceiling less than a foot above the top of his head. Three lamps in the shape of flat discs gave pleasantly warm light, somewhere between dark yellow and a tinge of orange that reminded him distantly of the light on the surface, but where it had always been a little dim because of the dense cloud cover.

There was a wide window on the left that seemed to be mirrored, because he could see himself in distorted form, next to Sönke and Karin, who came sneaking in behind him. Several uncomfortable-looking chairs stood in front of a wide table anchored directly into the rock wall in front of the window. On it, he saw all sorts of knobs and toggle switches that reminded him of World War II movies: archaic yet advanced with a penchant for aesthetics that had long since been lost to modern human technology and given way to ever tidier designs. Otherwise, there was nothing in the room except for two cabinets with smooth metal doors.

The alien walked to the left side of the long table and pressed some buttons, whereupon the work desk came to life. The window was suddenly no longer mirrored, nor was it really a window, but a large monitor showing an image consisting of three parallel lines on a red circle. The alien walked in obvious busyness to one of the chairs and turned his broad back to them. He seemed to be fiddling with something, and a moment later, the gloves, which now looked all the more like baseball gloves and made Nikos afraid to see the alien's real hand, flew off to the right and left. It tinkled and clicked as the alien made inputs, and then a blurry image appeared on the display, wide as a movie screen and far too narrow to resemble a normal image that would have looked familiar to Nikos — until he realized it was two shots being shown side by side.

The first shot showed alien soldiers in green, bulbous suits charging up a hill. In their hands, they held the clunky rifles he'd seen on the battlefield. The one holding the camera turned to his left, sounds of breathing drifting to Niko's ears from speakers somewhere. An alien tank — there was no other way he could describe the beetle-like, massive vehicle — plowed through deep mud. There had to be hundreds, thousands of soldiers and vehicles rushing up the hill. Then they had reached the crest, and with it, hell: the camera stared for a moment, unmoving, at an advancing battalion of Leopard 2 main battle tanks and soldiers, who immediately opened fire. Explosions tore the image apart, guttural screams rang out, and blood and mud sprayed in high fountains in all directions. The camera was thrown to the side, landing in the mud and showing one of the beetle tanks shredded and burned out by a direct hit. Screeching aliens jumped out of the remains, limbs severed and bodies burning. Nikos' mouth dropped open in horror as he realized the brutality that was being fought above. It seemed to take an eternity for the cameraman to lean down and whimper softly. It was a heart-wrenching sound that reminded Nikos of Bazaraki, his sister Nefeli's little cat, when he had once had dental surgery. All at once, the tanks of the First Armored Division were there, rolling through the picture and firing. A soldier with a hooded face — Nikos found the breathing mask and goggles, along with the combat helmet, terrifying all at once — pulled up his assault rifle and emitted a scar of fire. The camera's image was jerked upwards, so that for a moment, only the cloudy sky could be seen. Thick raindrops pelted the lens, then the camera, or the person on whose helmet it was mounted, landed in the mud, and the image showed a bare plain in a wide valley between huge mountain slopes. At the end of the valley, he saw a blue glowing crater that he knew from many reconnaissance photos: the mine. It clicked and the image froze.

The alien stood up and pointed to the second picture. It showed a gigantic shaft, kilometers wide and many kilometers deep, crisscrossed by bridges, cable pulls, and elevators. Everywhere it steamed and flashed. Gondolas went from side to side, connecting wide tunnels that reached into the roughly circular mine shaft like yawning mouths. Between them glowed a bluish hue, the color of rare ore.

"That's the mine," Sönke noted. "I wonder if that picture of the battle was a live shot. The guys are probably already in range of the target."

"I think the little one is trying to tell us something," Karin interrupted him, pointing at the alien, which got up from its chair and turned to face them. With nimble fingers, he pushed around on his chest, from which a square section suddenly detached itself and bulged forward. The alien reached into the opening and pulled out a plate-sized something, which he held out to them. It glowed blue. When no one stirred, he took a step forward and held it demonstratively in their direction once more.

"I think we should take this," Karin whispered, but without reaching for it, Nikos took it carefully. It was quite cold, and under its net-like, hard surface lay a blue layer of...

"That's the ore, isn't it?" Sönke uttered what Nikos was thinking at that moment.

"Looks like it, at least."

"Is this perhaps the power source for their suits? Is that why he led us here? To show us that the ore is vital to them?"

"I think so." Nikos swallowed and looked up at the alien, who at that moment was grabbing the ring latch of his helmet and releasing two bolts from thick eyelets.

"Oh shit!" crowed Karin, taking a step back. Nikos' mouth went dry all at once and he had to summon all his willpower not to recoil as well.

Then it was time. A hiss sounded and the alien's hands grasped the helmet from both sides and slowly pulled it up. When Nikos saw what was revealed, the blue artifact fell from his suddenly powerless hands.

Before them stood an alien, but also a human. The head was a little wider and rounder, like Mongols', the eyes smaller and sunken into deeper sockets, but there were two greenish eyes looking at them. Below them was a human nose with broad nostrils, a mouth with full, rosy lips, and a small chin that seemed to vibrate slightly. The entire face was no more alien to him than that of an Asian or vice versa. And that face showed sorrow.

CHAPTER 20

JACEK

"SHIT, that's not a trick of yours either? The AI?" Uffe asked with unmistakable unease in his voice.

"No. My name is T'Chall," the alien repeated. "I have had Sidhi give me a report, and I thank you for my deliverance."

"Uh, you're welcome," Jacek replied before Uffe could curse again.

"Even though I don't assume it was done out of pure altruism?"

"Um, not quite," he admitted, searching for a suitable explanation.

"Altruism is not quite our purview," Knut interjected. Out of his mouth, it sounded like great fun, not like they were standing in an unnatural storm on the edge of Lake Baikal in front of an alien that towered over them all by a head.

"That's rare in soldiers, especially in a special forces unit like Special Forces Command," T'Chall replied.

"How do you know our language?" Jacek tried to steer the conversation back to himself. He loved his team like family — they *were* his family — but if there was one thing he liked to keep them out of as much as possible, it was important conversations. At least as far as Uffe and Knut were concerned, who seemed to have lost any ability to take things seriously in their turbulent lives.

"Your language has been known to my species for a very long time, even before Britannic became mixed with Anglo-Saxon after the Saxons invaded the British Isles."

"Wait — that means you've been watching us for a long time?"

"Yes. We've been watching you since you were nothing more than a biological hope in the form of single-celled organisms in the floods of the seething primordial oceans, surrounded by volatile gasses and a toxic atmosphere," T'Chall explained calmly, as if they weren't standing in the howling, freezing wind of a dark storm.

"You've known all this time about us and our planet?" asked Hardy incredulously. "For... hundreds of thousands of years?"

"Evolution took millions of years," Pill corrected him.

"Billions more likely," the alien corrected them both. "And yes, we have been watching you in detail since the beginning of evolution on Earth. Every step from the first primates to our fateful arrival is recorded without a gap. We even know more about you and your history than you do, as we have records of every millimeter of the planet. No leaf has ever fallen from a tree without our knowing about it."

"I don't understand," Jacek said, trying to quell the whirlwind of thoughts forming around the words he heard from the alien, picking out clear questions and moving them around in his mind. "You have been watching us for so long. Why have we never caught onto this? Why have you never made contact?"

"Because," T'Chall replied, and suddenly, the peculiar helmet of his suit, which was in fact not a helmet, as the entire structure seemed to be of one piece, dissolved, and the alien revealed the face of a human. It was a little more elongated than Jacek had expected, and the eyes were almond-shaped like North American Indians. The skin was white and the nose long, the dark hair tied into elaborate braids that lay close to the scalp, but there was no doubt that a human stood before them. "It was we who brought you to Earth."

"Holy shit," Uffe murmured, and the others also gasped audibly even in the howl of the storm. "I don't believe it."

"You're human?" asked Jacek when he had enough saliva back in his mouth to form intelligible words.

"Yes and no. Our DNA is roughly identical, though mine has been heavily modified. But we could be called — depending on which scientist you ask — one and the same species."

"Wait, wait, wait!" Hardy took a step forward. "You said *you* brought us?"

"Yes, I did say that," T'Chall replied patiently. Jacek noticed that his lips moved out of sync with the words being carried into the storm. Apparently, his speech was translated into theirs in real time and took on the exact same sound, so nothing overlapped.

"But... How? Why?"

"We colonized a large part of the Milky Way by burying programmed amino acids in asteroids and hurling them through the endless reaches of space, after mapping the entire Milky Way using a dense network of probes. One of your scientists already had a similar idea. His name was John von Neumann, and he was a mathematician. He postulated self-replicating probes that explore the entire galaxy step by step, creating copies of themselves over and over again. This is similar to what my ancestors did five billion years ago. We believe that we were the first intelligent species in the Milky Way to evolve during the first life-friendly years of the universe. You were one of our first colonies, if you will."

"Wait, we're a colony of yours? But how can we be a colony if we don't even know anything about you?" Hardy asked.

"Well, there was just under two million years between the launch of the asteroid and the impact on Earth. Originally, the project called for the probes we sent after it to speed up evolution and tie the growing humans into our network, but in two million years, the politics and sentiments of a species do change a lot, and in the end, we decided on something like the Prime Directive. You must remember that at that time we didn't know how to get around the absolute limit of the speed of light."

"The Prime Directive?"

"*Star Trek*, man," Uffe grunted. "Prime Directive forbids all starships and members of Starfleet from interfering with the normal development of alien cultures and societies. Compliance with this directive takes precedence over the protection of starships and members of Starfleet. Casualties will be tolerated to the extent necessary to comply with this directive. Interference is specifically meant, in the case of a planet progressing in its development into a technological civilization, to provide clues about space, other planets, or civilizations."

All eyes were now on the little sniper with the huge alien rifle on her back. "What? I liked *Star Trek*! Get a life for once."

T'Chall smiled generously. Jacek found that there was something aristocratic about his facial expression and his entire slightly undercooled habitus. *Or something ancient, sublime.*

"I have to confess that I'm not familiar with *Star Trek* in any detail, but that's about the extent of it. Evolution is something very fascinating and has proven to be a basic constant in the universe. When an intelligent species like us manages to escape the great filter, it eventually encounters technological wonders that leave only one desire: to explore the essence and reason for existence. Evolution, though directed and pre-programmed in your case, is such a complex miracle that we no longer wanted to interfere, at least not after our jump start. There was also the question of whether we were very lucky not to fall victim to the great filter, or whether other civilizations of our DNA could succeed."

"What great filter?" asked Jacek. "What is it?"

"It's kind of like a natural barrier that every civilization hits at a certain point and then dies out."

"Something like artificial intelligence, nuclear bombs, or climate change?" asked Pill. "I read about that once."

"Yes. Each of these points is a great filter, but each great filter has at its core a single trigger, and that is the ability to fictionalize, as we have discovered," T'Chall explained, gesturing by turning one of his white palms upward with the six fingers. "Whether it's nukes, a killer virus, climate change, or artificial intelligence, these are all solely symptoms of a human trait: the ability to submit to common fictions. Someone established that there were many gods, and everyone believed it and adopted the priests' answers. Mythology replaced direct primate experience, shared belief in stories passed on. The pyramids could only be built by such large numbers of people because they thought that by working for the pharaoh – they thought they were doing something for their own salvation in the afterlife. Later, it was said that there was only one God, but that he was a redeemer of our sins and sent his son to you for this purpose. This story has endured through the millennia and has given meaning in life to an unfathomable amount of people. Religions are controversial, but fiction or not, haven't they, by that alone, done some good alongside all the undoubted bad? This ability to believe in fictions, however, is the great filter because it is the only link of a civilization. The world is exceedingly complex and impossible for one person to comprehend. That is why there are specialists like scientists for individual areas. But nobody understands, for example, climate change, only one of the fictions about it — be it that it exists or that it does not exist. People ignore the facts because their own world of experience doesn't match what they see, and there's no appeal in believing it."

"So all civilizations abolish themselves because they believe in fictions but can't grasp the complexities of reality and are caught up and destroyed by the consequences of their developments, be it dirt or technology?" asked Jacek, shivering.

"Yes."

"And that's how it went for all the civilizations you brought into the Milky Way with your amino acid asteroids via evolutionary tutoring?"

"Yes," T'Chall said, sadness reflected on his face. His large eyes lowered a little and the corners of his mouth twitched slightly. "Out of eighty thousand human evolutionary lineages, thirty thousand have reached the atomic age. Twenty thousand survived it, eighteen thousand perished from the great filter, and two thousand still exist. Most are somewhere between the Bronze Age and the Renaissance, if you will. You are among those closest to the great filter. We have estimated your survival at approximately one hundred years."

Jacek had to swallow. Hearing and seeing that the Tears, who they had thought were predatory aliens, were in fact humans from the depths of space, who were also responsible for evolution on Earth, was already a mighty mouthful to swallow. But to be told that the end of their civilization and their species was historically imminent added something on top that was almost too much for him to comprehend.

"We're going extinct?" asked Uffe lightly.

"Yes."

"And I thought it was your fault, with your ships and fighting in orbit and all."

T'Chall's mouth curled into a smile as he eyed the sniper. "We had no other choice. Those you call *Morphs want* to destroy you, and even if we don't make contact, we'll protect our species no matter where or how it evolves. I'm very sorry for what happened, but there was no alternative."

"The Morphs, why are you at war with them?"

"The Morphs are a dangerous swarm consciousness and the only other intelligent species we have ever encountered. They have only one sex and know nothing of two-way relationships and mutual respect, nor the concept of love or brood protection and care. They serve themselves and their reproduction and propagation, have never produced anything like philosophy or art. We have been at war for several thousand years already, trying to contain their expansionist efforts as best we can. Our technological superiority is matched by their sheer mass. Every Morph knows only one thing: the *advancement of the collective.* Concepts like leisure, relaxation, or war weariness are foreign to them. Not to us, however, and our robotized armies are getting more and more dangerously short of resources." T'Chall looked up at the storm clouds above their heads with a worried expression. "But we have found a way out. Better said, I have."

"The anti-technology spheres we caught you with?" asked Uffe, and the alien — human — raised his narrow eyebrows.

"Yes. I developed them — along with a large composite of artificial intelligences. They can let us regain the upper hand in this war, because they block not only all quantum mechanics-based technology — including your smartphones, for example — but the cohesion between the individual nano-replicators that make up the ascended Morphs."

"Ascended Morphs?"

"Yes. In biological form, they grow until adolescence, at which point their consciousness is transferred into a more efficient body of nano-replicators, whose individual replicators serve not exclusively as muscle but also as nerve replacements. The entire body is, in a sense, the brain." T'Chall made a throwing away gesture. "That's not important right now, though. I need to get to the crashed Morph ship that's near here."

"Why?" asked Jacek, looking south where the horizon seemed to glow an unhealthy red.

"I think there were some survivors who want to fix their reactor and overload it."

"They're going to blow themselves up?"

"Yes, and that would sterilize Earth forever. To the Morphs, any of our colonies is a threat to their expansion and the security of their civilization."

"I have one more question," Hardy spoke up again.

"All right, one last one."

"When you wanted to set up the anti-technology field in the Congo, why did your own people attack you?"

"Because I went against the orders of the higher-ups."

"The higher one?"

"It doesn't matter now. It was forbidden for several reasons. One is due to the violation of the Prime Directive, as you would call it, and the other is due to a distinct shortage of resources. We possess only a few of the self-replicating spheres, as they are powered by a rare ore found in only one place in the Milky Way. To procure it, we have violated the principle of non-interference for the first time since its inception. Currently, we are desperately searching for more of this ore, but have yet to find any. The higher-ups wish to protect our most important planets first."

Hardy turned his head and looked at Jacek, who got so cold

at the mention of ore that he felt like his back had turned into a piece of ice.

"We have a problem," he finally admitted as T'Chall was about to turn around. The alien human paused and turned to face him. "If you really can see and record everything, the Morphs have found a way to lock you out." Jacek wondered if it was wise to share classified information. What if they'd just been double-crossed? What if T'Chall was an illusion of the Morphs to test their loyalty to the Alliance? What if T'Chall wasn't human at all and was telling them lies? Perhaps his true form was a tentacled monster or a repulsive insect? Surely, with the technology they had mastered, such a thing would be a cinch. But he looked so human. And neither he nor the AI had shown any aggressive behavior. He himself had seen the Tear's own people attack him in the Congo for laying out the spheres. Surely that had to mean something? Perhaps Jacek had now reached a point where he could no longer stay out of it and do his job but had to follow his instincts.

"That would indeed be a problem," T'Chall said in a heavy tone. "What else are you not telling me?"

"The leadership of the European Union has received an offer of alliance from the Morphs. Our forces are to neutralize a strategic resource of the enemy for them — you — that they cannot get hold of themselves."

His tall counterpart's expression darkened more and more, turning into worry, which expressed itself with deep furrows in his white forehead.

"The ore," T'Chall breathed. "They've discovered a gap in the sphere network on Andualla and sent your army through a wormhole to destroy the ore mine."

"Yeah, I guess so," Jacek admitted contritely, feeling like a kid who had to confess a particularly bad prank to his father.

"The ore runs throughout the planet and is extremely flammable and reactive. You must withdraw your units immediately!"

"I guess that's no longer possible. They already went through the wormhole two days ago and I heard that Major General Theodor Steutner is in command. I've never met him in person, but they say he's not exactly the sort to back down once he's been given an order," Jacek explained, unable to believe that the political leadership had made a deal with the Morphs so easily. On the other hand, they were in distress and threatened with the annihilation of all humanity. There was probably too much on the table to go through all the facets of a decision first.

"This is a disaster." T'Chall sounded very concerned, and his face reflected a kind of crushed feeling that drove worry into Jacek's limbs. "I must contact the higher-ups and warn them, if it is not too late! We need to get to the crash site; I might be able to send a message to Saturn there."

"What if the message is too late and the ore is destroyed?" asked Uffe. The fact that she hadn't put a single curse in her sentence spoke to how worried she obviously was.

"Then I fear that this war is lost. It will not happen immediately, but little by little, without the ore and the spheres, we will be worn down by the overwhelming power of the Morphs. I also fear for the battle for Sol, because I overrode the orders of the higher-ups, seeing the installation of the spheres as the only way we can still save Earth."

"So, we fucked up," the sniper concluded, saying exactly what Jacek feared. They had blindly fallen into the trap of the Morphs and given the enemy of humanity — who had apparently spread across the entire Milky Way without knowing it — the key to their destruction.

"My energy supplies are low, so I may need your help. I don't know if the crashed ship's automated defenses are intact or how many Devourers are still alive," T'Chall said in a strained voice, his helmet closing again as if it had never been open.

"We'll help you," Jacek decided, looking to his team. All pairs of eyes were stuck behind thick snow goggles and their mouths behind scarves, but they all nodded in turn, and he could almost physically feel their determination.

THE SILENCE WAS tense to the breaking point, disturbed only by the flickering of the screen, which formed an optical contrast to the figures that stood frozen in front of each other. Nikos stood between Karin and Sönke, who stared at the alien, who was not an alien at all, but a human. Or a human alien. And, given the body proportions and long, nut-brown hair of their counterpart, he was pretty sure they belonged to a woman, one that was unusually bulky, yet compact, but that was almost certainly due to the different gravity conditions that prevailed here.

"We traveled across the Milky Way once just to meet other people?" asked Karin incredulously.

"And to slaughter them," Nikos added with a level of bitterness that frightened himself. "What's the game here?"

"I don't know," Sönke growled. "But I'm sure the Morphs knew exactly who we were raising our arms against."

"Hey-Kolpa," the alien woman said, and the way her lips moved was as familiar as if they were talking to someone from another country on Earth. Without the strange distorting effects of her suit, she sounded no stranger than an alien in her own country. All the stranger was the alien space they were standing in, and the knowledge that they were a few tens of thousands of light years from Earth.

"Hey-Kolpa," Nikos repeated lamely. "Is... is that your name?" He tapped his chest. "Nikos." Now he pointed. "Hey-Kolpa?"

The alien wiggled her head, raised one of her broad hands, and made a sweeping gesture that included her as well as him and his companions. "Hey-Kolpa."

"I think she means we're all human, so Hey-Kolpa probably means *human*," Karin interjected, having to clear her throat several times to give her voice form.

"Human," her small counterpart repeated, and the sound of the familiar word coming out of her mouth was both startling and intriguing. Before they could retort anything, she stomped her powerful legs back to the work desk and turned to the input devices. There were a few clacks and the still image of the mine from afar was replaced by a new transmission. It showed a blurred image from the perspective of someone who was currently running across a wide field. This time, there was also sound, interspersed with deep explosions and shrill shouts and screams. Soldiers from the local defense forces were running toward the mine crater, which was a glowing blue hole at the end of the horseshoe-shaped valley that was hemmed in by huge mountain peaks. The rain had subsided, leaving a wide plain of mud and grass that was now littered with fleeing units. The person filming turned his head and Nikos gasped in horror as he saw the straggling German, French, and Spanish armored units coming out of the woods. At least they weren't firing on the fleeing men, but they were doing something that horrified him even more: they were stopping.

The camera turned forward again, wobbling back and forth with each running step, showing the crater, its rims already burning from the constant artillery fire, sending thick columns of black smoke into the toxic sky.

"Oh, no, no, no," stammered Sönke.

"They don't want to..."

"Yes, I fear they do!" The soldier swallowed loudly and the alien woman turned to them, her eyes moist.

"Hey-Kolpa," she said sadly, wiggling her roundish head again.

"We need to get into radio range and inform the division command!" Nikos realized he sounded downright panicked, but he couldn't stop himself. "Now!"

"They must have seen that some of the bodies were human," Sönke objected, looking pale-faced at the screen, where the film-ender's escape continued amid the battered defense force.

"With such a quick advance? No, we must warn them. If they knew, they wouldn't..."

"Hey, what are you guys talking about anyway? Did I miss something?" asked Karin, upset. "You guys sound like we're about to have an even bigger problem."

"The tank units are holding back because now the final phase of the attack is beginning," Sönke explained sadly.

"And what is the final phase?"

"The MOAB. It will be flown over the target by two heli-copters and then dropped. It will fall into the mine shaft and detonate with its smart fuse in the depths. All of this," the soldier pointed to the image of the approaching crater, "will be destroyed."

"We need to get within radio range," Nikos insisted angrily, extending a hand in Sönke's direction.

"What?"

"The radio!"

"The radio was in the helmet," Sönke explained. "I still had a field radio, but it wasn't one for underwater."

"What a bummer." Nikos wrung his hands and took a step toward the alien, who eyed him out of her small eyes. There was fear and sadness in her gaze, but not because of him. He pointed at the picture and then at himself, reaching a finger toward the ceiling. "We need to talk to our people, let them know what's going on. We can stop this."

The alien looked up at him and seemed to be eyeing him intently. Finally, she wiggled her head again and stomped to the door.

"I think we're supposed to follow her," Karin said, rousing Nikos from his staring gaze that followed the filming man's flight from his fellows. He tore himself away from the frightening sight with flared nostrils and followed the others into the white airlock between the room and the corridor. Once again, they were trapped between the two doors and dense steam shot from the ceiling. The alien put on her helmet and also sealed her gloves back on the ring locks. Now she looked alien and even a touch scary all over again, but it wasn't like before because his mind projected the image of her human face behind the mirrored visor.

"How I wish I could talk to her," he murmured to himself. He had so many questions for her. Of all the things he had counted on, the possibility of meeting other people in the vastness of the universe was at the very back of his mind, if it had existed at all. What did that mean for his worldview? For the worldview of all the people on Earth? Clearly, they were not the only creation of this kind. What would this knowledge do to the world's religions once word got out? Could this knowledge unite humanity without requiring war as a means of cohesion? But the questions reached much deeper: was it possible to learn each other's languages? Sure, they both presumably possessed the same or yet very similar organs for sound production and hearing, but if eyes had evolved differently due to the different biospheres in which their evolution had taken place, green could be red here — at least that was what he believed. But then how did one explain a tree and what a human felt at the sight of it? The diplomats in Scotland, who had arranged the alliance with the Morphs, were probably allowed to think about such things anyway.

"This is taking too long," he said impatiently as the quarantine procedure dragged on endlessly.

"If the armored units have stopped, the helicopters are already on approach," Sönke said over the hiss of valves. "That means we only have minutes, I don't think..."

The hissing died away and the door to the hallway opened. The alien trudged ahead, poking her head out and looking right and left before giving them a beckon to follow her. They were led to a staircase up on the right, where the path forked. They kept to the left. It took what felt like an eternity before they reached a wide hall bustling with activity: Suit-clad aliens with rifles — at least twenty — stood in front of a rail system where a long transport sled waited, which they were about to enter. Their companion shooed them behind a large pallet of tied-down crates and barrels, and they crouched down, half-naked as they were. The aliens' guttural, rolling speech rang out in the distorted, tinny way their suits produced, then there was a squeak and a sound like a subway going off.

"Masma!" His companion reappeared and frantically beckoned him over. "Masma!"

Nikos stumbled out of their hiding place with Sönke and Karin and looked around cautiously. The tiny underground station was empty, the transport sled with the soldiers gone. From the tunnel on the right, a new sled raced up, a flat platform with low edges and a grooved loading area, stopping directly in front of them.

The alien flinched as voices sounded from the corridor they had come, and hastily pointed to the sled. Only when they had squatted down on the uncomfortable bed did she jump to them and hastily pressed some buttons on a small console just off the bow. As the vehicle began to move, a flurry of soldiers came in and jerked their rifles up with angry shouts. Their shots crashed into the edge of the tunnel, into which they plunged with a brisk rush – not a second too soon, for the bullets of their startled pursuers, for whom the sled was presumably intended, sent a cloud of splinters onto the track bed, which was completely in darkness. Only now and then did green circles whiz past them, glowing brightly enough to show how fast they were speeding through the tunnel. The driving wind was relentlessly cold and made Nikos shiver violently. As if automatically, he, Karin, and Sönke clung to each other so as not to lose at least the pitiful remnant of body heat.

"W-we're going to the m-m-mine, I think," Sönke jabbered into the darkness, barely loud enough to drown out the roar of the ride echoing through the narrow tunnel at uncomfortable volume levels. "They seem to be p-p-putting their r-r-remaining troops o-o-on down here."

"I can't believe that happened," Karin murmured, pressed against Niko's chest. She squatted like a chick between him and Sönke.

"W-we've been had," he agreed with her, wondering what the Morphs were really up to. What was the point of it all? He was about to add something else when the sleigh shook violently and dense dust trickled off the walls onto them, making them cough violently. The sled slowed to a screeching halt as a muffled rumble echoed through the tunnel like a bass set too low just below them. The truck bed vibrated so hard, it masked even the shuddering of Nikos' limbs.

"The MOAB!" cursed Sönke. "It must have been the MOAB!"

"Oh, no," Nikos breathed. Too late. They were too late.

The alien, sitting at the small console about an arm's length in front of them, looked around slowly, as if the ceiling might collapse on her at any moment. Then she pushed a lever forward and the ride continued. It took many more minutes, which felt like hours to him, before they finally reached another station. To the right and left, the dark tracks made deep indentations in the rock. They were littered with fallen chunks and smaller stones that must have broken out of the ceiling in the detonation. Two slain aliens lay next to a ripped open weapons cabinet. The tunnel led further but ended abruptly after a few meters in a large hole, behind which it glowed blue.

"This must be the mine," Nikos shouted, jumping up to leap onto the rail bed.

"Nikos, don't!" shouted Sönke after him, but he had to see and would not be stopped. With long strides of his burning legs, he ran across the tracks until he reached the end of the tunnel and stood at the edge of the central mine shaft. Before him spread an apocalyptic scene that made his blood run cold. About a hundred meters above him was the dirty sky, where the shadows of helicopters could be seen. Fires raged blazingly at the edges, but also deeper in the shaft: everywhere around it burned, illuminating the struts, cables, bridges, and nacelles of the gigantic hole in the ground where they had been torn and broken off, from the force of the bomb his fellows had dropped. Large chunks of the ore had been blasted away, and the predominant blue he had seen on the video recording had given way to the greedy blaze of yellow-red flames that, as far as he could see into the depths, had infested the craggy walls like a disease. They ate ever forward with a terrifying speed. The ore must have caught fire.

"Holy shit," a voice whispered. It was Karin, standing beside him, her eyes wide. The strong wind blowing through the churning thermals of the burning, mile-deep shaft tugged at her hair. Another figure appeared between them, clearly smaller and stronger. It was the alien. Her helmet gave no indication of any reaction, but the rigidity with which she stood gazing at the burning inferno gave utterance to a definite language. She did not move, even when he turned to her. He had wanted to say something, to reassure her, to express his hope that the ore, which was not the Tears' raw material for war, as the Morphs had claimed might, might yet somehow be saved. But that would have been a lie, for what he saw suggested much more that there was some kind of chain reaction, and that the ore kept igniting.

"Nikos! Karin!" cried Sönke behind them, and the sound of his voice was positively panic-stricken, so that he wheeled round reflexively to see his friend, who had remained on the sledge, wildly rowing his arms. "Come here!"

He exchanged a glance with Karin and took off running, nearly crumpling on the rough rock between the tracks and reaching the front of the sled. Gasping for breath, he was about to ask what was going on when he heard the familiar rattle of assault rifles from the left corridor that led off into the darkness in front of the two slain aliens in the waiting area of the track. The tinny screams of the aliens mingled with the deafening gunfire, then all at once, the sounds of battle died away. They were replaced by heavy boot steps from the section on the opposite side.

"Hey-Kolpa!" cried Nikos excitedly, turning to her native

companion who was still standing behind them at the edge of the ripped open tunnel, looking down into the inferno of the mine as if she were frozen in place. "Hey-Kolpa!"

She turned, far too slowly to match his driving excitement. The overlapping sounds of trampling boots swelled into an increasingly menacing echo that boomed from the passageways on her right and left, collapsing in the middle over her sled.

"I think there's about to be a slaughter here between our people and them," Sönke shouted in alarm. "We have to leave, and we have to leave now!"

"No," Nikos replied in a firm voice. Anger, frustration, and an almost painful compassion mixed with guilt took control. "No."

Sönke looked at him, aghast. "Oh no, I know that look."

"You want to tell me what's going on?" Karin wanted to know, glancing uncertainly back and forth between the two of them and the exits of the tracks.

"He's about to do something stupid!"

"Hey-Kolpa," Nikos called out again, watching with relief as the alien stomped through the front remnant of the tunnel to join them. Her steps were no longer driven and full of drive now, but lame and depressed. He helped her onto the sled, and as he grabbed her under the arms of her suit, he didn't realize that he had just touched an alien for the first time — even if only indirectly. She didn't really seem to notice it either, and plopped down powerlessly on the bed of the truck when, all at once, there was a noise. Soldiers came pouring out of both entrances to the small underground station. On the left, a dozen armored infantrymen with patches of EU forces on their arms. Looking fearsome and familiar at the same time with their futuristic-looking face masks, they fanned out and took aim at their small group as a large group of local soldiers in green suits and mirrored visors appeared on the right, also bringing their weapons to bear. Separating them was the track and the transport sled, on which Nikos, Sönke, Karin, and the alien squatted, raising their arms excitedly.

"Don't shoot!" shouted Nikos to the soldiers. "Don't shoot!"

"Take cover, man!" one of the soldiers yelled in German. Since they all looked alike and only their breathing masks were visible, he didn't understand who had spoken to him. The aliens on the other side began shouting wildly as well, and the hint of deadly force was so palpable that the hairs on the back of his neck stood up. Nikos wheeled around, looked at the alien soldiers, and realized with widened eyes that they were lowering their weapons one by one. All sights were on him and his two half-naked companions.

Of course, he thought. *They didn't know either.*

"Wait, please, don't shoot!" he repeated, his voice rolling over in the direction of the armored infantrymen. "You don't understand. They're human beings!"

"What are you talking about? Get the fuck down!"

"I order you to lower your weapons!" roared Sönke suddenly, rising beside him. The soldiers gave each other indecisive looks — at least that was how Nikos interpreted their movements. But they did not lower their weapons. "I am Captain Sönke Teunen, Military Counterintelligence! I order you to lower your weapons now!"

"We're about to open fire. I'll give you three seconds, man!" the soldier who had spoken earlier blared back. The men took a step forward and adjusted the barrels of their weapons toward the stunned aliens on the other side, who stared paralyzed at the three humans and their compatriot, not yet noticing the threat of the weapons pointed at them.

"You don't understand, these are..." Nikos raised his voice in another desperate attempt to stop the looming disaster just as movement came to the armored infantry. At first, it looked as if time had been stopped, for instead of nervously leaping from target to target, the men and women in their battle suits froze, only to gradually lower their weapons as if in slow motion. Sporadically, they tore their masks and goggles from their faces and stared open-mouthed as if they had collectively seen a ghost. And that was exactly what they did.

Nikos sadly narrowed his eyes and turned to his left. There he looked down into the face of the alien with her nut-brown hair and cheeks wet with tears, looking with a motionless, sad expression at the soldiers of the First Armored Division. Silence fell as everyone in the half-destroyed station realized what had happened and tried to grasp the possibility of the impossible. He removed the breathing mask that had been dangling from his neck, pulling the rubber over his head, and looked at the useless device before looking back to the alien. Now they had even more in common than being of the same species: they would die at the hands of this planet's microbiome.

"Who's in charge?" asked Sönke into the silence.

"I-I."

"Identify yourself, soldier!"

The man who had spoken, standing further to the left of the row with his breathing mask off, took a hesitant step forward as if he had to relearn how to walk. "Sergeant Major Reinhard."

"Alright, Sergeant Major, have you set up a radio chain?"

"Yes, we placed amplifiers every hundred yards."

"Good, do you have a field radio with you?" Sönke wanted to know.

The soldier nodded without taking his eyes off the alien and pulled a thick radio from his back. Sönke stalked from the cargo sled and strode to the man without anyone stirring. The rushing blaze of the inferno of flames that reached them through the tunnel grew louder and louder in the silence, as if someone had turned up the volume.

"This is Captain Sönke Teunen, MAD. Connect me to Major General Steutner, priority code D-D-U-1-1-8, now!"

There was a pause, then Sönke spoke into the archaic-looking radio again. "General, you must call off the attack immediately, I repeat: call off the attack immediately!"

CHAPTER 22

JACEK

T'CHALL LED them in a direct line toward the object of the Morphs. Jacek understood that after only a few hours, where-upon he suggested that they take the lead from now on, as he thought it would be much faster to use the buggies, as they certainly had a head start on the other teams. True, it pained him to take the vehicles away from his comrades — after all they had casualties with them — but if T'Chall was right, it was a matter of life and death for humanity.

The life and death of mankind. Until a few hours ago, that had meant Earth and its inhabitants, who thought themselves alone in a dark, cold universe. Now it meant the end of some two thousand human civilizations, one of which was as old as Earth. Grasping the magnitude of that fact was more difficult than easy for Jacek the more time he had to think about it. The weight on his shoulders had doubled and every step he took felt like his body weighed a ton. Before the mysterious alien had become a human, he had been worried about his comrades and how they were going to manage the extraction from Ulan-Ude; now he was marching toward the place he had volunteered to go last, and he had to try and make up for a big mistake that had been made far away in Brussels. Not that he thought he would have decided differently or better, but it just so happened that everything had changed, and he and his team now found themselves in the midst of developments that seemed too big and too huge. At least too big and too huge to be able to change anything. But someone had to try. Usually, *someone* was synonymous with anyone but oneself, but that luxury didn't exist for him, and he didn't want to be one of those who shirked responsibility.

Under his guidance, they took a new course slightly westward toward the north shore of Baikal, which they reached a few hours later. The storm had already grown into a hurricane here, making the march most uncomfortable and giving them a taste of what to expect as they continued to approach the object. He even quietly doubted that they could manage to reach the eye if the winds continued to increase as rapidly as they had been. At the edge of the lake, which from above looked like a bathtub lying in the dark, from which much of the water had been drained, having previously been filled to the brim, they stopped. After a moment's consideration, they decided to slide down the long, sloping icy rock ramp on their packs. The risk of injury was not inconsiderable; they could get stuck, slash something, or pick up too much speed and smash on the icy surface, but there were no alternatives.

So, they slid and it was downward at a rapid pace. T'Chall raced feet first in front of them, many times heavier, gaining more and more ground until, finally, he hit the ice like a comet. Fortunately, it didn't break and the alien seemed unharmed as well, quickly scrambling back a few feet and catching them one by one with superhumanly fast movements of his arms and hands.

The buggies were still where they had left them, but were covered with a thick layer of snow, which they roughly removed.

Then Pill, Uffe, Hardy, and Knut sat down in one and Jacek and T'Chall in the other to distribute the weight halfway evenly. To keep from freezing to death, they wrapped themselves in the thermal blankets from their luggage and tossed the rest of their luggage onto the short loading platforms. As soon as the thick lug wheels with the snow chains turned and they sped south at full throttle, he noticed that the wind had died down a bit down here. Maybe it was the lower altitude, since they were at least half a kilometer lower than on the newly created plateau. Nevertheless, the storm was still a gale, and tugged fiercely at him and the whole buggy. The farther they went, the harder he had to counter steer when they were caught by a gust and nearly skidded.

"Would you like me to take the wheel?" offered T'Chall at one point, when Jacek's arms were already burning and threatening to give way.

"No, I'm fine, thanks."

"There's no shame in accepting help. Your comrades can take turns; you can't." Only now did he realize he was hearing his companion's voice in his earpiece, through which he normally received only the radio. He sounded calm and collected, though the howling of the storm seemed to give his words an urgency all their own.

"I know," he lied, yet knew it was a mistake. He was amazed at how hard it was for him to admit to himself that he needed help and that his willpower might not be enough to get them to their destination. On top of that, he had to be in possession of his powers there in order to function. He had been through a lot and had often been pushed or forced to his limits and beyond, but never had he asked for help. That was just not what a KSK soldier did. Regular soldiers asked for assistance, and this was the KSK. Admitting that he now found himself in the role of regular soldier almost made him laugh out loud. It wouldn't have been a happy sound, but rather one that was amused by fate, and that it always found a balance. It always showed one the other side, however much one might turn. When T'Chall didn't answer, he bit his lower lip and added, "All right, that would be good."

They changed places, and the shapeless white figure of the alien steered the buggy from then on without the slightest swerve.

"You can sleep soundly, Jacek Stratholm," he heard T'Chall's voice in his ear after he nodded off several times. One and a half marathon distance with baggage after a battle they had already covered the same distance before was beyond even Jacek's iron willpower and well-trained body. He was about to object that it wasn't necessary, and ask how the alien knew their radio frequency and his last name, but he was asleep before he could bring anything past his blue lips. There he was, wrapped in two thermal blankets whipped by the storm, lying in the passenger seat, being rocked back and forth, slipping into the realm of dreams, of which he was oblivious as his completely overworked body took the rest it needed.

When he woke up, it was the storm that woke him. The wind howled and whistled so loudly, it was like someone was yelling directly in his ear. His chest felt heavy, and when he opened his eyes, he could barely see anything because the snow was blowing so close in front of his glasses that he might as well have been lost in a sea of snowflakes. Only when he looked down did he realize that T'Chall's right hand was holding him by the chest — presumably to keep him from being blown away.

"We are very close," the alien announced in his ear. Jacek felt as if his entire body was made of concrete — frozen concrete — and was unable to speak. As if in a dream, he experienced being lifted up and pulled out of the buggy. He could not even protest, so cold was he and so exhausted were his muscles. The storm was gone and there was as little wind as if they were underground. Only now did he realize it wasn't snowing at all, but his glasses were covered in snow. He wiped the flakes away and flinched as he saw, far too close, the organ-like, pitch-black object piercing the sky in the eye of the storm. The crimson lights now pulsed permanently from the base of the towers on the ice to the peaks high above where the lightning bolts struck. It was abundantly clear that something was about to come to a final phase.

"Can you walk?" asked T'Chall, and Jacek caught himself saying "yes" already without having tried it. But when he was set on his feet, he couldn't feel his toes, but he could hold himself up. To the left was the second buggy, from which Pill and Hardy were just getting out to help Uffe and Knut, who were not resisting the assistance, which worried him. Things had to be bad for them. Without thinking, he ran to them and peeled himself out of his blankets.

"Hey, are they…"

"Are okay," Hardy reassured him over the radio. "A little hypothermic, but they're still responsive. We may have to use the stimpacks, though."

Jacek reached his comrades and put one of his blankets each around Uffe and Knut, who were already wrapped in their own and swaying as if they were still in the wind.

"Hey, hey, what's up with my girl and my crazy?" he asked anxiously, rubbing their shoulders one by one.

"I c-c-can't take it anymore," Uffe breathed weakly. Her words were like whispering in the wind.

"Jessy, we have to inject or we're not going to get anything done here, nor are we going to walk out of here upright," Pill said, taking him by the arm and turning him to face him. "I know you hate the stuff and have always forbidden us to use it, but it's part of the equipment of every medic in the field for a reason."

"Is good," he returned. "Is good."

"Really?" Pill sounded surprised. Jacek hated amphetamines and knew that every shot was a mistake with possible consequences. Maybe one ingestion wasn't life threatening, but dangerous was always the first time you did something that wasn't good. As it was with every drug and every tool. Once you used it and it worked, you never stopped.

"Yes. We'll all take it. That's an order," he directed grudgingly, and Pill nodded. His entire body language seemed to express relief. T'Chall, meanwhile, watched the mysterious artifact that seemed to be playing haphazardly with the weather, reaching for the sky like a citadel of evil on the horizon. Knowing that at any moment it could cause the Earth to be glazed over in a raging fireball made him shiver so badly that he didn't even notice the jab that Pill was jamming down his throat. What he did notice, however, was the effect: his eyes felt like they were about to burst, and his hands began to tremble slightly, and not because of the cold.

"We must hurry," T'Chall urged them on, not taking his eyes off the wreck of the Morphs, which did not look like a wreck at all to Jacek.

"We're ready." It was Uffe who had spoken and gave a wave. "Shit, every filthy fiber in my fucked-up body hurts, but that right there gives me enough energy for a whole war."

Jacek had to smile involuntarily when he heard her swear and something in him relaxed. At least a little. He followed her gesture and looked to T'Chall, who was holding the rifle's power cell in his hands, and lashed across the bed of the buggy. *I wonder if it was the same power cell.* Or had the suit produced a replica?

"There's hardly any energy left in it, since I barely have any to give off myself, but it should be enough for a few shots. Make sure they're worth it," the alien said, turning back around as the sniper had almost reverently taken the power cell. "Sergeant Major. Your ammunition is NATO standard 7.62 millimeter?"

"Uh, yeah," he replied quickly.

"Good, that's very small. I can make each of you five rounds without shrinking the mass of my suit to a critical point. With that ammunition, you should be able to handle anything we encounter there, though five rounds isn't much."

"That'll do it. If anyone's going to make every shot worth their energy, it's us."

"Good." Like a magician, T'Chall held his arm out to the right, palm up, and one by one, small rounds sprouted from the palm of his suit as if from nowhere. Hastily, Jacek went forward and took them to distribute them among his team. The gloves made him quite clumsy, but he managed to remove the first five cartridges from his magazine and insert the new ones, which were in no way different in appearance or profile from the normal ones.

"Once we are inside, I will know what to do. I have examined several of the Devourers' ships and am familiar with their technology. I need you to protect me while I work. I don't know how many more of them are up to mischief in there. Maybe it's just one, maybe it's many. Either way, we have to try. I'm able to cut a hole in the hull with my suit, but I'll use up just about all of the suit's power. If I can no longer communicate with you, you know why."

"We just injected everyone with a horse dose of fenethylline, we'll figure it out," Pill announced, sounding psyched, like he couldn't wait.

"Alright, let's go." T'Chall ran with lunging strides across the snow-cushioned sheet of ice, and Jacek and his team followed him with the power of the drug cocktail in their bloodstreams, softening the heavy muscles and driving the brain almost frenetically to further performance. Like silent shadows, they flitted through the silence of the smooth icy landscape that had been torn open before them with brute force. A few minutes later, they reached the debris field of ice chunks of various sizes that lay in front of the ice wall that had been built up. Like gauntlet runners, they circled the white obstacles, which could often only be made out a short time before they blurred with the surroundings. T'Chall didn't see Jacek again until they reached the chunks of ice around where the Morph's debris had broken through. He stood in front of the ice, holding his arms forward as if to push the obstacle away with sheer force. Then suddenly, red lances of glistening light shone from his palms and apparently moved on their own, drawing two parallel semicircles in the ice that met at their apexes. A few seconds later, they were standing in front of a circular passageway and their boots were washed by molten water. The artificial tunnel was about ten meters long and ended at a black wall — the hull of the alien ship.

T'Chall didn't wait but gestured for them to stay in place before running inside and coming to a stop as a white glowing outline in front of the black shell. Red light wafted through the tunnel again, flickering like a candle.

"Really doesn't feel right going in there," Pill murmured, craning his neck next to Jacek's to look up at the lightning-maltreated, red-pulsing tip of the Baikal object.

"Looks like Minas Morgul, and I bet it doesn't get any better in there," Uffe agreed with him.

"If it was just orcs we had to deal with, I probably wouldn't have a problem. At least I know them from TV."

"Hey, at least we've got a white knight with us who can shoot lasers out of his hands like Superman!" Knut interjected into the conversation, grinning broadly after pulling the snow-and-ice-encrusted scarf from his mouth.

Pill and Uffe looked at him, shaking their heads.

"The lasers are coming out of Superman's eyes," the sniper corrected him. "Did you read those disgusting smut magazines from your locker when you were a kid instead of every regular comic book?"

Knut shrugged. "I've just always liked breasts more than quick-change artists who only have to put on glasses to be unrecognizable."

"Guys," Jacek hissed as T'Chall waved them out of the tunnel. "Here we go!"

He ran ahead, into the ice and toward the alien standing in front of the black wall, which seemed to start moving in the light of Jacek's switched-on flashlight. The previously solid black material bubbled in a square area, forming concentric wave patterns that changed shape faster and faster before the entire section melted like mercury. Without hesitation, T'Chall climbed through the square opening he had created in the ship's hull and disappeared into the darkness.

CHAPTER 23

NIKOS

WHEN NIKOS STUMBLED to the surface of Planet X, he was accompanied by the train that had picked up him and the others in the underground station. It formed a dense cocoon around them. The walk back to the dirty daylight had taken about twenty minutes and started out difficult. No one had known what to do. Both parties had stalked each other, until, finally, he had been able to persuade Lieutenant Fatahi, the commander of the platoon of armored infantry, to be the first to lay down his arms. Fortunately, the local troops had reacted positively — apparently as shocked by the fact that they were human as they were — and had not opened fire. Considering that they had been attacked for no reason and out of nowhere, their behavior could only be considered exceedingly admirable — as was that of the young lieutenant with the dark eyes. After a short conversation, Sönke had been able to persuade him to disregard the current orders and take new ones on his own responsibility: to stop the fighting and to bring the little alien human, whom Karin had since called "Hey-Kolpa," to Steutner to convince him to stop all fighting immediately. Apparently, the major general was not content with destroying the mine; he wanted to make sure that everything related to the mine was really razed to the ground. Sometimes he wished Germans wouldn't be so damn thorough. There was still fighting in some of the tunnels, which they could tell from the loud weapons fire and the flashing lights in the corridors. Every now and then, they passed bodies of defenders in their closed suits. Many soldiers of the First Armored Division and the Brigade Blindée were also wounded or dead and were being carried out on stretchers by comrades and medics. It was an opaque maze of corridors and caverns of various sizes through which the lieutenant led them. Many paths had been rendered impassable by the domino effect of the ignited ore, but eventually, they made it to the top.

A cocoon of soldiers from Fatahi's platoon ran body to body to shield them from prying eyes — though Nikos didn't think anyone had shown much interest in them. Soldiers everywhere were running about in apparent chaos, the wounded being transferred and carried back and forth between tanks and trucks. Much of the decimated formations were already re-aligned toward the wormhole that lay far in the distance among the woods.

"Lieutenant," Sönke hissed over the crackle of the thermal blanket the soldiers had put around him just like Nikos, Karin, and Hey-Kolpa. They had wrapped the little native in the blanket so that only her head peeked out, looking as human as anyone else. From the outside, she should look like nothing more than a smallish soldier. Nothing that would have drawn any special looks in the heat of battle. "We have to get to the general!"

"The command post is over there," the young lieutenant replied, nodding in the direction of the truck, which Nikos only recognized after some searching among all the vehicles. The truck was deliberately barely distinguishable from the others so as not to provide an obvious target for attack. The rear view, however, revealed that there must be a more solid outer wall under the tarpaulin. Without hesitation, the officer steered them between two Leopard 2s that were aiming menacing guns in the direction of the smoking mine, past a line of trucks that were being loaded with wounded. Their moans and wails stung Nikos, though he couldn't even see their pained faces. How bad it must be for the hundreds of men and women who, tied to their stretchers, couldn't even look into the friendly faces of the medics, only into those gruesome breathing masks and goggles?

In front of the General Staff truck, they were stopped by a group of soldiers. One of these, wearing dark armbands, raised a hand. "No entry for your platoon, Lieutenant. Take another route."

"I must speak to the general," Fatahi replied firmly.

"You're not authorized. Go back."

"Listen, Corporal," the lieutenant said in a clenched voice. "I order you to get out of the way. Now."

"I'm very sorry, Lieutenant, but there are clear orders from the General Staff. I'm afraid I'm going to have to turn you away."

"It's mission critical that you let us through," Fatahi insisted, and his soldiers began to grow restless, especially as the guards began to look curiously at what they were hiding in their midst. Nikos began to get nervous, for every minute that passed increased the danger of someone seeing through them.

"Give me the information and I'll pass it on, I promise," the corporal suggested.

"Men," Fatahi shouted in response, and with a brief gale of rustling, all the soldiers in the platoon snatched up their rifles and pointed them at the guards before they could react. They began to shift nervously from one foot to the other.

"Lieutenant, are you insane? This is treason!" murmured the lance corporal in a mixture of surprise and bewilderment.

"You can file a complaint, but I'm not waiting another second. People's lives are at stake!" Fatahi gave Nikos and his companions a wave and they didn't need to be asked twice. With careful glances, they scurried past the soldiers and to the stairway at the rear of the command vehicle. Before he could get a grip on the door handle, he turned back to Fatahi.

"Thank you. You're doing the right thing."

"I know," the young officer replied simply, nodding.

Nikos yanked open the door and climbed into the large command module, which was still fully occupied. Steutner and his Spanish colleague stood in front of a monitor further back and interrupted their conversation to see who was disturbing them unannounced.

"Why weren't you announced?" the general blared as Nikos strode clumsily between the female and male soldiers at the workstations with Sönke and Karin in tow, who were carrying Hey-Kolpa between them, directly toward the commander of the operation. "It's *you*. Where have you been, man? We thought you were dead already!"

"I almost was. Sir, you must cease all hostilities immediately!"

"So? Your friend has already demanded that over the radio too, I'm told." Steutner snorted contemptuously and shook his head. "You're a civilian and you don't understand anything about command hierarchies or combat tactical considerations, so I'm not going to start listening to advisors from the TV now. Just because you've read a few calendar sayings by Sun Tzu doesn't make you a military genius."

"What?" asked Nikos, irritated. "What are you talking about?"

"I want you to turn around and get out of here. Our operation is entering its final phase and I don't want to make any mistakes, so get out!"

"Sir, you don't understand."

"So, what don't I understand? I'll give you three seconds before I have you removed, and that's only because you found out about the tunnels and you're a smart little guy who knows when to clear the field," the major general replied with the stern look of a hawk circling over his prey.

"The locals, they're human!" blurted Nikos. At first, he had thought about the easiest way to say or show it, but now he thought it best to tell the truth. That was always the best way to communicate something anyway.

"I know."

Nikos was about to continue speaking, when he realized what the general had just said. "Excuse me?"

"I know they look like us. I first dismissed the scattered reports from the front as battlefield fighter gibberish. Then I had one of their dead brought in and looked into an all-too-human face," Steutner explained. "It's a strange thing."

"I... strange thing?" Karin snapped. "You can't be serious, man! We just attacked other people!"

"Oh, come on." The tall general snorted. "Other humans on an alien planet, that raises a lot of questions, but none that change anything about our mission objective and what it means to our species. And in case you haven't noticed, Ms. *Journalist,* we've been fighting other humans on Earth for thousands of years. Would you stop a war there too simply because it's against other humans?"

"Yes!" she and Nikos said simultaneously, while Sönke remained conspicuously quiet.

"That's some naive civilian talk. What makes these aliens that look like humans any different a reason to end a war than humans that come from Earth, huh?"

"What is the mission of the Bundeswehr, General?" Sönke spoke up for the first time.

"Don't lecture me, boy!"

"What is the Bundeswehr's mission?" the captain repeated stoically, and Steutner gritted his teeth. Nikos expected him to wave at any moment and soldiers to drag them out.

"Get out of here, now!"

"Article Eighty-Seven A of the Basic Law, Paragraph Two," Sönke quoted, interrupting the general so that their voices became tangled. "*Except for defense, the armed forces may be used only as expressly permitted by this Basic Law.* This is a war of aggression, Major General."

"Which refers to a military strategic target whose destruction is in the defense of our country," Steutner insisted, his eyes narrowing into slits. "Why don't you have your breathing masks on anyway?"

"Not a military strategic target," Nikos interjected without answering the question. Instead, he turned and beckoned Hey-Kolpa, who approached with a downcast look. The native seemed powerless and discouraged, as if she were sleepwalking. Nikos pulled away her thermal blanket, and when the general and his Spanish colleague, who had been watching the war of words with a stony expression so far, saw who she was, they gasped. All the soldiers in the room turned in their chairs and pistols were drawn.

Nikos was already expecting the general to yell "Are you insane?" or something of the sort, but instead he remained calm and eyed the small woman with the broad, strong build with a furrowed brow. The latter seemed to regain a little of her strength and raised her eyes to meet the general's.

"What is the meaning of this?" the German wanted to know.

"Hey-Kolpa," Nikos said, directed at the native, and knelt down to be level with her. He pointed to her chest and drew a square with his fingers. She nodded and pressed a spot on her suit, whereupon once again the square piece with the blue glowing mesh lifted off and pushed forward. She took it in her short fingers and held it out to the general, whose face lit up blue above his breathing mask.

"What is the meaning of this?" he repeated, more quietly this time, as if his mind were not quite on the matter.

"That means the ore wasn't just a military target. It seems to be something of a lifeline for the people here. They use it for their underground cities, as a power source for their suits, without which they can't survive. If this mine was the only one on the planet, we've just destroyed the livelihood of their species, and according to the Morphs, there's only this one mine," Nikos huffed with the fury of exasperation. "The Morphs knowingly sent us into battle to wipe out another human world."

Steutner's nostril began to twitch. "How do I know any of this is true?"

"Trust your eyes and let your heart give you the rest of the answers," Nikos suggested, ignoring that it might sound corny or maudlin. "The Morphs haven't given us any information. If they knew enough about the locals to tell us about the factions here and the location of the mine, they almost certainly knew we'd be fighting humans here. They didn't tell us, though. Why not? Why do they only talk to us when they need us to weaken their enemy, at the first opportunity they see to use us? Why do they let us slaughter other humans?"

"I'm afraid that even if all this is true, it's too late now," Steutner said seriously. He no longer sounded angry, but now thoughtful. "If we call off the attack, the Morphs will see this as a reason for us to renege on our alliance agreements."

"We can work around that and gain new allies at the same time."

The general considered and exchanged a look with the

Spanish general. "We contact the Tears, admit our guilt and that we were deceived, transmit the secret coordinates of the wormhole to them, and they can destroy it from orbit because the area around the wormhole is a gap in the anti-tech network. This cuts off all communication with Earth, and neither Army Command nor the Morphs will be able to learn what happened on the other side of the Milky Way anytime soon. At least that will keep them from jumping to conclusions. At least that must be the hope we're leaning on. Otherwise, I've cut off two divisions from their homes and sent them to their deaths."

"It's a risk," Sönke admitted. "But it's the right thing to do. If there's a way to get us back to Earth, then..." Nikos' friend was shaken by a violent coughing fit and sniffled audibly. "Then these are the Tears, who didn't enslave these people here, but made a deal with them for ore mining, it seems. That speaks well for them, doesn't it? Surely they could have taken the ore for themselves instead of equipping the planet with a protective shield to keep themselves out."

Steutner was silent for a while, then pointed to a soldier with red hair to his left. "Attach the radio repeater. We're sending a message into orbit."

Nikos breathed a sigh of relief and turned to Karin, who hugged him as if a huge weight had fallen from her shoulders. When they detached from each other again, a thin film of blood ran from her nose.

"You're bleeding," he said, placing a finger under his left nostril.

"Oh," she said, wiping it off and looking at her red-smeared index finger. No one said anything about it, because they both knew what it meant, and talking about it wouldn't change anything.

"Already online, Major General," the soldier at the monitor

announced. "Telecommunications has installed everything to optimize coordination with the Ari."

"Let's get this show on the road, then. Unencrypted, full transmit power, ninety degrees up or whatever — I don't care." Steutner leaned over the combat analyst's shoulder and pointed to some symbols on the screen that Nikos couldn't make out.

"This is Major General Steutner of the First Panzer Division of the German Armed Forces, Commander of Strike Force Alpha, European Union. We have been sent here under false pretenses. We are ceasing all combat operations with the local people immediately." Steutner gave his Spanish second-in-command a wave, and she turned to another soldier and hastily gave instructions. "We request assistance for the wounded on both sides, and as a sign of our sincerity, we are sending the coordinates of the wormhole through which we were able to penetrate on behalf of your enemies. We assume you will know what to do and await a response."

The major general took a step back and waited.

"Uh, General, I already have an answer," the soldier at the keyboard announced incredulously. Nikos went cold all at once. It hadn't even been two seconds since Steutner had stopped speaking. When he glanced over his shoulder at the combat analyst, his screen was black except for a number that was getting smaller.

"A countdown?" Steutner pursed his lips before abruptly beginning to yell, "Pull all units off the wormhole, now!"

The analysts became agitated and began talking wildly into their headsets until their voices merged into a confused jumble that filled the entire command cabin of the truck. Where there had just been the subdued calm of strategic coolness, panic now took hold. Nikos understood why: the countdown showed thirty seconds. The soldier's keyboard in front of the monitor clacked in protest as he hammered frantically on the escape key, but the screen no longer obeyed him. One by one, all the displays changed to the rapidly decreasing number.

Nikos ran to the door and threw it open, jumping into the mud and almost falling when his knees gave way under the massive weight the planet was putting on him. Hey-Kolpa, Sönke and Karin followed, shouting something after him that he couldn't hear. It wasn't until he had rounded the truck and climbed onto the hood that he paused and stared south. In his mind, he counted down the final numbers that must now be flickering across the monitors, and then it happened. Far in the distance, a single thin beam of light, which had to be a massive diameter on the ground if it was still so visible from here, pierced the cloud cover. It glowed a menacing red, vaporizing the clouds into dancing molecules. The beam appeared for barely three seconds and was gone as abruptly as it had appeared.

"I guess the wormhole just got destroyed," Sönke murmured, still standing in the mud next to the truck and staring incredulously at the horizon, where everything now looked peaceful again as before, as if nothing had happened.

A few moments later, the general came staggering out of the command post and sought them out.

"I don't know if that was a good decision, lad," he said in a worn voice.

"I don't know either, but it was the right one," Nikos replied, though a part of him felt lost in the knowledge that they were stranded on the other side of the Milky Way. Earth was now so remote that it was beyond the limits of human imagination in terms of distances, on a planet so toxic that his lungs already ached. Steutner nodded thoughtfully and pointed at the little Hey-Kolpa, who seemed visibly uncomfortable among all the enemy soldiers, more and more of whom were now coming from all directions and gawking at her in disbelief.

"I have instructed my soldiers to render aid to the locals and not to initiate any more combat operations except to defend themselves in an extreme emergency. I'm moving the wounded into the tunnels we control to protect them from the rain, which could start up again at any time."

"Thank you, sir," Nikos said.

"I'm not doing this for you."

"Thanks anyway."

Again, the general nodded. "Since you have a good hand with the locals, I suggest you see your way out of this situation. You're a civilian, not a threat."

"What were you thinking?" asked Nikos, exhaustion making his limbs heavy all at once.

"The way I see it, there's only one way to contact the Tears," Steutner replied, pointing north where a line as thin as a thread bisected the horizon between the planet's surface and the clouds.

"The orbital elevator," Sönke said promisingly.

"We have captured several vehicles from the ene..." the major general cleared his throat, "...locals. I suggest you take one and take your new escort to reach orbit."

Nikos wanted to shout *no!* to protest, to give voice to his screaming muscles that wanted nothing more than to rest.

"We'll do it, sir." He looked at Sönke and Karin.

"We'll do it," they confirmed, and all eyes turned to Hey-Kolpa, who had followed the general's gesture toward the orbital elevator and nodded hesitantly.

CHAPTER 24

JACEK

"STAY calm and don't let the amphetamine make you do anything stupid, alright?" Jacek waited for his team members' confirmations, took a deep breath, and dove into the alien object. The cone of light from his flashlight brushed across a charcoal gray floor that merged seamlessly into walls that were rounded and oval toward the top. It was uncomfortable to stand here, as the floor was not straight. If he held his rifle steady, he could see that the walls formed honeycomb patterns between which dark mercury seemed to pour, constantly moving and flowing restlessly in all directions. Beneath his boots too, everything seemed fluid, looking dark and solid only directly around the soles.

T'Chall waited until they had entered and dropped four small marbles from his hands, which buzzed at an uncomfortably high frequency and flew off into the darkness.

"These are small probes scanning the corridors and rooms. I should have a map of the entire ship in a few minutes," he whispered from the suit, and the fact that their companion apparently didn't dare raise his voice in this place, despite being inside an utterly incredible piece of technology, made Jacek shiver. "The Devourers know we're here, so be vigilant."

"How do they know?" asked Hardy quietly.

"All of the Devourer's materials are made of intelligent, programmable nano-assemblers that form an artificial neural net similar to their own replicator bodies. A Devourer can latch on to the ship and sense it as if it were its own body."

"Sounds promising," Uffe grumbled as T'Chall turned and started running. First, they went through a slightly curved corridor, stumbling around like toddlers who hadn't yet learned to walk. The tapering ground made it difficult to keep their balance and was so obviously not made for human locomotion that the strangeness of the place was not merely visible, but palpable. The walls seemed to have eyes and ears. At any moment, Jacek expected an ambush by the tentacled monsters that were the Morphs. He had only seen this one image, but it had reminded him of a grim mix of the worst horror films in movie history. Nothing about this place seemed remotely made for human physiology: no straight surfaces, no aesthetics whatsoever, or comprehensible shapes to offer guidance. The ceiling could have been the floor and vice versa, and nothing he saw offered anything like a clue as to what it was. His flashlight, for example, illuminated a long string that jutted horizontally into the hallway from the left wall and looked like it was hanging down – except that it didn't follow gravity. After a few minutes, which seemed like hours to him as they crept through the hulking corridors on silent soles and in tense silence, T'Chall stopped.

"The probe data is there. I only recorded a single Morph before he destroyed one of the probes. He was in the upper decahedron when it happened. From what I can tell, the ship was hit by an electromagnetic lance that disintegrated all the assemblers."

"All but one," Jacek said, and T'Chall nodded in a very human gesture.

"I now know where to access the onboard systems. The procedure is complex because I have to feed my mind into the ship and only have as much time as my AI will allow me once I am attacked by the enemy system. While I do that, my suit will continue to function, but it will be motionless as long as Sidhi and I are in the on-board system." T'Chall looked at them in turn, and his face seemed both concerned and as if to convey hope. "You must ensure that the Devourer does not kill me in that time, or there is no chance of preventing the reactor overload. The energy level has already reached a critical peak."

"Count on us," Jacek assured him, gripping his G36 a little tighter so that his gloves creaked.

"Thank you. Follow me." The Tear took off running, setting a much faster pace this time. Though his long legs made it look like it was an easy jog, Jacek and his team almost had to run to keep up with him. This once again presented them with challenges as they stumbled frequently, trying to find their footing on the uneven ground. At some point, they turned right into a small passageway. The honeycomb patterns in the walls here pulsed a dark red that seemed to fight the cones of light from their flashlights like spectral poison as they restlessly painted and scanned the walls, floor, and ceiling. The corridor finally ended in a room whose ceiling was impossible to find. It was either so far up that their high-powered flashlights couldn't reach it, or it was the unformed blackness that swallowed the light. To Jacek's eyes, it was the latter, as there was something greedy about the darkness that felt entirely unnatural.

"What's that?" asked Uffe, standing with her huge alien rifle in front of two triangular contraptions, between which there was an open area that was black, unlike the ever-moving mercury floor.

"Careful!" T'Chall warned her so fiercely that she flinched back as if she had been burned. "This is a molecular analyzer. It independently breaks down anything that goes on the scanning surface into its basic components and creates a computer model."

"Sick shit," the sniper growled, making a sour face. "It's like a chamber of horrors."

"This way!" the Tear urged them, waving. In front of a hole the size of a child's crawl tunnel, he made himself small and climbed in. His shoulders just fit into the dark opening — then he was sucked in and disappeared.

"Great," Jacek murmured, climbing in next. It was as if his body became a projectile, except he didn't feel any acceleration forces as he hurtled through the darkness. He just knew he was shooting straight up, with no clue to that knowledge as he couldn't even see his hand in front of his eyes, it was so dark. Then it was over again; he was spat out into a new darkness and hit the ground hard. Quickly, he turned his flashlight back on. He took two steps to the side to make way for his comrades, who one by one also came shooting through the tube and swept the space they were now in with his flashlight.

If the hallways had already been eerie and strange, this room was even worse. Although there was a floor that was level and a ceiling that was as flat as a board, everything else just didn't want to be right to his eyes. For one thing, there were the walls, which he could identify solely by the fact that the light there disappeared into an eerie lack of contour. For another, there were a lot of fixtures, both on the floor and the ceiling, as if someone had folded two rooms together. Both halves looked like people could walk between them and work on the fixtures, except that the fixtures had no controls, openings, levers, or anything to interact with. Some of the columns extended from the ceiling to the floor and were riddled with deep scratches, as if a predatory cat had ravaged them. The size of the scratches made him shudder and hope that he would never encounter this feline.

A Morph inside the ship, he thought, noticing for the first time how warm it was inside the ship as a drop of sweat fell from his forehead onto the butt of his assault rifle. *It can't be long before he comes and descends upon us.*

"I'll begin now," T'Chall announced, and as soon as the first syllable of his sentence sounded, five cones of light jerked onto his suit, which began to glow under the onslaught of photons. The Tear stood in front of a waist-high fitting that had a single hole on top, into which he inserted his right hand at that moment. A moment later, his helmet closed again.

"How long will it take?" asked Hardy, but T'Chall stopped answering.

"All right, let's form a circle around his position. Two meters apart, take cover behind the fittings, and don't forget to scan the ceiling. With its tentacles, I'm sure the Morph isn't as limited by gravity as we are. Well, Uffe?"

"Yo, Joss?"

"Don't point your new gun at me, or I'll whip your ass."

Uffe grinned broadly in the light of her flashlight, eyes wide. "He was swearing, you guys! He cursed! That's gonna give me a wet streak in my panties."

"You're disgusting. Besides, you're wearing a diaper, if I know you," grumbled Knut, who was just slinking around a baggy protrusion and looking around.

"Better safe than sorry. Was too cold for me to squat in the ice too."

"Quiet now," Jacek intervened. "Concentrate and don't let the stimpacks get to you."

Silence quickly fell after they spread out behind columns, fixtures, and strange protrusions. Shortly after, they lit their phosphor flares and threw them toward the walls. They bounced off the center of the room they were standing in, only a few feet away, bathing everything in deep red light. Their familiar roar lent something grounding to this unreal place that calmed Jacek a little, even if the sight of the torches bouncing back from a contour-less darkness still worried him.

A long silence followed, so tense that Jacek could hear the blood pulsing in his ears. The attack came out of nowhere and so quickly that it seemed like a dream. One moment he was still blowing a bead of sweat from the tip of his nose and following the cone of light from his flashlight as it was lost in the black of the invisible wall. Everything seemed still and unmoving, then the blackness began to move and suddenly possessed erratic twitching appendages. Before he realized what was happening, a shadow raced across the ceiling and landed between him, Hardy, and Pill. The Morph looked like a creature from nightmares, with more than half a dozen tentacles that appeared blunt and were constantly changing shape. They converged in a compact torso, at the front of which a glowing red opening was ripped wide open like a mouth torn open into an endless scream. From the rear of the torso stood twitching strands back and forth, seemingly weightless. The constant changing of the limbs in shape and texture made it exhausting for the eye to follow them. This brief impression lasted only a fraction of a second, then the Morph shot toward Hardy, who just managed to fire a shot. The muzzle flashed brightly, illuminating the Morph for a gruesome moment, then two of the tentacles thrust forward, shredding the sergeant major's chest. He was hurled across the room as if by a pile driver and crashed into one of the armatures, from which he slid lifelessly. Jacek screamed angrily and fired two well-aimed shots into the torso of the alien, which showed no reaction as the shells dislodged large chunks from its back. Red sparks crackled in the darkness where they had torn the wounds. Pill fired several volleys at once as well, and while the first shredded one of the tentacles, the rest — normal armor-piercing ammunition — ricocheted ineffectively, producing nothing but sparks.

Jacek also continued to rake the alien, even if his bullets did nothing at all, but at worst, he could at least distract it from T'Chall, who still stood motionless like a statue against the pillar that had swallowed his arm up to the elbow. Only a few feet separated him from the Morph — only a few feet decided the fate of their planet. The torn mouth from which the spherical red glow radiated jerked to the side, fixing the white suit like the eye of a hawk. From somewhere, more gunfire — presumably from Knut — shredded one of the Morph's tentacles. The alien's body twitched faster and harder and changed: it shrank. Neither the holes nor the two tentacles ending in stumps were visible — it seemed, on the contrary, to be perfectly intact again, only a third smaller and thus not much bigger than Jacek. The mouth-like eye — or whatever it was — was still staring at T'Chall. All of this had happened in less than two seconds, and he could sense more than really understand that the alien was preparing to pounce, and that pounce was what would kill the Tear. He reacted reflexively and dashed between the two hostile aliens as the Morph rushed forward simultaneously. Out of the corner of his eye, he saw Knut come out from behind a pillar, screaming loudly and shooting, but as if casually, the monster wiped him away with one of its tentacle limbs and severed one of his comrade's legs.

Jacek still managed to hold his rifle in front of him with both hands like a protective barrier, then they crashed into each other. The impact was like being run over by a truck and hurled him back, past T'Chall. A brutal pain in his abdomen nearly robbed him of consciousness, and it wasn't until he was in flight, wondering why the alien was stuck to him, that he saw the wide tentacle that had pierced him.

Through bloody teeth, he had to grin as he understood that the monster had latched on to him and fumbled with a trembling hand for his combat knife. He found it as they simultaneously crashed to the ground, somersaulting in a wild mix of arms, legs, and tentacles.

"Let him go, you ugly piece of shit," someone shouted in a growly voice. Uffe, it had to be Uffe. Jacek cried out as the Morph detached itself from him and pulled the bloodied tentacle from his body. The hole left behind was the size of a child's head, and the sound of things falling to the ground that shouldn't be falling out of him told him he didn't stand a chance. As if to emphasize that fact, two more tentacles shot forward and pierced his shoulders before he was thrown around. The Morph used him as a shield against Uffe, who he was now looking at. Only in a blur could he make her out, her small stature, the huge weapon as the life drained out of him.

"I know how this gun works, Jessy," she said in a clipped voice. "Do you trust me?"

"Did..." Jacek coughed, letting a gush of blood bubble over his lips before he could speak again. "Always have."

"Good." Uffe pulled the trigger and two glowing blue bullets, downright disappointingly puny compared to the mighty weapon that fired them, dislodged themselves, skittering apart and circling Jacek before converging behind him and hitting the Morph, which was blown to tiny bits in an explosion. Before he even hit the ground, Uffe had dropped the rifle and leapt to him. Half she caught him, half they fell together. She held his head in her hands, the only part of his body that didn't feel cold. He was so weak that he could not find strength enough to speak.

"Hey, that looks really bad," she said, her eyes moist. "Real bad. Pill! PILL!"

"I'm here," the medic replied breathlessly, kneeling down beside her. The look in his eyes as he looked Jacek up and down told him what he knew anyway. That he would one day die in the heart of an alien starship was something he had never imagined. However, he did like it better than passing away with Parkinson's in a hospice. Besides, they had given Earth another spark of hope. What more could a commando soldier ask for?

"Do something!" growled Uffe in Pill's direction.

"I can't do anything!"

"I don't care, do something!"

"I can't, I..."

"Take care of Hardy and Knut," Jacek said, only to find that his lips had not moved, and no sound had escaped his body. No one had heard him, for the words had not cleared the hurdle between thought and speech, had seeped away powerlessly halfway as the pure wish of a brain gradually shutting down. His neurons, cut off from the blood supply, fired in different places, sending the strangest images to his mind's eye: distorted memories of his childhood mingled with missions in crisis zones. A crying face, then a piece of bread he looked at. A cat with a sad face peeking out from behind a mud wall, staring at him reproachfully.

"It is done," a third voice mingled with the two angry soldiers discussing. Jacek knew it belonged to T'Chall, but he could no longer see him as his field of vision became more restricted and blurred. "I've broken off the overload. I've spoken to the higher-ups at Saturn, but they can't get me out because the Morphs are in orbit around..."

"I don't give a fuck, man!" hissed Uffe. "We've got three seriously injured people here! Do something for them!"

"I can't," came the apologetic reply. He sounded kind of

embarrassed and depressed, Jacek thought. Why was everyone so down? He could already feel the last sparks of life pouring out of him.

"There has to be something! You're a fucking magic alien for all I know!" Uffe's voice grew shriller. He'd never heard her speak like that before; she almost sounded like a hysterical mother — the very image of a woman she took so much trouble never to show.

"I can't, I could only..."

"What?" she huffed. Pill had already disappeared. *I wonder if he is taking care of Knut and Hardy. I wonder if they will survive.* He hoped so very much.

His field of vision was smaller than the head of a pin when he heard the last words of his life. They were so spectacularly unspectacular that they formed a fitting conclusion to his life. More than that, the alien's words were something like the shortest fitting description for his life and work as a KSK soldier; after all, he had heard this phrase endlessly during training and before his missions.

"You won't like it."

EPILOGUE

THE VEHICLE STEUTNER provided them with looked like an elongated caterpillar with a long comb of antennae on the roof. The interior was small and squat, even by local standards. Hey-Kolpa sat at the wheel in front of the curved windshield, which was as narrow as the frame of a motion picture that contracted from top and bottom to center in the final shot. Fortunately for Nikos, Sönke, and Karin, there were two benches that ran lengthwise through the cabin to the rear door. This way, they could sit crosswise and make sure that their heads didn't constantly collide with the compartments that were attached to the ceiling. It was amazing how familiar everything looked in the vehicle. Steering wheel, side mirrors, restraining nets, storage compartments, seats with seat belts — all things that existed in vehicles on Earth. The differences were there, of course: the steering wheel wasn't round but a curved rectangle, the dashboard looked alien, and the seats seemed to him like little tubs that you sank into rather than actually sitting in. Nevertheless, it amazed Nikos how similar people who apparently existed far apart from each other developed, and apparently, functionality and technology.

They didn't speak much on the way, aside from a few attempts at translation between him and Hey-Kolpa. He figured out that her name was *Krashkanadu*, at least he was pretty sure of that, and that either her planet, species, people, or country was called *Andualla*. Which was true was impossible to say, but then again, he wasn't a linguist. All these questions could still be asked by the experts if they succeeded in their mission and ever saw Earth again.

Sönke and Karin fell asleep after the first hour, were rocked back and forth in their harnesses and seemed to slumber like newborns. Nikos regularly wiped the blood from their noses and upper lips and held them when a coughing spasm shook them and they vomited blood. In between, he gave them antibiotics and fever-reducing painkillers given to them by a paramedic and smeared their skin with cortisone cream. He could also feel the fever spreading through him and the first red pustules on his skin burst and festered. His immune system was running at full speed to cope with the foreign pathogens — a battle it would slowly lose. The broad-spectrum antibiotic he had swallowed might have helped a little, but that didn't change the fact that it might be powerless against the foreign bacteria of the local microbiome.

In between his short stints as a nurse, he kept crouching behind Hey-Kolpa, whose real name he had already forgotten because it sounded so complicated, and his head felt like a balloon about to burst. She kept talking into some kind of radio she pulled from the dashboard, which hung from the end of a coiled cord. Sometimes she sounded excited, sometimes defensive, and sometimes quite calm and matter-of-fact, though the rolling, guttural sound of her speech always had an undertone that sounded coarse and aggressive, much like Russian or German. He wanted to ask her who she was talking to, to shake her so she would come out with details of what she expected, and yet he could do purely nothing. Nikos was condemned to listen and watch, without any influence on her actions or intentions. Now it was up to him to blindly trust her, as she had done with him, to end the battle between their nations. She had put her life on the line to do the right thing, and he had respected her for it. Now that he was in a similar situation himself, he admired her.

After several hours, they came to a road whose asphalt had a conspicuous green tinge and which was probably not paved at all. But it was upgraded, and they made faster progress until they finally reached a military post. Armored vehicles blocked the two-lane road in a wedge shape, and two dozen or more soldiers in green suits similar to Hey-Kolpa's aimed their rifles at them. As soon as their car stopped, Nikos could see some deviation through the windshield. The soldiers wore yellow badges on their upper arms, and their torsos were protected by olive-green armored vests – at least, that was what he interpreted the oddly beefy garments as.

Hey-Kolpa seemed nervous but not surprised and pressed a toggle switch, whereupon the side door was unlocked, and three soldiers entered. The beefy little figures shouted excitedly and with jagged movements told Nikos to sit down next to Sönke and Karin, who were awake by now and raised their arms with eyes wide with shock. Each of the three got a rifle pressed to their chest and had to stare into the mirrored visors of the alien soldiers for what felt like an eternity. A fourth figure came and argued with Hey-Kolpa. They both debated wildly until the radio on the armature chirped. She took it off and held it out to the alien. Meanwhile, Nikos, Sönke, and Karin were being searched by their guards, who were not exactly squeamish about the job. At least they didn't talk aggressively at them like the one talking to their local companion, and to Nikos' surprise, they retreated after a short while. The roadblock was lifted, and they were allowed to pass — with the difference that there was now an armored military vehicle in front of them and possibly one behind them as well.

The forest, through which they drove straight ahead as if pulled by a string, was lined to the right and left by the massive mushrooms whose lamellar dust lay all over the road and its edge. Since the pavement was dry, the flake-like formations were kicked up like snow by the tires of their front vehicle, matching the bizarre strangeness of the view in front of the windshield. The orbital lift was becoming more of a line with each passing hour, becoming a thick stalk connecting ground and clouds, impressive if only for the sheer gigantism of such a structure. The road seemed to lead directly toward it, and a short time later brought them to a widely cleared area protected by high walls. Once again, there was a sweep of military personnel protecting the huge gate through which they were eventually waved.

As soon as they had passed through — from now on without escort — the sight of the surroundings changed dramatically: a gigantic area was completely leveled and cleared of any vegetation. In its center, the base of the orbital elevator grew out: massive and hundreds of meters wide at its base, the behemoth of metal ran toward the veritable elevator, which disappeared into the clouds like a dash. At the end of the ground station, six cabins clung to it like ulcers. But also impressive were the many railroad tracks that ran through the wall from the southwest and disappeared into great gullets at the base of the ground station. Here, apparently, the infrastructure had been put in place to transport the ore, on a scale that was impossible to comprehend. Everything looked a little old and crude, yet functional in an ugly way.

Hey-Kolpa steered her car through a large gate at the foot of the building and they were swallowed by the darkness until they reached a huge hall. If everything looked deserted from the outside, inside, it pulsed with activity: hundreds of workers and dozens of large machines were loading massive containers with the hieroglyphs of the natives. The containers were in turn loaded by cranes onto a system of wide conveyor belts that ran in a star shape toward elevators in the center of the hall. Hey-Kolpa drove a little further and was stopped by a worker holding up a yellow sign and redirecting her to the right. There, a small car with a yellow siren clamped in front of her and she followed it to a small passenger elevator. The local parked so close to it that the side door was right up against the elevator door.

The people here don't know what happened, Nikos thought abruptly, and the knowledge that all these workers still had no clue that their livelihoods further south had been destroyed and they were facing the end gave him a painful stab of sorrow. When Hey-Kolpa opened the door, she shooed him and his two companions out with hurried movements before wiping blood from her nose with the back of her hand.

Once inside the car, she flipped a few toggle switches and up they went. The ride was short, and the doors released them onto a small platform, which they rounded to the left to enter another elevator. This one was slightly larger and had a total of six of the locals' uncomfortable-looking chairs that tilted back forty-five degrees. There was a control panel with one arrow pointing down and one pointing up, and the walls were transparent. Hey-Kolpa pushed the up arrow, and nothing happened until a voice sounded from the small speaker above the control panel and she answered something. Then the ride started.

Their cabin took off leisurely and was pulled through a dark tube until, a few minutes later, they glided out of the ground station and sped upward. Quickly, the cleared area below them became smaller and its dirty brown surface indistinct like a pastel painting. A second elevator followed them, slightly offset, but it was considerably larger and more massive and had no windows. Nikos guessed it must be an ore shipment.

"That was really easy," crowed Sönke, exhausted. He sat beside him and gazed with half-closed eyes over the land, which looked beautiful in its yellows and browns. Nikos felt reminded of a deciduous forest lying preserved in eternal autumn. "And it happened so fast."

"I believe we were smuggled in quickly and secretly and most of the residents and military personnel don't know about it. Hence the secrecy and speed," Nikos replied, shaken by a coughing fit, at the end of which he spat in a handkerchief with blood and some dark bits that didn't look like they should leave his body. They didn't have much time left, he sensed.

"They obviously have hope that our trip into orbit can save them. That gives me hope too," Sönke returned wearily. "The fact that there's a personnel cabin must mean that there have already been encounters between them and the Tears. That's a good thing, right?"

"Yes," Nikos agreed with him and continued to listen to his friend without understanding his words. Shortly after, he fell asleep.

When he awoke, they were already well above the cloud cover and the sky was beginning to turn black when he peered up through the transparent wall. A glance at the clock showed him that he had been asleep for over twelve hours. He glanced to his right and saw Sönke sleeping so motionlessly that he checked his pulse and breathed a sigh of relief. To his left, Karin lay with her head against his shoulder. He stroked her hair and carefully maneuvered her to the other side, where Hey-Kolpa sat with her eyes open, wagging her head as their eyes met. By now, he understood the gesture for a nod and waved at her. From his bag, he retrieved the medicines and the water bottles and handed out the pills to his friends, for which he woke them each briefly. They all — the native included — looked pale and sick, with open patches on their faces and fever-wet foreheads. At their current pace, it would surely be days before they reached orbit, and they had to hold out for that time.

After his friends were taken care of, he stood at the window and looked at the yellowish cloud cover below them. From their height, he could see the swirls formed by the formations that shifted into each other like cotton wool. No land was visible, only flashes here and there and dark discolorations where rain announced itself. As he let his gaze wander upward into the space that lay above the fragile and thin-looking layer of gas that formed Planet X's atmosphere, he felt small and insignificant. His gaze was lost in a mixture of longing and wistfulness that mingled with the exhaustion of his struggling body. It was only when something bright flickered on that he was roused from his trance. A flash of light in bright colors flared in the black nothingness above them and faded away again. Several bright dots, which he had previously thought were stars, shot toward the spot like little flies of fire, but the flash of light did not return.

With aching limbs, he staggered back to his seat and stroked Karin's hair, who immediately leaned back against him. Blood ran from her nose onto his chest, but it was insignificant, and he fell asleep again a short time later. In between, he kept waking up, seeing, as if in a dream, that the planet was only a pale glimmer below them and their cabin was shrouded in deep blackness. At some point, an endless time later, the elevator stopped abruptly. A huge structure — a spaceship? — in the shape of a dark drop or tear grew outside the window into a monstrosity of incomparable proportions and seemed to want to swallow them. It roused the others, who groaned reluctantly and presented a frighteningly sick sight. There was a hiss and a creak in the cabin, then the doors suddenly moved aside, and Nikos rose from his chair with the last of his strength, at least to face the aliens upright before delivering the general's message to them. He prayed he still had enough breath left in his body to negotiate a peaceful way to deal with their guilt, but he could already feel his body losing the battle against the alien germs.

Light flooded the open door, then disappeared, revealing a room of brilliant white. A human figure stood there, taller than even Nikos, its face contorted into a smile. He beckoned him closer like an ethereal dream figure and he followed the invitation. As soon as he stepped through the doorway, the figure took a step to the side, revealing five people standing in a loose semicircle.

"You guys?" asked Nikos incredulously, eyeing Jacek, Uffe, Pill, Hardy and Knut, who came up to him and took him into their midst. They squeezed his shoulders, patted him on the back, and all talked in confusion.

"I... Is this a dream? How can this be?" he stammered in disbelief, having to keep blinking to make sure he was really seeing what he was seeing. Had the aliens drugged him? Was he dead?

"We wonder," Jacek replied with a warm smile. "But we're here."

"But how? What happened?"

"It's a long story." Jacek pointed to the tall human standing next to the elevator doors, commanding a swarm of small humanoid robots by hand signals. Stretchers grew from their metallic hands, and his companions floated out on them shortly after.

"A story for next time, big guy," Uffe said, grinning, but her exuberant expression hid other emotions he knew from his time in Athens. It was an attempt to mask a deep-seated fear and worry. "First, the Tears need to get you back on your feet."

"Yeah, next time," Nikos sighed wearily, smiling weakly. *There will be a next time; that's a start at least.*

THANK YOU FOR READING THE COUNTERSTRIKE

WE HOPE you enjoyed it as much as we enjoyed bringing it to you. We just wanted to take a moment to encourage you to review the book. Follow this link: **The Counterstrike** to be directed to the book's Amazon product page to leave your review.

Every review helps further the author's reach and, ultimately, helps them continue writing fantastic books for us all to enjoy.

———

You can also join our non-spam mailing list by visiting www. subscribepage.com/AethonReadersGroup and never miss out on future releases. You'll also receive three full books completely Free as our thanks to you.

Facebook | Instagram | Twitter | Website

Want to discuss our books with other readers and even the

authors? Join our Discord server today and be a part of the Aethon community.

————

ALSO IN SERIES:
THE ARRIVAL
THE COUNTERSTRIKE
THE EXTINCTION

————

Looking for more great Science Fiction?

They've plundered their way across the galaxy and just found the score of a lifetime. All they have to do is steal from the most ruthless crime lord in the galaxy. What could possibly go wrong? Yan and his band of rogues are intent on plundering their way to fame and fortune. When they stumble across the score of a lifetime, they quickly go all in for one last job. With everything on the line, there's no way they can fail. At least that's what they're hoping. In the end, they just might have gotten into something bigger than they ever imagined possible.

GET MOST WANTED NOW!

―――――

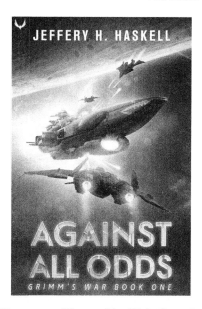

Wrong crew. Wrong ship. Right Captain.

Idealistic navy lieutenant Jacob Grimm just wanted to honor his mother's sacrifice in the last great war. When he's forced to return fire and destroy a squadron of ships to save his own, he thinks he's the hero... Until they discover the ships are full of children. Disgraced and denied promotion, Jacob's career is over. That is until the head of ONI needs a disposable officer to command a battered destroyer on the rim. There's just one problem, *Interceptor* hasn't had a CO in months and the ship is a mess. Worse, the system he's assigned to is corrupt and on the verge of all-out civil war with the Alliance. However, no one told Jacob he was disposable. Pirates, smugglers, and Caliphate spies complicate the situation and one captain with an old ship can't enforce the law, let alone stop anyone. The single greatest discovery of all time is about to change intergalactic politics forever. If Jacob doesn't find a way to succeed, then it won't just be the end of the Alliance, it will be the end of freedom for humanity.

GET AGAINST ALL ODDS NOW!

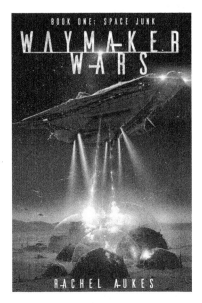

Captain Jack Hale and his crew of ragtag scavengers live by a code. They do the job, get paid, and keep their heads down. Salvaging a distant section of the asteroid belt seemed like the perfect job. But when he and his crew stumble across a mining camp filled with dead bodies, their plans for a quick payday quickly go out the airlock. Especially when they find a scared little girl who knows the truth about the massacre. When Captain Hale refuses to turn over the survivor to those behind the slaughter, he and his crew become outlaws. Fugitives in a system controlled by an alien AI. The odds are against him, but Captain Hale has an ace up his sleeve, or rather, in his blood. The secret might just give him an edge to beat Sol Corps at their own game, though exposing it will draw out an old and even more dangerous enemy. The sins of his past may just be what saves the future for all mankind.

GET SPACE JUNK NOW!

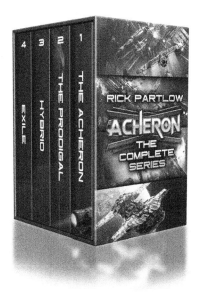

AFTERWORD

Dear Readers,

Thank you so much for staying with me through the second part of Annihilation. In this book, I have endeavored to answer some of the most burning questions for you: Who are the aliens? What are their motivations, and how is Earth changing? Please forgive me for not being able to answer *all* the questions this time either. That won't happen until Part Three — this one will be a conclusion for now. Whether it will be *the* conclusion of the story, however, remains to be seen.

You can support these sequels by reviewing this book on Amazon. This can be kept short and simple — anything is better than being part of the silent crowd. Our books live on your voice!

If you'd like to never miss a new release and get to know me better, you can sign up for my monthly newsletter here: www.joshuatcalvert.com

Thank you and my warmest regards,

Joshua T. Calvert
  Jodphur, November 1, 2021

CAST OF CHARACTERS

Andualla: Planet X/P3X-888.

Bachara Al Ghabra: Colonel, British Land Forces.

Bazaraki: Cat of Nefeli, Nikos' sister.

Costas: friend of Nikos.

The Prince: Leader of the collectors in ruined Athens.

Eleni: prisoner of the Gatherers, Runner.

Evangelia: friend of Nikos.

Francois Vienne: French Prime Minister.

Franziska "Uffe" von Ufzhausen: sniper, corporal.

General de Brigada Sara Camacho: Deputy to Major General Steutner, Commander of the Spanish component of Operation Rolling Thunder.

Général De Divison Jean Joret: Deputy to Major General Steutner and Commander of the French Division 7e Brigade Blindée, Operation Rolling Thunder.

Inspector General Werhahn: highest-ranking soldier in the Bundeswehr.

Major General Steutner: Commander of Operation Rolling Thunder.

Georg Driedler: Brigadier General, Commander of the Special Forces Command.

Giorgos: Collector's prisoner, runner.

Günther Leopold: Chancellor of the Federal Republic of Germany.

Henry Wilson: NATO diplomat.

Ioannis: son of Nikos.

Jacek "Jessy" Stratholm: Sergeant Major.

Karin Getzsch: Journalist for the ARD.

Konstantina: ex-wife of Nikos.

Lieutenant Fatahi: Lieutenant in the German Armed Forces, part of Operation Rolling Thunder.

Lutz "Knut" Ammon: ABC, Sergeant Major.

Major Brandt: Major of the German Armed Forces, commander of their Command Company One of the KSK.

Maria: friend of Nikos.

Nefeli: sister of Nikos.

Nikos Antoniadis: Head of a kindergarten in Nea Ionia, Athens.

Colonel Ferdinand: Colonel in the German Armed Forces, Jacek's attending physician.

Patroklos: best friend of Nikos.

Paul "Pill" Koslowski: sergeant, medic.

Reinhard "Hardy" Feldmann: Sergeant, Telecommunications Technician.

Rooney Schneidfelder: ARD cameraman.

Sidhi: Suit AI of T'Chall.

Sönke Teunen: Captain of the Military Counterintelligence Service MAD.

Theresa June: British Prime Minister.

Viktoras: former nurse and employee of the Prince.

GLOSSARY

.357 Magnum: revolver.

7e Brigade Blindée: French armored division.

A400M: transport aircraft of the European Union.

NBC equipment: protective equipment against nuclear, biological and chemical warfare agents.

Abnormality: term used by some survivors in Athens for unexplained phenomena.

for **AEK:** popular football club from Athens.

AG36 Grenade Launcher: under barrel **grenade** launcher for the G36.

Amphetamines: stimulants that can be used to enhance performance and euphoria in its users.

Angara Mountains: mountain massif in the north of Lake Baikal.

Angoya: settlement north of Lake Baikal, Russia.

Apollon Smyrnis: football club in Athens.

Augmented Reality: computer-based enhancement of the perception of reality.

Barrett M82 caliber .50: most powerful sniper rifle,

also used by the Bundeswehr under the designation G82. Used with armor-piercing ammunition to take out "hard" targets such as vehicles, drones and radar systems.

Battlenav/GPS Battlenav: wrist display with GPS function and tactical battlefield analytics.

Bomblet projectile: cluster munition that destroys a large area at the expense of direct penetration.

Calw: home barracks of the Special Forces Command in Calw.

Containment zone: sealed-off quarantine zone around a piece of alien debris.

Crash cage: protective cage around a vehicle used for protection in the event of rollover or other accident.

Dassault Aviation: French aircraft manufacturer. Manufacturer of the Dassault Rafale.

Decahedron: ten-sided polygon.

Deploy: pull mechanism for pulling the auxiliary parachute of a parachute on the container, with which the main parachute is pulled out of the container with a delay.

The zone: cordoned off urban area of destroyed Athens.

EADS Harfang: European Union reconnaissance drone.

EPA: One-man pack. Daily rations of a Bundeswehr soldier.

Erste Panzerdivision: German armored division of the Bundeswehr.

EUSFOR: European Science Force. Newly established research and development department of the EU.

Fenetylline: amphetamine (see amphetamine) used for soldiers in war zones who have to exceed performance limits for short periods of time.

G29 Sniper Rifle: Special Forces sniper rifle.

G36: standard assault rifle of the Bundeswehr.

Ghillie suit: camouflage suit for snipers that allows the sniper to blend in with the environment.

Gia Sas: Greek for 'Good day'/ 'Hello.' (polite form).

Gia Sou: Greek for 'Good day'/ 'Hello.'

HK 417: assault rifle of the manufacturer Heckler & Koch.

HK P12: pistol.

Hypothermia: dangerously low body temperature.

JEMCOM: Joint European Military Command, based in Switzerland.

Jump run: direction of flight of the aircraft when dropping parachutists.

Kato Patissia: district in Athens, north of the center.

Kichera: village in Siberia, north of Lake Baikal.

Kursumlija: town in the south of Serbia.

Kyria: Greek for 'woman'/'lady.'

Runners: prisoners and volunteers sent by the collectors through the crater to the shard.

Leopard 2: battle tank of the Bundeswehr.

MAD: Militärischer Abschirmdienst. Military intelligence service of the Federal Republic of Germany.

Metformin: diabetes drug.

Midias: street in Athens.

Microbiome: the totality of all microorganisms of a planet/ecosystem.

MOAB: Massive Ordnance Air Blast: largest conventional bomb in the arsenal of the US armed forces. Colloquially known as the 'Mother Of All Bombs.'

MRSI method: Multiple Round Simultaneous Impact: Method/launch pattern of artillery guns that allows up to six projectiles to impact the target simultaneously.

Nea Ionia: northern district of Athens.

Operation Iron Dome: defense operation of European forces in northern Scandinavia.

Panagía mou: Greek for "Holy Mary!"

Panzerhaubitze 2000: self-propelled artillery gun of the Bundeswehr.

Parea: Greek for "clique," the "circle of friends," which in Greek culture has a similar status to the family.

PTSD: post-traumatic stress disorder.

Pull height: height at which the parachute (canopy) is opened.

Puma: infantry fighting vehicle of the Bundeswehr.

Rotor drone: drone with rotor drives.

Gatherer/Stinger: organized gang in the ruins of Athens that raids other survivors and steals supplies from them.

Skatá: Greek for 'shit!'/ 'damn!'

Sklithra: Greek for 'splinter.'

Stimpack: see Fenetyllin.

Strike Force Alpha: merger of two European divisions involved in Operation Rolling Thunder.

Terra Incognita: unmapped (unknown) area or land mass.

Ti Kanis: Greek for 'How are you?'

Tracking: targeted fall of a parachutist in a specific direction.

V-LAP-Munition: Velocity-enhanced Long-range Artillery Projectile. Langstreckenartilleriegeschoss.

Wachtmeester: (non-commissioned) rank in the Dutch armed forces.